The Jewels of Paradise

Donna Leon has lived in Venice for thirty years and previously lived in Switzerland, Saudi Arabia, Iran and China, where she worked as a teacher. Her previous novels featuring Commissario Brunetti have all been highly acclaimed; including *Friends in High Places*, which won the CWA Macallan Silver Dagger for Fiction, *Through a Glass, Darkly*, *Suffer the Little Children*, *The Girl of His Dreams*, *Drawing Conclusions*, *Beastly Things* and, most recently, *The Golden Egg*.

Donna Leon

The Jewels of Paradise

arrow books

Published by Arrow Books 2013

2 4 6 8 10 9 7 5 3

Copyright © Donna Leon and Diogenes Verlag AG Zurich 2012

First published in Great Britain in 2012 by William Heinemann

Arrow Books
Random House,
20 Vauxhall Bridge Road, London SW1V 2SA

www.randomhouse.co.uk

Addresses for companies within The Random House Group Limited can
be found at: www.randomhouse.co.uk/offices.htm

The Random House Group Limited Reg. No. 954009

A CIP catalogue record for this book
is available from the British Library

ISBN 9780099580270

The Random House Group Limited supports the Forest Stewardship
Council® (FSC®), the leading international forest-certification organisation.
Our books carrying the FSC label are printed on FSC®-certified paper.
FSC is the only forest-certification scheme supported by the leading
environmental organisations, including Greenpeace. Our paper procurement
policy can be found at www.randomhouse.co.uk/environment

Typeset in Palatino by
Palimpsest Book Production Limited, Falkirk, Stirlingshire

Printed and bound by
CPI Group (UK) Ltd, Croydon, CR0 4YY

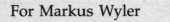

For Markus Wyler

Oh mio fiero Destin, perversa sorte!
Sparì mia vita e non mi date a morte.

Oh, my proud Destiny, perverse Fate!
To destroy my life, but not give me to death.

Agostino Steffani,
Niobe, Act 2, scene 5

1

Caterina Pellegrini closed the door behind her and leaned her back and then her head against it. First came the slight trembling of her legs as tension began to relax its hold on her muscles, then the deep breaths that helped relieve the tightness in her chest. The desire to wrap her arms around herself in an expression of wild, uncontrollable glee was almost irresistible, but she beat down that temptation, as she had beaten down many in her life, and stood with her hands at her sides, leaning against the door and telling herself to relax.

It had taken great patience, but she had done it. She had put up with a pair of fools, smiled at their manifestations of cupidity, treated them with the deference they so evidently did not deserve, all the while manoeuvring them into giving her the job she wanted and which they held in their gift. They had no wit, but they had the power to decide; they had no grace of spirit, but they could say yes or no; they had little understanding of her qualifications and a badly disguised contempt for her learning, but she had needed them to choose her.

And they had, both of them, and none of the other applicants she had thought of – not without a wry consciousness of how much her language had been affected by the historical period in which she had spent her academic and professional life – as her rivals. As the youngest of five sisters, Caterina was endowed with a healthy sense of rivalry. Not unlike characters in a Goldoni play, the sisters were: Claudia the Beautiful; Clara the Happy; Cristina the Religious; Cinzia the Athletic; and, last born, Caterina, the Clever. Claudia and Clara had married fresh out of school; Claudia had divorced within a year and upgraded to a lawyer she seemed not to like very much, while Clara stuck to her first husband and was happy; Cristina had taken vows and renounced the world, then gone on to take advanced degrees in the history of theology; Cinzia had won some medals in diving at the national level, but then had married, borne two children, and grown fat.

Caterina, the clever one, had studied at the *liceo* where her father taught history and had consistently won the yearly prize in Latin and Greek translation while picking up Russian from her aunt. From there she had spent an ignominious year as a vocal student at the Conservatory, then two years studying law at Padova, which disappointed, and then bored, her. The lure of music returned then, and she had chosen to study musicology in Florence and then in Vienna, where her thesis advisor, learning of her fluency in Russian, had arranged a two-year research grant for her to accompany him to St Petersburg to help with his research on Paisiello's Russian operas. That concluded, she returned to Vienna and finished a doctorate in Baroque opera, the degree and her possession of it sources of delight and pride to her family. This qualification, after only one year of trying to find a job, had earned her a sort of internal exile to the South in the form of a position as lecturer in counterpoint at the Conservatory of Music Egidio Romualdo Duni in Matera. Egidio Romualdo Duni. What scholar of Baroque opera would not recognize his name? Caterina had always thought of him as Duni Who Also Wrote, the man who had written operas with titles identical to those of more famous or more gifted composers: *Bajazet*, *Catone in Utica*, *Adriano in Siria*. Duni had left as little trace in Caterina's memory as he had on current opera production.

A doctorate from the University of Vienna, and then a job lecturing first year conservatory students in counterpoint. Duni. There were entire weeks when she thought she might as well have been lecturing in mathematics, so far did this subject seem from the magic thrill of the singing voice. This dissatisfaction did not bode well, something she had known almost as soon as she arrived. But it had taken her two years to decide to leave Italy again, this time by accepting a position at Manchester, one of the best centres in Europe for the study of Baroque music, where she had spent four years as a research fellow and assistant professor.

Manchester had appalled Caterina by its physical ugliness, but she had been content enough at the university, digging into the music – and to a lesser degree, the lives – of a handful of eighteenth-century Italian musicians whose careers had prospered in Germany. Veracini, Handel's great rival; Porpora, Farinelli's teacher; the practically forgotten Sartorio; Lotti, a Venetian who, it appeared, had been everyone's teacher. It was not long before she began to see the similarity between their destiny and her own: in search of the work and fame they had failed to find in Italy, they had emigrated north. Like some of them, she had found work, and like most of them, she had suffered homesickness and longed for the air, beauty, and possibility of joy offered by a country she realized, only now, that she loved.

Salvation had come, as is so often the case, by chance. Each spring, the wife of the head of her department gave a dinner for her husband's colleagues. The

4

Chairman always made it clear that it was a casual thing: come if you're free. Older and wiser heads knew that the invitation had the same weight as a ukase from, say, Ivan the Terrible. Not to go was to cast aside all hope of advancement, though to attend was to sacrifice one evening of life to tedium so encompassing as almost to be fatal. Heated exchange of insult and vituperation, even blows, would have been a source of delight, but the dinner conversation was rigidly governed by caution and a tight-lipped politeness that failed to camouflage decades of rancorous familiarity and professional jealousy.

Caterina, aware of her own incapacity to be bland, avoided conversation and devoted herself to the study of the personal and sartorial peculiarities of her colleagues. Most of the people at the table appeared to be wearing the unwashed clothing of their larger-sized friends. The shoes appalled her. And then there was the food. Though she sometimes discussed the other subjects with Italian colleagues, none of them had the courage to mention the food.

Her saviour was a Romanian musicologist who had spent the last three years, so far as Caterina could judge, in an alcoholic stupor: the fact that he was drunk in the morning and drunk in the evening never prevented him, however, from smiling amiably at her when they passed in the corridors or library, a smile she always gladly returned. He was possibly sober and unquestionably brilliant during his classes, where his analysis of the metaphors in the libretti of Metastasio broke new ground, and his explication of the Viennese court poet Apostolo Zeno's correspondence concerning the foundation of the Accademia degli Animosi was a source of wonder to his students. He often wore cashmere jackets that fitted him very well.

On the night of her salvation, the Romanian was seated across from her at the Chairman's dinner, and Caterina found herself smiling back into his wine-dulled eyes if only because they could speak easily in Italian. Most of the other people at the table had learned Italian to facilitate their reading of opera libretti; thus few of her colleagues could hold a conversation in that language without descending into wild declarations of love, terror, remorse and, upon occasion, bloodlust. Caterina preferred to converse with them in English. While she considered the use of the language of opera libretti as dinner conversation, Caterina studied the people at the table. Revelation occurred: how well a phrase such as, *Io muoio, io manco*, expressed her current feelings. Even *Traditore infame* would not be far off as a description of many of her colleagues. And was not the Chairman himself *Un vil scellerato*?

The Romanian set down his glass – he didn't bother with food so had no fork to set down – and broke his silence to ask, in Italian, 'You want to get out of this place?'

Caterina's answering glance was filled with curiosity,

as was her voice. 'Do you mean this dinner or this university?'

He smiled, took his wine glass, and looked around for another bottle. 'This university,' he said in a completely sober voice.

'Yes.' She picked up her glass, surprised to hear her own admission and struck by its force.

'A friend has told me that La Fondazione Musicale Italo-Tedesca is looking for a scholar.' He sipped, smiled. She liked his smile, though perhaps not his teeth.

'La Fondazione Musicale Italo-Tedesca,' she repeated. There was something with a similar name at home, she recalled, but she knew little about it. Dilettantes, amateurs. Surely he was speaking about something in the German-speaking world.

'You know it?'

'I've heard of it,' she said in the tone she'd use if someone asked her if she'd heard about the infestation of bedbugs in New York hotels.

He finished the wine and held up his glass. Looking at it, he said, surprising her with the angry vehemence with which he spoke: 'Italy.' The glass was from Italy? The wine?

'Money,' he added in what she thought he intended to be a seductive voice. 'Some.' When he saw how little effect this had on her, his smile returned, as if she'd just agreed with him about something he had believed for a long time. 'Research. New documents.' He saw the jolt this gave her and glanced towards the head of the table, where the Chairman sat. 'You want to end up like him?'

In a voice that slipped towards possibility, she smiled and said, 'Tell me more.'

He ignored her and looked in vain at the bottles on the sideboard. Perhaps he had already reached the point where the trip back and forth was impossible for him.

He placed his empty glass next to that of the woman to his right, who had turned to her other neighbour. He switched glasses.

'Idiots,' he said in a suddenly loud voice. They were speaking Italian, so the slurring of his speech, though it did nothing to lower the volume of his voice, at least managed to disguise the hard dentals of that word. No one so much as glanced in his direction.

Taking his napkin he wiped methodically around the edge of his neighbour's glass; only then did he take a long drink from it.

Seeing that he had all but emptied what had now become his glass, Caterina leaned across the table and poured her white wine into the small quantity of red at the bottom. He nodded.

His smile faded and he muttered, 'I don't want it. Maybe you'd like it?'

'Why?' she asked, confused. Did he mean her wine?

'I told you,' he answered, giving her a sharp look. 'Aren't you listening? It's in Venice. I hate Venice.'

So it was the one at home: a job in the city. She

didn't know everything, but she knew a lot: how serious could this place be if she'd never heard anything about it save the name? Italians cared little for the Baroque. No: only Verdi, Rossini, and – God help us all, she thought, as a small shudder walked a descending cadence down her spine – Puccini.

'You're talking about Venice? The job's in Venice?' His eyes had continued their retreat from focus all the time he had been talking, and she wanted to be certain that this possibility existed before she opened her heart to hope.

'Hateful place,' he said, making a sour face. 'Disgusting climate. Horrible food. Tourists. T-shirts. All those tattoos.'

'You've said no?' she asked with wide-eyed wonder that begged for explanation.

'Venice,' he repeated and swilled his wine to wash away the very sound of it. 'I'd go to Treviso, Castelfranco. Friuli. Good wine.' He looked into his glass, as if to ask the contents where they had come from. Finding no answer, he turned back to her. 'Even Germany. I like beer.'

Having spent many years in the academic world, Caterina did not doubt that this would sufficiently explain his acceptance of a job.

'Why me?' she asked.

'You've been nice to me.' Did that mean half a glass of white wine or the fact that she had spoken to him with respect and had smiled at him occasionally during the last years? It didn't matter. 'And you're blonde.' That at least made sense.

'Would you recommend me?' she asked.

'If you get me a bottle of red from the sideboard,' he answered.

2

Greater changes had resulted from stranger things, Caterina reflected, calling herself back from memory. The research job was hers, and she was back in Venice, though hired only to complete a single project. She looked around at the office where she was to wait for the Acting Director. If an office could be a small, high-ceilinged cubicle with two tiny windows, one behind the desk and one so close to the ceiling as to provide some light but no view, then this was an office. The desk and chair added to that possibility, though the absence of computer, telephone, and even paper and pen suggested more a monk's cell than anything else. The location – in what had once been a two-floor apartment at the end of Ruga Giuffa – could be used to argue either case. But it was a cold day at the beginning of April, and the room was warm: it had to be an office that was meant to be in use.

What little she had been able to learn about the Foundation before applying for the job had prepared her for this dismal little room: nothing in it – and nothing not in it – surprised her. The internet had provided some information about the Foundation: it had been established twenty-three years before by Ludovico Dardago, a Venetian banker who had made a career in Germany and was a passionate lover of Baroque opera, both Italian and German. He had left money for the creation of a foundation to 'disseminate and promote the performance of the music of composers who travelled and worked between Germany and Italy during the Baroque era'.

However modest the rooms, the location was propitious, only a ten-minute walk from the major collections of the Biblioteca Marciana, where manuscripts and scores were to be found.

When she thought about the events that had brought her to this room and viewed her situation in a certain way, Caterina concluded that she had been hired for a bit part in a bad nineteenth-century melodrama: The Rediscovered Trunks? The Rival Cousins? For more than a year, two cousins, descended from different sides of a mutual ancestor's family, had been embroiled in dispute over the ownership of two recently rediscovered trunks that had once belonged to their mutual ancestor. Both possessed archival evidence proving their descent from the former owner, a cleric and musician who had died without issue. Unable to find legal redress, and with great reluctance, they had finally consulted an arbitrator, who suggested that, in light of their refusal to divide equally the still-unknown contents of the trunks, a neutral and competent researcher be hired, at their shared expense, to examine the historical record and any documents contained in the trunks for any evidence of a preference for one side of the family over the other. In the event that such a document was found, both agreed – in a contract drawn up by the arbitrator and signed in front of a notary – that the entire contents of the trunks would become the exclusive possession of the person whose ancestor was so favoured.

When the arbitrator, who had some weeks ago invited her to Venice for an interview, had explained all of this to her, Caterina had decided that he was joking or had taken leave of his senses, possibly both. She had, however, smiled and asked him to explain a bit more fully the particular circumstances, adding that this would help her more clearly to understand the duties the position might entail. What she did not tell him was how the sight and smell and feel of Venice had so overpowered her that she knew she wanted the job, regardless of the conditions, and to hell with Manchester.

Dottor Moretti's explanation contained elements

of myth, family saga, soap opera, and farce, though it contained no names. The deceased cleric, he told her, was a Baroque composer who would easily be within her competence; he had died almost three centuries before, leaving no will. His possessions had been disbursed, but two chests believed to contain papers and – perhaps – valuables had finally been found and brought to Venice. One undisputed element in all of this was the claimants' descent from the relatives of the childless musician: both had produced copies of baptismal and marriage certificates going back more than two hundred years.

Here Caterina had interrupted to ask the name of the musician, a question that obviously startled Dottor Moretti by its rash impropriety. That would be revealed only to a successful candidate, and she was not yet to be considered that, was she? It was a small snap of the whip, but it was nevertheless a snap.

Would the candidate, she asked, be told the name of the musician before beginning to examine whatever papers might be found?

That, Dottor Moretti had explained, would depend upon the nature of what was found in the trunks. Another snap. The two heirs, he surprised her by saying, would interview all likely candidates. Separately. No longer able to contain herself, Caterina had interrupted again to ask Dottor Moretti if he were making this up. With a look as sober as his tie, the arbitrator had assured her that he was not.

Her task, he had gone on to say, would be to read through the documents that were believed to be in the trunks and that were likely to be in Italian, German, and Latin, though others might well be in French and Dutch, perhaps even English. Any passages referring to the deceased musician's testamentary wishes or to his affection for or involvement with various members of his family were to be translated in full: those papers relating to music or other areas of his life did not have to be translated. The cousins would expect frequent reports on her progress. It seemed that Dottor Moretti experienced a certain embarrassment in having to say this. 'If you send these reports to me, I will forward them.'

When Caterina expressed a certain difficulty in understanding why no one knew the contents of these trunks, Dottor Moretti told her that the seals appeared to be intact. Assuming this to be true, the chests had not been opened for centuries.

Caterina had the good sense to say that all of this sounded interesting, adding that, to a researcher, it was fascinating. As she spoke, she ran through the names of composers, but since she didn't know either his nationality or where he had died – or lived, for that matter – there was little chance of identifying him.

She must have impressed Moretti, for he told her he would like her to speak that afternoon to two men he suggested she treat as gentlemen. He asked only one thing of her, he added: once she learned their family names, she could easily trace them back to the composer. He trusted she would not do so until the decision about the position had been made, then explained, before she could ask, that this was a request from the two presumptive heirs, 'men with a certain fondness for secrecy'.

Caterina said she would begin research only if granted the job and would not pursue it in any way were she not chosen.

That same afternoon, she had met the contesting heirs, introduced to them, separately, by name. They met in 'the library', which turned out to be a room holding photocopies of the libretti and the scores of the operas and orchestral works of the dozen or so composers who had most delighted Signor Dardago. The library had a large table and book- shelves on which the photocopies no longer made the attempt to stand upright. There were just three or four books on the shelves, lying flat as though placed there in haste. She looked more closely and saw that one of them was a historical novel about a castrato.

Nothing either of the men said or did suggested that they were anything but gentlemen: the evidence that such an attribution was mistaken had come that evening from her parents, with whom she was staying and who, in the best Venetian way, told her what was common knowledge about each of them.

Franco Scapinelli was the owner of four shops selling glass in the area around San Marco. He was also – though nothing that happened during the interview would have suggested this – a convicted usurer who was forbidden from owning any business in the city. But who could forbid a man from giving his sons a hand in their shops? What sort of law would that be?

The other contender, Umberto Stievani, owned water taxis, seven of them, and declared, according to a friend of Caterina's father – a friend who happened to work in the Guardia di Finanza – a yearly income of just over eleven thousand Euros. The combined income of his two sons who worked for him as pilots did not reach that of their father.

During the interviews, both men claimed great interest in the manuscripts and documents and whatever else might be contained in the chests, but as Caterina listened to them she realized their interest was not in any historical or musicological importance the purported documents might have. Both had asked if any manuscripts would have value, meaning would anyone want to buy them. Stievani, no doubt because of his time spent among taxi drivers, had used the elegance of their language to ask, *'Valgono schei?'* Caterina wondered if money could be real to him only when named in Veneziano.

They must have approved of her, for here she was less than a month later, both her position and her apartment in Manchester abandoned, standing in an office at the Fondazione Italo-Tedesca, eager to begin work. And she was home again, her spirit salved by the sounds and smells of the city, by the enveloping familiarity.

She took a closer look around the room. Three small prints hung to the left of the window behind the desk. She moved across the room, not a difficult thing to do, and took a closer look at these bewigged men in their plastic Ikea frames. She recognized Apostolo Zeno by the length of his wig and the long white scarf popping out from his robes. Familiarity with prints of the bewigged Handel made it easy to recognize him. And farthest to the left was Porpora, looking as though he'd stolen his wig from Bach and his jacket from a naval commander. Poor old Porpora: to have been such a high flyer and then to have died in penury.

Caterina examined the window behind her. About the size of one of the prints, 15 x 20 centimetres, it had to be the smallest window she had ever seen. It might even be the smallest window in the city.

She put her face close to the glass and saw the shutters of the apartment on the other side of the calle: green, weather-stained, shut, as if the inhabitants were still asleep. It was ten in the morning, surely time that respectable people – hearing herself think it, gente per bene, she felt as though she were channelling her grandmother's voice – would be up and about, off to the office, off to school, busy, doing, working.

Caterina, a victim of the work ethic, had always thought she must be a throwback to some Northern

European invader, a blond-haired Goth whose genetically fuelled lust for industry had lain dormant for generations, centuries, only to burst into bloom with the birth of the last child of Marco Pellegrini and Margherita Rossi. How else explain the atavistic desire for serious work that had driven her even when she was a child? Or her response when offered a job as city counsellor for music education by the mayor, an old friend of her father? She saw no sense in diverting money from one school to another, nor in overseeing music instruction in schools that had no books, no musical instruments, and teachers of music who, though unable to read musical notation, found perfectly legible the intentions of the politicians who offered them the jobs. She had refused.

Thus her flight to Vienna and years of study, more digging through the archives in St Petersburg, and then her galley years in Matera after the desire to return to Italy had become too strong to resist. Then renewed flight to Manchester, and now this, whatever 'this' was.

A light knock at the door pulled her from these reflections. '*Avanti,*' she called. Thinking it would be a friendly gesture to be seen approaching whoever was there, Caterina started towards the door just as it opened and a woman the age of her mother entered the room. Like her mother, this woman was short and tended to roundness, as did her soft-skinned face, above which rose a structure of intertwined braids and tresses that sent Caterina's memory to a production of Cherubini's *Medea* she had seen many years ago at the Teatro Massimo in Palermo, in which the costume designer had clearly confused Medea with Medusa and had topped the head of the soprano with a loose-fitting helmet of snakes, whose twining and twisting had done a great deal to aid her performance by distracting the attention of the audience from her singing. Unlike those of the singer, this woman's serpents were motionless.

'Dottoressa Pellegrini?' the woman asked, and Caterina wondered if she had perhaps expected to find someone else in the room. The woman gave a very small smile and extended her hand. 'I'm Roseanna Salvi, Acting Director of the Foundation.' Caterina had been told that Dottor Asnaldi, the former Director, had left a year before, and his assistant was now in charge until a permanent replacement could be found.

'How very kind of you to come and find me, Dottoressa Salvi,' Caterina said, taking her hand. She addressed her both with her title and in the formal *Lei*.

The contact was fleeting, quite as if Dottoressa Salvi were fearful to entrust her right hand to this other woman for more than a second. She whipped her hand behind her back, embracing it safely with the other.

'Would you care to take a seat?' Caterina asked, deciding to act as though this had always been her office. She turned to her desk and only then realized that there was just the one chair in the room.

Caterina smiled, hoping for a mirror-smile on the other woman's face. Nothing, only attentive politeness. 'Dottoressa,' she said, 'perhaps you could take the chair.'

Her hands still hidden, the other woman said, 'I'm afraid I have to correct you, Dottoressa.'

Here it came, Caterina thought. Territoriality, competition, beat down the newcomer, get the pecking order established: so much for female solidarity. Saying nothing, she smiled again.

'There's been a misunderstanding. I'm not a doctor. Not of anything.' As she spoke, Not-Dottoressa Salvi's face relaxed, and her hands came out from behind her back.

'Ah,' Caterina said, impulsively placing a hand on the other woman's arm, as if to provide comfort. 'No one told me. In fact, no one's told me anything, really.' Then, to ease the situation she said, 'Call me Caterina, please. And no "Dottoressa".'

Signora Salvi smiled, and the snakes surrounding her head turned into mere curls. 'And I'm Roseanna,' she said, avoiding the informal *tu*, no doubt leaving the decision to the Dottoressa.

'Can we call one another "*tu*"?' Caterina asked. 'Since we're working together.' She didn't know if that was precisely true, but at least they did work in the same place, and that was close enough for collegiality.

As usually happens when one person suggests grammatical informality, the mood of the conversation eased with the establishment of equality. Signora Salvi turned towards the door and said, 'Let's go to my office.' Then, with a smile, she added, 'At least it has two chairs.'

In Signora Salvi's office, two doors away from her own, Caterina noticed that the second chair was almost the only difference; that and a larger window looking out to the courtyard behind the building. There was a table just as small as Caterina's. No telephone here, either, but on the table stood something Caterina had not seen for more than a decade: a typewriter. Electric, assuredly, but still a typewriter. Caterina would have been no more astonished had she seen a woman on the street in a crinoline and bloomers. She drew closer and looked at the keyboard. Yes, the letters were all there.

Signora Salvi saw where her attention rested and said, her shoulders raised in a shrug of resignation or apology, 'We don't have a computer any more, so I've been using that.' Remembering her role as hostess, she offered a chair to Caterina. She pulled her own to the side of her desk so that the typewriter was not between them, and sat down.

Each of them waited for the other to break the silence and set the mood until finally Caterina gave in to her simple curiosity – elementary school children did their homework on computers, people used them on trains. 'How is it that an institution like this doesn't have a computer?'

Signora Salvi looked at the typewriter, then at Caterina. 'It was stolen.'

'What happened?'

'Someone broke in one night – it was about three months ago – and took the computer and the printer and some money that was in the drawer,' she said, pointing towards the back of the desk.

'How did they get in?' Caterina asked, thinking of her own tiny window.

'Through there,' Signora Salvi said, indicating the considerably larger window at the back. 'It must have been easy. All they had to do was get into the court-yard, prise open the shutter and break the glass. They didn't take anything else, so far as I could tell. But that's because they couldn't get into the other offices. All of the doors were locked.'

'Were the police here?' Caterina asked.

'Of course. I called them as soon as I saw what had happened.'

'And?'

'Oh, the usual,' Signora Salvi said, as if dealing with the police were part of an annoying daily routine. 'First they acted as though they thought I'd done it, and then they said it was kids stealing things to pay for drugs.'

'Is that all?'

'They told me to get the window fixed,' Signora Salvi said with some evidence of disgust. 'They didn't bother to ask what kind of computer it was or to take fingerprints. Or to ask anything at all, for that matter.' Then, sounding even more disgruntled, she added, 'And they didn't talk to anyone else in the building or to the others that share the court-yard.' She shrugged to dismiss the police, then smiled again.

'How do you get on without it?' Caterina asked, looking at the typewriter as if it were a votive statue of the missing computer.

In a confessional tone, Roseanna said, 'There was really very little in it. I keep the records of any new documents that are added to the collection and answer the letters we receive.' She gave Caterina a very small smile and added, 'The Foundation doesn't really do much, you know. And I'm here only three hours a day. I have to be here in case anyone comes to ask for information.' Her next smile showed signs of embarrassment as she said, 'But no one ever does. Well, once in a while, but not to ask questions: just to use the library.' She gave Caterina, who was busy trying to think of how anyone could possibly use such a library, a long, appraising look and then added in a softer voice. 'They're very peculiar.'

'In what way?'

Signora Salvi shifted around in her seat, and Caterina wondered if she had been made nervous by her own impulsive confidence, or perhaps didn't want to speak badly of the people who, in a sense, helped keep the Foundation running. Caterina smiled to encourage her.

'They look like the people who go and sit in the Marciana all day. I think some of them come here only to keep warm. In the winter, that is, because we're closer to wherever they live than the Marciana is.'

'Do they ask about the music?'

'Almost never. Most of them don't know what the Foundation's for. I don't know how they hear about it, or what they hear: I suppose they tell one another that it's warm and no one will bother them for three hours. But they come, and they sit there. Sometimes they bring a newspaper, or they find one that's been left. Or they sleep.' She gave Caterina a long look, as if assessing her trustworthiness, and then said, 'Sometimes, when it's very cold, I keep it open longer.'

'What are you supposed to be doing?' Caterina asked, curious to learn anything about this place where she was to carry out her research.

'I think, at the beginning – I've worked here only three years – the Fondazione really did what Dottor Dardago wanted: it made contributions to support performances of operas, and it gave money to people who worked on scores and research.' Here she gave a smile Caterina found quite engaging. 'It's all in the files: how much they gave and who they gave it to.' She stopped. 'Then things changed.'

'What happened?'

'The first Director made some bad investments, and the endowment shrank. So the people who are interested in grants stopped asking us for help because we had none to give. Dottor Asnaldi came twelve years ago, and things just kept getting worse.

Then, two years ago, they had another big loss, and Dottor Asnaldi left.'

'Leaving what behind?' Caterina asked, though she had no right to do so.

Roseanna raised a hand and scratched beneath one of her curls, then said, 'There's an accountant who looks at the books every six months, and he says the endowment's almost gone. He thinks there might be enough to keep the office open for another year, at best.'

'And then?'

'And then we close it, I suppose,' Roseanna said and gave a small, disappointed shrug. 'If there's no more money . . .' she began but did not finish the sentence.

'Who decided this? Dottor Moretti?'

'Oh, no. Another lawyer, Fanno, the one who's in charge of the endowment.' Caterina did not recognize the name and did not think it important enough to ask who he was. From the little she had learned and seen, it was evident that the Foundation was not long for this world, not with no computer and no telephone, and with that castrato novel on the shelf. Though she didn't work for the Foundation, curiosity urged her to ask, 'Are there records of the correspondence going back to the beginning?'

'Oh yes,' Signora Salvi said. 'They're upstairs.' She pointed to the ceiling, as if to remove any possible uncertainty Caterina might have had about where upstairs might be.

'Upstairs?'

'In the Director's office.'

'I thought this was the Director's office,' she said.

'Oh, no. I mean Dottor Asnaldi's office – well, his ex-office.' Then in a smaller voice, she added, 'That's where the chests are. In the storeroom. They're safe there.'

3

Like Lot's wife, Caterina turned to salt; unlike the other woman, she turned immediately back into flesh and said, 'But that's im . . .' before she stopped herself, realizing that she had no idea at all where the chests were or could be, just as, in all of this, she had no idea of what was possible or not. The cousins had spoken of the chests as though they belonged in a bank vault, yet here they were, being kept in an apartment with rooms on the ground floor that had windows without bars. Further, it was an apartment thieves had already entered with no difficulty.

Caterina could not understand the Foundation's involvement with the chests. What Roseanna called the endowment was almost finished, the offices could have been in Albania, the heat and access to a place to sit drew a number of not-quite-vagrants to the library, and yet the Foundation was somehow, however peripherally, involved.

Hoping that none of this was visible in her expression, she continued, as though she'd paused to consider the exact word. '. . . impressive, really impressive. To have them safe in a storeroom.' It was the best she could do, and Roseanna smiled in response so Caterina went on, 'How did that happen?'

'The previous owners had the storeroom built into the wall; I don't know why. It was here when the Foundation first rented the apartment: Dottor Asnaldi used to joke about it: sometimes he'd put his umbrella inside and close all the locks.' Then, voice lower, Roseanna asked, 'They told you some of this, didn't they?'

'Perhaps not all of it,' Caterina answered. 'There was a certain lack of background in what I was told, if I might call it that.' Short of a direct request for information, Caterina could have given no clearer message.

'Since you're going to be working on the papers, I suppose you should know where they came from.'

Caterina thanked her.

'One of the cousins called Dottor Asnaldi at home about four months ago. I don't know how he got his number, and I don't remember which one of them it was. He wanted to know if the Dottore would be interested in reading some documents and writing a report on them. All I know is that he met with the two men – the cousins – but he turned down their offer. I never knew why.' Here Roseanna gave the smile/shrug combination that Caterina was beginning to recognize.

Caterina nodded, and Roseanna continued. 'But he called me because he'd left me in charge and said it might be a good idea to keep the papers here, in the storeroom: that's why they're upstairs.'

'I'm surprised they didn't ask the Marciana or the Conservatory, even a bank. That is, if they think the papers might be valuable,' Caterina said.

Absentmindedly, Roseanna ran her hand over the surface of her desk, as if feeling to see if it needed to be waxed. 'It's cheap,' she finally said. 'That is, cheaper.'

'Than?'

'Than the Marciana or the Conservatory or a bank. They offered to pay three hundred Euros a month, and that was in winter, when we had the heating bill to think about.' She opened her hands in a gesture replete with resignation. 'Dottor Asnaldi called me with the suggestion, and I agreed. The others would have cost much more.'

Given that the place had been broken into recently, a bank might also have been safer, though Caterina saw no reason to pass this idea on to Roseanna.

'I was in charge, you see. As Acting Director, I had to sign the contract.'

She seemed so proud of the title that Caterina said

'*Complimenti*', in a low voice, which caused Roseanna to blush.

Feeling that Roseanna's pause was a suggestion that she inquire, Caterina asked, 'What happened then?'

'Dottor Moretti convinced them they should find someone competent to read the papers.'

'Did he think this would settle all their problems and end their dispute?'

'Oh,' Roseanna said with a laugh, 'I don't think the person exists who could do that.'

That lightened the mood and gave Caterina the courage to try to satisfy some of her curiosity. 'Presumably, the trunks are safe up there.'

'Of course. The storeroom is really just a small closet, but it has *una porta blindata*. If you think about it, it's much more than most shops have.' Then, 'There's another, smaller cabinet: that's where the archives are kept.'

'The archives?' Caterina asked.

'The letters,' Roseanna said. 'But Dottor Asnaldi always called them the archives.'

'Where are they?'

Roseanna raised her eyes and gazed at the ceiling, reminding Caterina of the holy cards of Saint Thérèse of Lisieux so often found lying on the tables in the back of empty churches. The hair-snakes on her head, ironed flat, would have looked just like the saint's black veil. 'Upstairs.'

The unsummoned images came to Caterina of

Ugolino imprisoned in the Tower, Vercingetorix in the Mamertine – quickly cancelled because that prison was underground – Casanova escaping from the Piombi. First there was the Director's office, and now there were the archives. How many other things were hidden away on the next floor?

'Upstairs?' Caterina repeated unnecessarily.

'It's in the same room, but it's only a simple wall cabinet with a key.'

'What's kept in the archives?'

'Some scores that Dottor Dardago collected,' Roseanna explained.

'Are they part of the endowment?' Caterina asked, wondering why, if they were, they had not been sold to continue with sponsorship or, at least, alleviate some of the misery around them.

'No. Dottor Dardago left them to the Marciana, to be given to them if the Foundation ever ceased to function. I suppose he didn't want things ever to be sold off, piece by piece. The Foundation merely has the use of them for as long as it's in existence. That's always been very clear.' But then, in a lower, more confidential voice, she added, 'It's only a few things, really: a printed copy of an opera by Porpora and some musical scores.' When Caterina seemed about to ask, Roseanna said, sounding sad to have to say it, as if she were confessing to some minor vulgarity on the Foundation's part, 'No, only copies, and not even from the times they were written.' Then, after a pause, she added, 'I'm afraid Dottor Dardago was an amateur.'

To Caterina, this amateur's collection hardly sounded like something that belonged under lock and key, but her work did not concern the archive, and so she asked nothing further about it.

'How do you get there?' Caterina asked.

Roseanna's glance made her confusion obvious. 'The stairs.'

'Can a person go up there?'

Roseanna made as if to push away Caterina's question. 'I don't know if you can go up there yet.'

Like most people, Caterina disliked being told she could not do something. Like most professional women who had risen in a male-dominated profession by dint of skill and tenacity and superior talent that was never acknowledged and could seldom be admitted, she had learned to stifle her instinctive desire to shout at the source of the prohibition, though she had never learned to control the pounding of the heart that resulted from unexplained opposition.

After a few moments, Caterina asked, in a voice she managed to make sound entirely normal, 'Sooner or later, I have to go up, don't I? If I'm going to be working there.' Recalling something, she added, 'You mentioned that you receive letters. Would it be possible for me to have a look at them?' When Roseanna did not respond, she continued, 'It's possible that people who contacted the Foundation in the past – with real musicological information or questions, that is – might be the sort of amateur a researcher dreams of finding.' The only dream researchers had about amateurs and their suggestions were night-mares, but Roseanna need not be told this.

'We never know what will be useful,' she added with a broad smile meant to include Roseanna in that 'we'. 'Whose rule is it, anyway?'

Roseanna thought for a moment and then said, 'It's not a rule, really. It's just that the cousins are rather . . .'

'Secretive?'

This time her smile was bigger than her shrug.

Caterina smiled in return and said, unwilling to admit to no motive higher than her own mounting curiosity about the Foundation, 'All I want to do is save time by learning if there are any people who might eventually be able to help in the research.' As if confessing uncertainty to a friend, she said, 'I don't know if it will help me with these documents, but it might be useful to know who the interested people are: they often know a lot more than the experts do, especially in a field as narrow as this one.' It was lame, and she knew it, but Roseanna might not.

Apparently sufficient good will had been restored because Roseanna got to her feet, saying, 'I suppose you can.' Then, with a smile of solidarity, she added, 'Besides, I'm the Acting Director, aren't I?'

She led the way from her office, turning towards the back of the building. The hallway ended in a door. She took a set of keys from her pocket, opened the door, and started up a set of steps. Caterina followed. At the top, another door led into a small entrance corridor with wooden doors facing one another.

Roseanna opened the door on the left and let them into an office complete with barred windows. The desk was large, and a dark wooden cabinet was fitted into the wall to the left of it. On either side of the cabinet hung etchings of bewigged men. Even from this distance, Caterina recognized round-faced Jommelli. The other might have been Hasse. She liked him: any man who would marry Faustina Bordoni had to be a hero.

Roseanna nodded towards the wooden cabinet, saying, 'All of the correspondence is in there.' Caterina saw that the key was in the lock. Looking around for the storeroom, she noticed a pair of smooth metal doors, almost a metre high, set into the wall to the right of the desk and partly blocked from her sight by the desk and the chair.

Pointedly ignoring those doors, she asked, 'How far back does the correspondence date, Roseanna?'

'To the beginning.'

'What do people write about?' Caterina asked with genuine interest.

'Oh, all sorts of things. You'd be amazed. Some send us copies of manuscripts or scores and ask us to identify them or verify the handwriting, and some ask for biographical information about the composers. Or what we think of new CDs, or whether we think it's worth going to see a particular production. We've even been sent documents and manuscripts, but never anything of great importance. There's no telling. If you read through the files, you'll get an idea.'

'If it's no trouble,' Caterina said, interested in the letters and wanting to show Roseanna that she had come up here in good faith and not in the hope of learning the identity of the composer whose manuscripts might well be behind those thick metal doors, doors she continued to ignore.

Roseanna turned the key of the cabinet, latched her fingers expertly under the side of one door, and pulled it open. The other swung after it.

Caterina had met Roseanna only a brief time ago, but she had seen enough – the conservative clothing, the neatness with which the snakes were wrapped around one another – to know she could not have been responsible for the chaos inside the cabinet.

There were two shelves, each sized to hold Manila folders, and on each of them files lay splashed about. Some leaked papers, others appeared untouched; still others were strewn across the shelves as if flung by a heavy wind.

Roseanna's gasp was entirely involuntary. '*Maria Vergine*,' she exclaimed. No liar, Caterina thought, would say that. Then Roseanna gave her astonishment an upgrade and whispered, '*Oddio*.'

When she reached for the files, Caterina said 'No, Roseanna. Don't touch anything.'

'What?'

'Don't touch anything,' she repeated.

The other woman looked at her with open curiosity.

Then, 'I don't want the police here again,' she said with sudden energy.

Caterina leaned closer to the shelves. 'But look at it. Someone's been through those papers.' Remembering no doubt what she had seen in the cinema, she asked, 'Who else has a key to this room?'

'I do. That's all.'

'Dottor Moretti gave me one to the building,' Caterina said, wondering how difficult it would be to get into this office. 'So no one else has one?' she asked. From Roseanna's expression she saw she had gone too far. She tried to modify the effect by continuing, as if naturally, 'It must be a terrible shock for you, Roseanna. To have someone come in and do this.' Her tactic of excluding Roseanna as a possible suspect was as crude as it was obvious.

Caterina ran through what she knew about the police: their first suspects would be anyone with keys to the building. Or, learning that the disturbance – she didn't even know if it had been a theft – concerned correspondence about centuries-old music and the men who wrote it, they would simply leave. That is, if they came in the first place.

In her most placatory tone, Caterina said, 'You're right, of course. This is not for the police.' That made them partners and equally complicit.

'What's missing?' Caterina moved away from the cabinet, as if to give physical evidence of her trust in Roseanna's competence. Her sister Cinzia had been involved with an anthropologist for some years and had passed on to her sisters what she had learned from him about dominance displays in simians. Caterina thought of this as she moved back from the desk, leaving access to the cabinet entirely to Roseanna.

The Acting Director gathered the files on each shelf into a stack, tapping papers back inside the folders. She put the first pile on the desk and beside them those from the shelf below. Then she opened each file and straightened the papers until she had them in an order she seemed to like.

She returned to the top file on the first stack and began to page through the letters; Caterina, to disguise her impatience, went and studied the second portrait to see if there was a name printed at the bottom. Beside her, Roseanna methodically opened one file after another, fingering through the papers in each.

Caterina returned her attention to the men with the wigs.

'Caterina,' Roseanna said.

'Sì?'

'I don't understand this,' she said hesitantly.

'What?'

'Nothing seems to be missing.'

4

'What?' Caterina asked, amazed that someone would have gone to the trouble of breaking in and then not have taken anything. What she had seen did not suggest vandalism. Nothing had spilled out of the cabinet, nothing had been destroyed. There were signs of a hasty, careless search: nothing more.

Roseanna gave her a Manila folder. Neatly typed (yes, typed) on the flap was 'Sartorio, Antonio, 1630–1680.'

'What's in it?' Caterina asked as she handed it back without opening it.

'The letters we've received over the years concerning him,' Roseanna said, hefting it in her right hand as if she could judge by the weight.

'Everything seems to be here,' Roseanna said. 'And in this one,' she added, passing another file to Caterina. 'But I can check.'

Caterina began to read the top letter in the file she held, which was in German and addressed to the Director of the Foundation by title and not by name. The writer began by saying that, the last time he had been in Venice, he had been unable to find Hasse's grave in the church of San Marcuola and asked, in a peremptory manner, why the Foundation had not seen to the placing of a memorial plaque in the church. The writer was a member of the Hasse Society in . . .

Caterina pulled her attention from the letter and asked, 'What did you just say?'

'I wanted to check if anything's missing from the Porpora file.'

'How?' Caterina asked, suddenly interested.

Roseanna turned back to the cabinet and reached inside. She placed her hand on one of the decorative knobs on the inlaid panels that ran perpendicular to the shelves. She gave it a sharp twist, and the panel tilted forward and down, revealing a vertical drawer the width of the panel, about ten centimetres. Reaching in, she pulled out a student's notebook, on its cover the bronze equestrian statue of Marcus Aurelius.

She set the notebook on the desk, opened it near the front, and pressed it flat by running her hand down the centre. She placed the file she was holding beside the notebook and removed the letters. Methodically, she paged through them, each time putting her forefinger on an entry in the notebook: it was too far from Caterina for her to read. When she had checked every letter, Roseanna turned to her and said, 'They're all here.'

'May I?' Caterina asked and picked up the notebook.

'Porpora' was written at the top of the page on the left, and below it were columns that listed the date of the arrival of the letter, the name and address of the person who sent it, and the date the letter was answered.

'Why do you keep it?' Caterina asked in a voice she made as neutral as she could.

Roseanna pursed her lips in embarrassment, carefully avoiding Caterina's gaze. 'I've always kept permanent records of things, even my gas bills. It's just a habit of mine, I suppose. This way, if anything goes missing or gets misfiled, I've got a record that it did arrive. I've kept it since I started here.' Head lowered, she added, 'I began it with all the correspondence that was already here and kept adding to it over the years.'

Caterina stopped herself from asking if the Foundation had a website or email address or any evidence that it was functioning in the current millennium.

She thought of the letter complaining about Hasse's grave: such things did not lead to burglary. 'Can you remember anyone asking a strange question or making a threat?' she asked.

'Some of the letters are strange,' Roseanna said. Then, as if hearing a playback, she slapped her hand over her mouth.

Caterina didn't bother to fight the impulse and laughed out loud. 'You should have seen some of the people I took classes with.' Swept away by memory, she added, 'Or from,' and that set her off again.

Roseanna resisted, then gave in and said, laughing, 'If you think they're strange, you should see the people who come here. Not the ones who come to sleep: the ones who come to ask questions.'

Still laughing, Caterina waved a hand in the air. She knew, she knew. She'd spent a decade of her life with them.

'The ones who write letters are usually better,' Roseanna told her. 'There's an elderly gentleman in Pavia who still listens to phonograph records. He writes and asks for suggestions about which ones to buy. Would you believe it?' Roseanna shook her head at this. This was a woman who still used a typewriter, Caterina thought.

Caterina took the notebook and, knowing that Roseanna's list would be in alphabetical order, paged back from 'Porpora' to 'Hasse'. The letters in the file dated back twelve years; for Caldara a bit more than that, though there were only two letters.

She flipped back towards the end, passed 'Sartorio' and found 'Steffani'.

'Why is it that the entries for Steffani start so recently, Roseanna?'

'Oh, he's been forgotten for a long time,' Roseanna answered.

'I see,' Caterina said. She remembered seeing his portrait in a book she had once read: round face and sagging chin, bishop's cap with white hair sneaking out on both sides, long fingers caressing the cross he wore across his chest. The man had been dead for almost three centuries. Caterina closed the notebook and set it on the table. As she did, her eyes were drawn to the photo of the statue. Marcus Aurelius. Emperor. Hero. Blamed by generations of historians for having passed the throne to his son Commodus, as if they thought he should have remained childless. Childless. Without heirs.

Illumination flashed upon her, forcing out an involuntary grunt, as though someone had punched her in the stomach. 'Marco Aurelio,' she pronounced. 'Of course, of course.'

Startled, Roseanna turned to her. 'What's wrong? What's the matter?' She dropped a file on the table and put her hand on Caterina's arm. 'What's wrong?'

'Marco Aurelio,' Caterina repeated.

Roseanna looked at the cover of the notebook. 'Yes, I know, but what's wrong with you?'

Caterina rubbed her forehead, then tapped her fingers lightly against her head a few times. 'Of course, of course,' she repeated. Then, to Roseanna, she said, 'The trunks belonged to Steffani, didn't they?'

The other woman's mouth dropped open. 'Who told you? They said no one was to say anything until the person they chose started to work on the papers. How did you find out?' When Caterina remained silent, Roseanna took her arm again, this time with greater force. 'Tell me.'

Caterina pointed to the notebook. 'That told me,' she said.

It was obvious that Roseanna had no idea what she was talking about. She picked up the notebook and paged through it, as if Caterina had seen the answer written inside. 'I don't understand,' she confessed.

'I remembered,' Caterina said. 'Things I read when I was at university. His first opera was *Marco Aurelio*.' Roseanna gave no sign of recognition, but how many people would know this? 'And I remembered reading that he had no direct heirs, and no one ever knew what happened to his possessions after his death.' The Church was mixed up in it, too, she recalled but could not remember the details.

Roseanna went and sat behind the desk. It was the Director's desk and the Director's chair, yet she looked like anything but a Director. She leaned forward and propped her chin on her hand. 'Yes. You're right. It's Steffani.' She pronounced it with the accent on the first syllable, as an Italian would. As Steffani had not.

'I don't see what difference it makes,' Roseanna went on in a voice grown suddenly brisk. 'Really. You would have known as soon as you started reading and found his name in the papers. It's those two men,' she said, her voice growing warmer. 'Everything has to be secret. No one can know anything. If one of them saw that the other one's hair was on fire, he wouldn't say anything.' Her tone was a mixture of anger and exasperation. 'They're terrible men. One's worse than the other.'

'The cousins?' Caterina asked.

Roseanna raised her head and gave an angry flip of her hand. 'What cousins? They're just two men who smell the possibility of money. That's the way they're related.' Then, after a moment's reflection, 'And in mutual suspicion.'

'Are they really his descendants?' Caterina asked. 'Steffani's?'

'Oh, they are, they are.'

'How do they know that? Or prove it?'

Here Roseanna gave a snort, either of disgust or anger. Then she gave Caterina a sudden, assessing look and said, 'It's the Mormons.'

'I beg your pardon?' Steffani, she remembered, had been a clergyman, so where'd the Mormons come from? 'He was a priest, wasn't he? And long before the Mormons.'

'Oh, I know that,' Roseanna said. 'But that's how you can find your ancestors. By asking them.'

Caterina, who took very little interest in her own ancestors, could hardly imagine asking the Mormons to look for them. 'What have the Mormons got to do with this?'

Roseanna smiled and waved her fingers before her face to suggest a lack of mental stability. 'It's what they believe, or at least what Dottor Moretti told me they believe. They can go back and baptize people in the past.' Her expression showed how much faith she put in this possibility.

Caterina stared at her for a long moment. 'You think you can marry them in the past, too, and inherit their money?'

It took Roseanna a moment to realize this was a joke, then she laughed, losing a decade as she did. She wiped her eyes and said, her voice a bit rough after laughing so hard, 'It would be convenient, wouldn't it?' She considered the possibilities and said, 'I suppose I could marry Gianni Agnelli.' Then, with a careful attention to fact that made Caterina admire her, she added, 'No, he lived too long. I'd want someone who died young.'

Caterina stopped herself from naming a candidate or two and returned to the business at hand.

Wiping away a few vagrant tears and still smiling, Roseanna said, 'Dottor Moretti told me they're very good at tracing people's ancestry, and they're generous about giving the information.'

'How do they do it? This is a Catholic country. And parts of Germany are, too.' This rang another historical bell: Steffani had been mixed up in the squabbles between the Protestants and the Catholics. How long ago it was, and how futile such things seemed now. Before his time, people died disputing how many angels could dance on the head of a pin, or whether the Host was real flesh or merely a symbol. During his lifetime, the wars still went on. She shook her head at the thought of it: how many millions had died for those angels and for that flesh/non-flesh Host? Centuries later, and the churches are empty except for old people and kids with badly tuned guitars.

'What's wrong?' Roseanna asked.

'Nothing,' Caterina said. 'I was just trying to remember what I read as a student about Steffani.'

'There are books about him in the Marciana, I'm sure,' Roseanna said. 'I haven't read about him, but some of the others are fascinating. Gesualdo killed his wife and her lover, and he was a hunchback, too. Porpora went bankrupt, and all I ever read about Cavalli said he sat around all day, writing operas.'

Caterina gave her a long look, as if seeing a different person, but said nothing.

'I like this music, so I started reading about it, and about the composers. The Conservatory has books, but they wouldn't let me use the library.' From her tone, it was difficult to tell whether she was offended. But then she smiled. 'At the Marciana, when I told them I was the Assistant Director here, they let me use them.'

'Good for you,' Caterina said with a blossoming smile.

'Thank you,' Roseanna said in a voice best suited to confession. 'And their lives were interesting.

Besides, if I work here, I should know something about what we're doing, shouldn't I?'

First the woman wanted to marry the richest man in Italy, and now she struck a death blow to every political appointee in the country. What would she want next? A functioning political system? The Philosopher King?

'Tell me more about the Mormons,' Caterina said.

It looked as if Roseanna might have preferred talking about the music, but she said, 'Dottor Moretti's used them before. He said they have files going back hundreds of years: you can trace your family back all those generations.'

'So these two cousins can trace their ancestry back to Steffani?'

'To his cousins, they could: that's how they're descended. The Mormons have copies of parish registers from all over Italy, and they sent Dottor Moretti copies of all of the documents: birth certificates, death certificates, marriage contracts.'

Caterina thought of the two cousins: she doubted that they would be more computer savvy than Roseanna. 'Who did it for them?' Caterina asked. 'The online search?'

'Not them. The Mormons did it all.'

'Interesting,' Caterina said. 'There was no will, was there?'

'No one could find one, so the Church claimed everything; some things were sold to pay his debts, and the rest was lost until the trunks turned up.'

Caterina sat back in her chair and studied her feet. The cousins had no interest in the contents of the trunks, save for what price they might bring; if they were the papers of what her profession would call a major minor composer, dead almost three centuries, what was their value? The Stabat Mater was a masterpiece, and the few opera arias she knew were wonderful, though strangely short to the modern ear. She'd gone down to London to see *Niobe* a few years ago and found it a revelation. What was that heartbreaking lament, something about *'Dal mio petto'*? With a key change towards the end that had driven her wild when she heard it and then again when a musician friend had shown her the score. But her personal excitement would hardly influence the price put on a manuscript. A page of a score by Mozart was worth a fortune, or one by Bach, or Handel, but who had ever heard of Steffani? And yet the cousins were willing to hire a lawyer/arbitrator and pay her salary? For two trunks they thought were full of papers?

Some English poet she had read at school said that Fortune went up and down like a 'bucket in a well'. So did the fortune of composers as taste changed and reputations were re-evaluated. The roads to concert houses were littered with the bones of the reputations of composers like Gassmann, Tosi, Keiser. Every so often, some long-dead composer would be resurrected and hailed as the new master: she had seen it happen with Hildegard von Bingen and Josquin des

Prez. For a year or so no concert hall was without at least one performance of their music. And then they went back to being dead and written about in books, which is where Caterina thought they both belonged. But if what she had heard in London was any indication, Steffani did not belong there, not at all.

'Are you listening, Caterina?' she heard Roseanna ask.

'No, I'm sorry,' she said with an embarrassed grin. 'I was thinking about something else.'

'What?'

'That no one much values Steffani's music these days.' She said it with regret, thinking of the beauty of the arias and the mastery shown in the Stabat Mater. Maybe it was time for a return to the stage for the good Bishop?

'It's not the music those two are after,' Roseanna said.

'What is it, then?' Caterina asked, wondering what else might have lasted and come down through the centuries.

'The treasure.'

5

The word astonished her. 'Treasure?' she repeated. 'What treasure?'

'He didn't tell you?' Roseanna asked.

'Who?' Caterina asked. Then, 'Tell me what?'

'Dottor Moretti. He must know about it,' Roseanna said, sounding surprised. 'I thought he'd have told you when you accepted the job.'

Caterina, who had been strolling along a beach, looking idly at the shells underfoot, was swept away by an unexpected wave. The water, she realized, was deeper than she had expected. She thought of the two cousins, and there came a sudden vision of sharp fins slicing through the waters. To escape this fantasy, she put her hand on Roseanna's arm and said, 'Believe me. I don't have any idea what you're talking about.'

'*Ma, ti xe Venexiana*?' Roseanna asked, exaggerating the pronunciation of the words.

Caterina nodded: she had been away from home so long that Italian now came more easily to her than did the language she had heard at home as a child, but still dialect was the language of her bones.

'You're Venetian and you don't know anything about those two?' she asked, leading Caterina away from the idea of treasure.

'The usurer and the man with the fleet of water taxis who has almost no income?' Caterina said, and Roseanna gave her a look that was the equivalent of a stamp in her passport. To know that much about them was to be Venetian.

'What else do you know?' she asked Caterina.

'That Stievani's sons and nephews drive the taxis. And make a fortune. All undeclared, of course.'

'And Scapinelli?'

'That he's a convicted usurer but still works in the shops of his sons. Who are not angels, either.'

Roseanna considered all of this for some time and asked, moving even further away from any mention of treasure, 'Is your mother Margherita Rossi?'

'Yes.'

'And her father played in the Fenice orchestra?'

'Yes. Violin.'

'Then I know your family,' Roseanna said and sighed. 'Your grandfather used to give my father opera tickets.' She did not sound at all pleased at the memory, or perhaps her displeasure resulted from the obligations imposed upon her by that memory.

Caterina had the sense to remain quiet and wait and allow Roseanna to decide how to tell things. 'They're very bad men,' Roseanna said and then added, by way of explication, 'They come of bad families. One side was originally from Castelfranco; the other's from Padova, I think. But they've been here in the city for generations. Greed's in their bones.'

Suddenly tired of what sounded like melodrama and overcome with impatience, Caterina said, 'And what about treasure? Where does that come from?'

'No one knows,' Roseanna said.

'Does anyone know where it is?' Caterina asked.

Roseanna shook her head and abruptly got to her feet. 'Let's go for a coffee,' she said, and headed for the door without waiting to see if Caterina followed her.

Outside, Caterina stopped in the *calle*. It had been years since she had been in this part of the city, so she had no idea which bars still served decent coffee.

Roseanna stood for a moment, moving her head from side to side, like a hunting dog testing the air for the temperature or passing prey. 'Come on,' she finally said, turning to the right and, at the first corner, right again. 'We can go to that place in Campo Santa Maria Formosa.'

There were two of them, Caterina remembered, the

one with the outside benches that remained in place until the really cold weather arrived and the one opposite it, along the canal, that she had been told – and thereafter always believed – had once been the room where the bodies of the dead in the parish were kept before being taken out to the cemetery on San Michele.

They walked down Ruga Giuffa, making small talk: admiring this or that, pointing to a perfume they had once tried but got tired of. Because they were Venetian, they also commented on the shops that were gone and what had come after them: the wonderful place that sold bathroom fixtures replaced by the cheapest of fake-leather bags and belts.

After crossing the bridge, Roseanna continued straight across the *campo*, to Caterina's relief avoiding the bar alongside the canal. In front of the other bar, Roseanna stopped and asked, 'Inside or outside?' This time, it was Caterina who tested the temperature before saying, 'Inside, I'm afraid.' But before they went in, she pointed to the near corner and asked, 'What happened to that *palazzo*?' As Caterina recalled, the building, as Steffani's chests were now, had been at the centre of a contested inheritance, but in this case rumour said it concerned first and second wives, a far more deadly game.

'A hotel,' Roseanna said, making no attempt to disguise her disgust. 'They hacked it up inside and brought in cheap imitation furniture, and now tourists can tell themselves they're staying in a real

Venetian *palazzo*.' She pushed open the door and went into the bar. Caterina saw that there was nowhere to sit and delighted in the fact. She had had enough of *gemütlich* coffee houses with velvet benches and whipped cream everywhere: alongside the strudel, inside the cakes, on top of the coffee. Here a person stood, drank a coffee in one swift gulp, and went back to the business of the day.

Roseanna called the barman by name and asked for two coffees, which arrived almost instantly and were as quickly consumed. Roseanna did not speak, nor did Caterina: so much for the idea of an intimate conversation. Back outside, Caterina glanced at her watch and saw it was just after eleven, so she turned left and headed towards the bridge that would take them back to the Foundation. 'You still haven't told me about the treasure,' she said, deciding that push had come to shove.

Roseanna, walking beside her, nodded, then said, 'I know. It's so crazy I'm almost embarrassed to talk about it. And I don't know how much you're supposed to be told.'

Caterina stopped before the bridge and pulled Roseanna aside to keep her out of the way of the people passing by. 'Roseanna, I know who it's all about, and I know what type of men the cousins are, and now you've told me there's some sort of treasure: it doesn't take much imagination to understand that's why they're so interested in the trunks and the papers.' Tired of all the secrecy, she spoke before she thought. 'What do they think the applicants who didn't get the job are doing? Not telling people about all of this?'

As often happened with her, the more she thought about the situation, the more her anger grew. What in God's name do these fools think is in the trunks, the manuscript of Monteverdi's lost *Arianna*? A missing papal tiara? Saint Veronica's veil?

Roseanna started to speak, but Caterina ignored her. 'You're the one who mentioned it, who used the word "treasure". I didn't. So tell me what this is all about.' Her heart was pounding, sweat stood on her forehead, but she stopped because she realized there was no threat she could make. She needed the job: the scholar she had once been was curious to follow the paper trail that led back to Steffani.

Roseanna moved away from her but made no attempt to go back across the bridge. She looked down at her shoes, shifted her bag from one shoulder to the other. 'First, let me tell you there were no other applicants. Only you.'

'Then why did they tell me there were?' Caterina all but bleated.

'Capitalism,' Roseanna said.

'What?'

'To beat your price down.' She smiled, and Caterina saw the force of her logic. 'If you thought there were a lot of people after the job, you'd be willing to let them pay you less than you're worth.'

Caterina raised a hand to cover her face from the embarrassment of it.

Roseanna latched her arm into Caterina's and turned towards the bridge, pulling Caterina along beside her. 'All right,' she said. 'I'll tell you what I think is happening.'

The story she told was at times unclear, her telling of it filled with backups and turnarounds, with omissions and additions, and corrections and afterthoughts, with what she had heard at the Foundation, read, and imagined. In essence, it filled in some of the gaps left in the story Caterina had been told by Dottor Moretti and had inferred from her meetings with the cousins. Letters from Steffani existed in which he spoke of the poverty of his life. When she heard Roseanna say this, Caterina tried to recall ever having seen a letter from a Baroque composer – indeed, any composer – who complained of the excessive richness of his life. But there also existed a letter – Roseanna had indeed put in her time reading at the Marciana – written in the last year of his life in which he mentioned some of the objects in his possession, among them books and pictures and a casket and jewels. The catalogue of the more than five hundred books he owned listed first editions of Luther, which would be of enormous value today.

'Is that the treasure?'

Roseanna stopped and pulled her arm free to raise it, along with the other, in a gesture of complete exasperation. 'My God, listen to me. We don't even know if there are papers in the chests – or what's in them – and here I am, talking about treasure. The whole thing's crazy.'

Caterina took great comfort from the other woman's unconscious use of the plural. And yet Roseanna had a point in saying that they were all crazy: Caterina was swiftly approaching the same view. If the cousins had learned of the possibility of unearned wealth, Caterina had seen enough of them to know they would be driven wild by the thought of 'treasure'.

As to the chance that any papers in the trunk would lead to the discovery of a treasure, Caterina was less certain: it was unlikely that any treasure – whatever it was – would still be resting, safely undiscovered, in the place where it had been put. Realizing that her speculations led nowhere, Caterina asked, 'What else did you find out?' Producing her easiest and most relaxed smile, she coaxed, 'I had to do a lot of that sort of reading while I was in school; it's comforting to know that someone else finds it interesting.'

Roseanna, who had been spared the experience of reading back issues of *Studies in Early-Baroque Counterpoint*, gave Caterina an uncertain glance and said, 'I understood only the historical parts, not the musicological.'

'Good,' Caterina said with a smile, 'the historical part's usually more interesting.'

This earned her another puzzled glance, enough to warn her to treat her profession with greater seriousness. 'What else did you read?'

'One of the articles said that his possessions went

to a Vatican organization called Propaganda Fide and disappeared, then these two trunks turned up a few years ago when an inventory was made. Somehow the cousins managed to have them sent here: I was never told how that happened.'

Caterina saw there was little to be gained from trying to penetrate the mysteries created by the cousins. Thinking out loud and returning to the question of the trunks, Caterina said, 'If they were autograph scores, then the music would have a certain value.'

'What does "certain value" mean?' Roseanna asked.

'I have no idea. That usually depends on how famous the composer is and how many of his manuscripts are on the market. But Steffani's star isn't in the ascendant, so no one's going to be paying a fortune for whatever might be there.'

Nudged by curiosity, Caterina asked, 'Did Dottor Moretti tell you when they'd come to open the chests?'

'Noon,' Roseanna said and looked at her watch. Then, sounding like a guilty schoolgirl and not at all like the Acting Director of the Fondazione Musicale Italo-Tedesca, she said, 'We better get back.'

6

They had been in Roseanna's office only a few minutes when they heard the front door open and close. Footsteps approached, and then Dottor Moretti was in the doorway. Just as she remembered him: dark grey suit with a faint stripe of lighter grey, dark blue tie with a stripe so discreet as to reveal itself only under torture. Caterina was certain he would be able to comb his hair in the reflection from his shoes, were it not that a man such as Dottor Moretti would never comb his hair in public. He'd give it a discreet tap, perhaps a faint stroke in the wake of a heavy wind. But a comb? Never.

He was a tidy man, not tall and not short, a few centimetres taller than she. His hair, neither dark nor light, was thick and cut short, already turning white at the temples. The oval lenses of his gold-framed glasses were so clean that she wondered if he wore a new pair every day. His nose was narrow and straight, his eyes a very pale blue, hardly the eyes of the cliché Italian, though perhaps those of the cliché Veneziano. Caterina doubted, however, that dialect ever passed those lips: in the few conversations they had had, he had used an easy elegance of language, as if he had chosen to speak as an adult from his very first words. She had no idea of what part of the country he came from, and his speech provided no clue.

A grey woollen topcoat was folded over his arm, and the other hand held the briefcase she had noticed before: smooth brown leather with twin brass locks that looked as though someone gave them a very careful buffing at least once a week. Caterina, a great admirer of men's clothing and often of the men who wore it, coveted the bag.

Dottor Moretti looked to be in his early forties, though from the faint wrinkles around his eyes his age might be greater. He seemed to smile only when a remark amused him; Caterina had found herself, when last they spoke, trying to make him smile, perhaps even to laugh. It had taken her no time to realize that he was responsive to language used well; as to his feelings about music, she had no idea.

'Signore,' he said with a small bow to both of them that, had another man made it, would have been faintly ridiculous. As made by Dottor Moretti, it was a show of respect and attention, meant perhaps to be read as a man's declaration that he lived to serve these ladies' wishes. Caterina, remembering that he was a lawyer, dismissed that idea and chose to read it as an old-fashioned gesture from that marvel of marvels, an old-fashioned man.

'Dottore,' she said, getting to her feet and extending her hand. 'A great pleasure to see you again.'

'The pleasure is once more entirely mine, Dottoressa,' he said, releasing her hand. He turned immediately and offered it to Roseanna, who rose from her desk to take it, saying only, *'Buon giorno, Dottore.'*

Dottor Moretti set his briefcase on the floor against Roseanna's desk. She gave a half-wave, half-shrug that presented the surface of her desk as the one place where he might sit in this two-chaired room. Caterina was interested to see how he would react. He did not surprise her: he folded his coat, placed it neatly on the desk, then leaned back against it and folded his arms.

'I'm glad you're both here,' he began. 'Signor Stievani and Signor Scapinelli should arrive at noon. This gives me the chance to speak to you before they get here.'

'To tell us what?' Roseanna asked. So far, Caterina noted, nothing she said to Moretti had required her to choose between the polite or the familiar form of address. Linguistically, then, they could be friends, they could be enemies, they could be lovers. Roseanna's manner with him, however, suggested equal parts of interest and deference, effectively eliminating the second possibility.

Ignoring her question, Dottor Moretti continued. 'They're very eager for Dottoressa Pellegrini to begin work.'

'Today, I hope,' Caterina said. Did he think she had stopped in to borrow a cup of sugar from Roseanna? 'Yes.'

'The sooner she reads through it all, the sooner they can stop paying her salary,' Roseanna observed in a dead level voice entirely free of irony or sarcasm. Time is money, she was Venetian: that's the way things are.

Again ignoring Roseanna's comment, Moretti asked Caterina, 'Do you have any objection to beginning so soon, Dottoressa?'

She smiled. 'Quite the opposite, Dottore. I'm very eager to begin and discover what treasures . . .' she began, giving the briefest pause, '. . . await us in those chests.'

His glance was quick, and he turned it immediately into a smile. 'I compliment you on your energy and eagerness, Dottoressa. I'm sure we all look forward to the results of your research.'

'That can't be all those two want,' Roseanna said. Dottor Moretti gave her a long, assessing look, as if surprised at this unwonted frankness in front of the researcher who, like him, was meant to be entirely neutral. He bent down and snapped open his briefcase. He pulled out some papers and handed one to

Caterina, keeping another for himself. 'I've spoken to the two . . .' and here he gave a pause even more infinitesimal than Caterina's '. . . gentlemen, about the procedure for the research.'

'Procedure?' Roseanna asked before Caterina could speak.

'If you'll take a look,' he said, raising the paper and peering over the top of his glasses at Caterina, 'you'll see written what I've already told you: that they want written reports.' He glanced back at the paper and read aloud, '". . . with a summary of the documents read and translations of any that might refer to our deceased relative's desires regarding the disposition of his worldly assets."'

Caterina enjoyed the words, which the cousins must have learned from Dottor Moretti: 'deceased relative', 'disposition of his worldly assets'. Ah, what a marvel language was, and blessed they who respected it.

'The Dottoressa is not to have private or personal contact with either of the two . . .' again that pause '. . . gentlemen. In the event that she has information to convey, or in response to any request from either of the two parties that she provide further information about the documents, it must be provided to me and the two parties at the same time. Further, all emails must go through me.' He glanced at Caterina, who nodded in understanding and acceptance, deciding to wait before asking about the computer on which she was meant to send these emails. Before leaving Manchester, she had returned to the university the laptop it provided to all researchers and had only her own desktop, which she had no intention of bringing from her apartment.

'And,' he went on, looking up and through the lenses of his glasses as he said this, 'in the event that either of them should request a meeting to explain any of the documents, they must both agree to the time and place, and I'm afraid I must be present at any such meeting.'

With a small smile, Caterina said, 'I hope your fear does not result from the thought of my presence, Dottore.'

This earned her one of his smiles. 'Only from the thought that my presence might not be as enjoyable as theirs is sure to be,' he replied.

Caterina returned her attention to the paper he had given her. Was a lawyer supposed to speak of his clients this way? The cousins might have enough money to pay a man wearing a suit like his, but they seemed to lack the price of his respect. They must be very sure of Dottor Moretti's ability to find the best person to lead them to whatever treasure there might be, but then she remembered what Roseanna had said about Caterina's being the only person interviewed, and she wondered how concerned the cousins were about anything except price. Further, was she meant to be complimented or flattered by the slighting way he spoke of them, as if to suggest he was being open and honest with her?

'I see there are other conditions,' she said, holding

up her copy of the paper. 'What's this about having to read any papers in the order in which I find them?' she asked tersely. 'Of course I will.' She felt her voice growing sharp and paused a moment to try to relax. 'How else would a scholar go through papers?' Her visceral resentment told her a good deal about the way she felt about the cousins.

'Unfortunately,' Dottor Moretti began, putting on a serious face, 'I did not make the list of requirements, Dottoressa, nor is it in my competence to question them. They were given to me, and it's my task to persuade you to follow them.'

'Of course, I'll follow them,' she said, 'but these gentlemen might consider the fact that they are paying me for my expertise, and part of that is knowing how to deal with documents.' In the face of his silence – neither obstinate nor patient; just silence – she went on, 'I have only a general histor- ical context for any documents I might find,' she said. 'I'm at home in the music of the period, but I foresee needing to do research beyond reading the actual documents.' He said nothing, and so she concluded, 'I would like to establish that as one of my conditions.'

'One?' he asked.

She held up the paper and said, 'I haven't finished reading this yet. There might be more.'

Roseanna broke in and said, 'Perhaps they're hoping that there will be a folder on the top with neat lettering on the outside, saying, "Last will and testament". And below it in a different hand, just to save time: "List of everything of value and where to find it".' If she was trying to make a joke, one glance at Dottor Moretti's face showed she had not succeeded.

'You've told me he died intestate,' Caterina said. 'I can only hope I do find a will among the papers, or something in which he makes his desires known. But I'd still have to read the rest of the papers, of course, to see that he did not subsequently contradict this.'

If she had expected surprise or disagreement from Dottor Moretti, she was mistaken. 'Naturally,' he muttered and then gestured towards the paper in her hand, as if to suggest she finish reading it.

'And this,' she said, tapping at the paper with her finger: 'that I will not write anything – article or book – about any personal information contained in the trunks and that I will not speak of it in public or private. Not until I am given permission by both of the heirs, as well as by you.' She paused briefly and then asked, feeling a flutter of anger at what she saw as petty, ignorant obstructionism, 'I assume this does not apply to my reports?' Her smile was falsity itself.

Dottor Moretti used the universal gesture of surrender and held up both hands in front of his chest. 'I don't make the rules, Dottoressa: I only transmit them.' Then, with a small smile, he added, 'If you'll continue reading, Dottoressa, you'll see that this prohibition does not extend to any musicological information that might be contained in the documents.'

'Meaning?' she asked.

'Meaning that you have the exclusive rights to edit any scores that might be found, whether of orchestral or vocal music, that you judge to be of artistic importance.' He pointed to his copy, and she found the sentence on hers.

She kept her face impassive as she read, though this hope had at least partially animated her willingness to toss over the job in Manchester: most musicologists would have traded their first born for this opportunity. Two chests possibly filled with the papers of a once-famous composer of the Baroque period. They could contain operas, many of his famous chamber duets, unpublished arias. And she would be the one to write the articles and edit the scores. Boosey & Hawkes, she knew, had begun to publish Baroque music: she also knew she could not find a better company. If anything could launch her career, this was it.

She nodded, as if this were a normal part of any job she'd ever had. Then she asked, 'And if I were to publish any of the other papers?'

He lowered his hands and said, 'I do civil law, Dottoressa: breach of contract is something my office deals with every day.'

'What does that mean, Dottore?' Caterina asked, conscious that her tone had changed.

'To do so would be a breach of contract, Dottoressa, in which event a case would surely be brought against you. It would be a very long and it would be a very expensive case.' He left it to her to assume that, though the length would concern them both equally, perhaps the cost would be more of a burden to her.

'How long would a case like this take to pass through the courts?' she asked, then explained. 'If I might ask for the sake of curiosity.'

He let the hand that still held the paper fall to his side. 'I'd imagine the least it could take is eight or nine years. That is, if the verdict were appealed.'

'I see,' Caterina said, preferring not to ask how much it might cost. 'I'm perfectly willing to agree to the conditions.'

His whole body seemed to relax, and she wondered if he had some personal interest in controlling the information in the trunks. What could he and the cousins fear would be hidden in those documents? What scandal might have survived all these generations, quietly ticking away inside two locked chests? Caterina gave herself a mental shake and dismissed the idea: to think like this was to enter into the world of paranoia in which the cousins seemed to live.

Before Dottor Moretti could thank her for agreeing, she held up a hand and said, 'I want to make something clear.' He leaned forward, the very picture of attention. 'I want to repeat that I am not a historian, so it might be necessary for me to spend time reading about the historical background in the Marciana to get some sense of what was going on when these documents were written. Is that understood?'

Dottor Moretti smiled. 'Your letters of recommendation said you were an eager student and researcher, Dottoressa. I'm happy to see signs of it now.' His smile broadened. 'Of course you can read. It will be of invaluable use, I hope, in helping you to put any events mentioned into their correct historical context.'

Roseanna broke in to say, 'I doubt that they'll like paying for historical context.' In response to Caterina's glance, she said, 'You've met them: they have blunt minds. They think in numbers and yes and no.' She looked across at Moretti.

'I think you're right, Signora, that they won't grasp the need for this,' he said. Then to Caterina: 'You're a scholar. Of course you have to do the background reading: otherwise it makes no sense for you to read anything. They won't like it, but I think I have sufficient influence with them to encourage them to allow it.' Then, after a pause, 'I think it's both essential and prudent that you do it.'

Caterina was struck by his use of that word, for Dottor Moretti, more than any other thing, was a prudent man. For Caterina, however, the term was descriptive: it could as easily be a vice as a virtue. She hoped it was a virtue in the lawyer.

Her reflections were interrupted by a loud knocking at the front door.

Dottor Moretti looked at his watch and said, looking at Roseanna, 'You were right, Signora: it's just noon. Indeed, our two guests do think in numbers.'

7

Roseanna got to her feet, saying, 'Dottore, might I ask you to open the door for our guests?' It was Monday, Caterina recalled, the day the library was closed to visitors, so they would have it to themselves. It was the only room she had seen with more than two chairs, and so the only place where all of them could meet. She had not seen the cousins since the interviews in that same room, when she had met with them to present her qualifications.

She and Roseanna went down the corridor to the library. The room was warmer than either her office or Roseanna's had been; the heat, unfortunately, brought out the scent of the bodies and clothing that had been present in the room during the last weeks. Roseanna went immediately to the windows and threw them wide, then returned to the door and opened it: Caterina felt the draught sweep past her and out the door. 'Keep them open as long as you can,' Roseanna said and went to receive the visitors.

Caterina, in the accidental role of major-domo, went over to the windows and stood in the draught cutting into the room. When the footsteps approached, she shut the windows and moved back to the table. In less than a minute, Roseanna came through the door, followed by Moretti, carrying his briefcase. Caterina wondered whether the cousins would force themselves through the door side by side or stand outside to fight about who went first.

Her fantasy was wasted. Signor Stievani came in first, closely followed by his cousin, the usurer. Or would it have been better to say that the tax evader came in first, closely followed by his cousin, Signor Scapinelli? Caterina smiled with every indication of pleasure and shook hands with both men, then turned to the table and pulled out a chair for one, just as Roseanna pulled out the one opposite for his cousin. Neither of the cousins seemed surprised by her presence.

With casual authority, Dottor Moretti moved to the head of the table, waited for everyone else to sit, and then took his place. He nodded to both men and began *in medias res*. 'I've already explained the conditions of her employment to Dottoressa Pellegrini. You are both already familiar with what they are. She has no objections to any of the requirements. In fact, she was just about to sign the agreement as you arrived.' So saying, he looked at Caterina, who took the pen he handed her and signed the agreement, then passed it back to him.

Dottor Moretti opened his briefcase and pulled out a blue folder. He slipped the agreement into it and replaced it in his briefcase, which he set back on the floor, where it made a surprisingly heavy thump. 'If either of you, Signor Scapinelli or Signor Stievani, has anything to say to the Dottoressa, or to either Signora Salvi or to me, then perhaps you could do so now?'

While he spoke, Caterina studied the two men, trying to judge whether her first opinion – negative – would find confirmation in this second encounter with them. So far, however, all they had done was sit, each carefully avoiding the sight of the other by giving their attention to Moretti.

Caterina realized that Stievani must be older than his cousin, perhaps by as much as a decade. He had the rough skin of a man who worked outside and had never thought to protect himself from the sun, skin that reminded her of the leather of Dottor Moretti's briefcase, though the lawyer had taken better care of the briefcase than Signor Stievani had of his face. Or his hands, for that matter. The knuckles of both were swollen, the fingers twisted at odd angles, perhaps from arthritis, perhaps from decades of work on boats in cold weather. She was surprised to see that his nails were neatly trimmed and filed, surely the work of a manicurist.

His nose was long and straight, his eyes clear blue under sharply arched brows. But the face was bloated and puffed up, perhaps from alcohol, perhaps from disease, removing the possibility of beauty, leaving the wreckage of a man.

When she glanced at Signor Scapinelli, her attention was drawn, as it had been the first time, to his eyes. Her memory flashed, to the vision Dante had given of the usurers. She forgot what Circle he had consigned them to – the seventh? The eighth? They sat, for all eternity, on the burning sands of Hell, flapping at falling flames the way dogs swat at flies. Around their necks hung bags, small purses that held their meaningless wealth, and Dante described the way their eyes, even in that place, feasted on the sight of those bags. Their eyes, she decided, must have been eyes like Signor Scapinelli's: deep set, never still, with dark half-moons below them.

She had watched him notice Dottor Moretti's briefcase and the gold frames of his glasses, had seen him tote up the cost of his suit, and she felt a shiver of embarrassment that she had done much the same. To save herself from her own harsh accusations, she offered the excuse that she had done it in a complimentary way, in admiration of his taste and not in envy that he had the means to permit himself that casual elegance.

Scapinelli's clothing disguised his wealth, had

perhaps been chosen to achieve that end. His jacket was faintly threadbare at the cuffs, and a button had been replaced. His hands were as large as his cousin's, though much better cared for, as were, strangely enough, his teeth, where she saw evidence of a great deal of work and expense.

He was round-faced and balding and walked with the ponderous splay-footed tread of the obese, though he was not a fat man. Caterina had no clear idea how closely related the two sides of the family might once have been, but all resemblance had been worn away by the passing of time, and now the only way these men looked alike was in the possession of two eyes, a nose, and a mouth.

Scapinelli, she was reminded when he caught her glance and moved his mouth in a quick rictus, had the distracting habit of smiling at inappropriate times, as if his face were on a timer or programmed to respond to certain expressions. Strangely, the smile never came in reaction to anything funny or witty or ironic. The last time, she had attempted to figure out what the key was, but had abandoned the task as hopeless and let him smile at will.

One might dismiss him as a happy fool because of those smiles, but that would be to make a mistake, for above the vacuous smile rested those reptilian eyes.

He spoke first, in the rough voice she remembered and speaking in Veneziano. 'Good. If she's accepted all the terms, then she can go to work.' What was next? Caterina wondered. They put a time clock by the front door, and she stamped in and out every day?

Dottor Moretti spoke again. 'Before she does, Signor Scapinelli, there are a few things that remain to be settled.'

'Like what?' Scapinelli asked with a pugnacity Caterina thought unnecessary.

'You gentlemen have agreed – I think very wisely – that Dottoressa Pellegrini is to have complete freedom to expand her research.'

Signor Scapinelli opened his mouth to speak, but Dottor Moretti ignored him and continued. 'She is to send me written reports of what she reads and is to pay special attention to anything that might be regarded as your ancestor's testamentary dispositions,' Dottor Moretti said. 'Which reports I will forward to both of you with great dispatch.'

There he went again, using those wonderful phrases, she thought. If only Italians could be taught to think of 'testamentary dispositions' instead of 'making a will', they'd all have one drawn up by the end of the week.

'Yes. That's right. That's what's in the paper you gave us.' Signor Stievani broke in to say. Then the clincher, 'And she signed it.'

'We want copies,' his cousin concluded.

'And how, if I might ask, is the Dottoressa supposed to write these reports?' Dottor Moretti asked.

Scapinelli turned to her and said, 'We're not buying you one.'

Caterina turned to Moretti, leaving it to him to fight her corner for her.

'Most places of employment provide their employees with a computer.'

'She's hired as "*una libera professionista*",' Stievani said. 'She should have her own.' He spoke of her, Caterina thought, as though she were a blacksmith who should show up with his own bag of pliers, hammers, and horseshoes. They'd provide the fire – perhaps – but the tools were up to her.

In a softer voice, Dottor Moretti said, 'I think I can take care of that.' Four faces turned to him. 'A few months ago, our office upgraded the computers we give our younger associates. The laptops they were using are still in a closet in my secretary's office. I can have someone take out whatever refers to our office. I think access to the internet is built into these things.' He waited for comment, but then added, speaking directly to Caterina, 'It's only a few years old, but it should certainly be adequate for what you have to do here.'

'That's very kind of you, Dottore,' Roseanna said, apparently delighted that a man could so casually confess to imperfect familiarity with computers. 'On behalf of the Foundation I thank you for this largesse.' Ah, yes, 'largesse', Caterina thought, charmed to hear Roseanna rise to the level of Moretti's speech. She was also impressed with the way her graciousness was likely to prevent any embarrassing questions as to why the Foundation had no computer.

'What were you going to do with them?' Signor Scapinelli interrupted.

Dottor Moretti was momentarily confused by the question but then answered, 'We usually give them to the children of our employees.'

'You give them away?' Scapinelli asked with a mixture of astonishment and disapproval.

'That way, we can deduct them from our taxes,' Dottor Moretti said, an answer that calmed Signor Scapinelli's troubled spirit, at least to the degree that a usurer's spirit can ever be calm at the revelation of an unmade profit.

'You mentioned a few things that needed to be settled,' Caterina reminded him.

'Ah, yes. Thank you, Dottoressa,' Dottor Moretti said. 'We'd like to establish some parameters for the handling of the papers.'

'Parameters,' she repeated, for the first time unimpressed by his use of language.

'Yes. We have to settle how we will go about the actual opening of the chests and decide who will be there when you remove the contents and begin to work.'

'Let me say one thing,' Caterina declared. 'I don't care who's there when the chests are opened, but I can't have anyone present while I'm working.'

'"Can't"?' Dottor Moretti inquired.

'Can't because having someone there, looking over my shoulder – even sitting at the other side of the room – would slow me down terribly. It would double the time it will take me to do the research.'

'Simply having someone in the room with you?' Dottor Moretti asked.

Before she could answer, Signor Stievani said, sounding angry or impatient, 'All right, all right. If we're there when they're opened, and we're sure there's only papers in there, then there's nothing to worry about.' Perhaps a life spent on boats led a man to believe that papers could have no value, Caterina reflected.

'We don't want her spending the rest of her life doing this, you know,' Signor Stievani went on, addressing Dottor Moretti directly; he ignored the sarcasm and heard the statement.

'Quite right,' he agreed. 'Once the trunks have been opened, we're agreed that Dottoressa Pellegrini can stay alone in the room.'

'Then I work upstairs?'

'Yes, that's the room where the work will be done,' Dottor Moretti said. 'It's got the storeroom, and there's a wireless connection.'

'Why is that?' Caterina asked Roseanna, remembering that the stolen computer had been on this floor.

Looking awkward, Roseanna said, 'Well, it doesn't exactly belong to the Foundation.'

'"Exactly"?' Caterina asked. 'Then whose is it?'

Her embarrassment grew stronger. 'I don't know.'

'Don't tell me it's someone else's Wi-Fi you're piggybacking on?' Caterina demanded.

'Yes.'

'Do you think that's safe?' She did not bother to

ask what would happen if the line were to disappear or be secured by its legal owner.

The smile was not present in Roseanna's shrug. 'I have no idea. But it's the only line we have. Dottor Asnaldi used it, and there was no trouble at all.'

Trouble came from Signor Scapinelli, who interrupted to say, 'We're not paying for any of those things. You give her a computer, you figure out how she can use it.' Then, with undisguised contempt, 'This place doesn't even have a telephone.'

'And the computer doesn't leave that room, either,' Signor Stievani added.

Caterina turned towards the men and, after allowing her anger a few seconds to dissipate, said quite pleasantly, 'I'm perfectly content to use that connection. And the computer can stay here all the time. After all, what sort of secrets can be in papers that are hundreds of years old?'

8

Soon after this decision was made, Caterina noticed that both cousins grew restless. First Stievani looked at his watch, and then Scapinelli did. It took her just a moment to understand: they were afraid, if this went on much longer, that they might be expected to go to lunch with these people or, worse, expected to take them to lunch. Dottor Moretti must have read the signs at the same time, for he glanced at his watch and said, speaking in general to everyone at the table, 'I hope we've made all of the major decisions that concern us.'

He looked around and saw four nodding heads. Addressing them, he said, 'Then perhaps we can remove ourselves to the upper floor and see to opening the chests.' There was no reason for Caterina to be surprised, but she was. Though everything she had done since coming back to Venice had been aimed at this goal, she was still unprepared to hear it announced. The chests would be opened, and she would see the papers – the putative papers – she would hold them in her hands, and she would be surprised, of course she would be surprised, to learn that they were the papers of Agostino Steffani, composer and bishop, musician and diplomat.

They got to their feet. At the door, the two cousins were careful to see that Dottor Moretti stood between them: Stievani went first, the lawyer next, and then Signor Scapinelli. Women and children last.

Moretti led them only as far as the door to the stairway that led to the upper floor, where he waited for Roseanna to come and unlock the door. This done, she stepped aside to allow the men to pass in front of her.

Once they were inside the Director's office Roseanna went to the metal doors of the storeroom and dealt with three separate locks – Caterina had failed to notice the third lock set almost at floor level. With no ceremony whatsoever, Roseanna pulled open the metal doors and stepped back to allow the others to see the chests that stood, one behind the other, the back one about twenty centimetres taller than the other, in the closet-sized storeroom. Caterina had seen scores of similar trunks in antique shops and museums: unadorned dark wood, metal strips rimming the top and bottom and thus creating a border into which a secure locking mechanism could be anchored. The keys were missing from both keyholes.

Signor Stievani, by far the more robust of the cousins, took Dottor Moretti's arm, saying, 'Let's pull them out: you grab the other handle.' He bent over the smaller trunk and took hold of one of the handles.

Moretti was unable to hide his surprise, both at being so addressed by the other man and at the idea of being asked to help move the chest. He reacted quickly and well, however, set his briefcase down, and grabbed the second handle. From the ease with which they moved it, Caterina got an idea of the probable weight of the chest. They carried it from the storeroom and set it to the side of the desk. Then they did the same with the second chest, which seemed to Caterina to be much heavier and which they set down next to the first.

So there they were: the two chests containing the contested patrimony of the musician whose name she was not supposed to know. Both of them had what seemed to be wax-covered ropes tied around them, the first spanning front and back and the other going across the top from side to side. The first one ended in elaborate knots from which hung fragments of what must once have been a large medallion of red wax. The surface was pitted and scarred, and it was impossible to distinguish what might once have been impressed into it. Four nails held a faded rectangle of paper to the front of the smaller chest.

The bottom left corner had been torn loose from the nail, taking with it a corner of the paper. Barely legible, in faded brown ink, Caterina read, in the spidery handwriting of the times, '—fani 1728.'

Before Caterina could ask how they were going to proceed, Scapinelli demanded, 'And who's going to open them?'

Dottor Moretti surprised them all by taking from his briefcase a folding knife and a large ring of what looked like antique keys. Some were rusted, some polished bright, but all ended in serrated teeth and had obviously been made by hand.

'I showed a photo of the two locks to an antiquarian friend of mine, and he sent me these,' he explained. 'He thinks some of the keys will fit.' Caterina was pleased at this very un-lawyerly behaviour on Dottor Moretti's part. Could it be that he was enjoying their trip into the past?

'Both locks?' Scapinelli asked.

'He thinks so, and I hope so,' Moretti answered.

Caterina and Roseanna exchanged approving glances, but Scapinelli made a noise. Caterina wondered if he'd expected Dottor Moretti to have arrived certain about which were the proper keys.

Hiking up the right leg of his trousers Dottor Moretti half knelt in front of the first, smaller, trunk. Methodically, holding each by the seal, he cut the ropes and left them where they lay. He cut the seal free and handed it to Caterina, who placed it carefully on the desk. Then he went through the keys one by one, inserting them and trying to turn them. A few seemed to move in the lock, but none was successful until a key quite close to the end of the ring moved to the right two times with a grinding double creak. Moretti withdrew the key and pushed at the top; after a few seconds and some shifting side to side, he managed to raise it a few centimetres but immediately set it back in place and moved to the larger trunk.

Nailed to the front was a similar piece of paper, though this one was intact and read, 'Steffani. 1728'; there was no wax wafer attached to the ropes. Again, Moretti cut through the rope and let the pieces fall to the floor. This time the key was the third or fourth he tried, though it took considerably more effort to lift this lid. When he had raised it free of the metal band, Dottor Moretti settled it back into place and got to his feet. He opened his briefcase and dropped the keys and knife inside.

'They're ours, aren't they?' Signor Scapinelli asked, pointing to the keys. It was a statement and not a question.

'I'm expecting a judgment,' Dottor Moretti said in an English only Caterina understood, but then he reverted to Italian and added, 'The keys belong to my friend, who has asked for them back.' He gave Signor Scapinelli a friendly smile and added, quite affably, 'If you and your cousin prefer, I can ask him how much he'd charge if you'd like to keep them.' He turned to Signor Stievani and said, 'Have you a preference?'

'Don't provoke me, Avvocato,' he said. 'Leave them open and send the keys back.' With a wave towards the metal doors, he added, 'Anyone who could get through those wouldn't have much trouble with these locks.' He might be a tax-evading fraud, Caterina told herself, but the man was no fool.

She looked at her watch and saw that it was almost one. 'Signori,' she began, a term in which Roseanna was included, 'I think we should make some logistical decisions. You're agreed that the trunks will stay open. But as you saw, I can hardly move them back into the storeroom myself.'

She let them consider that. She was not going to make a suggestion, knowing the greater wisdom of letting herself accede to one of theirs, so long as it was what she wanted.

She watched their reactions. Roseanna followed the same tactic by shaking her head to show she opted out of the decision and left it to the men to decide; Dottor Moretti was there in his legal capacity and so refused to express an opinion; neither cousin wanted to make a suggestion, probably fearful – or certain – that the other would block it. Finally Stievani said, 'The chests have to be locked in the storeroom at night.' He looked at all of them, not only at his cousin. When he saw consensus, he went on. 'So why don't we let her look through them to see if there's only papers? Then we put the chests back in the cupboard, and when she's done every day, she puts the papers back in the trunk and locks the cupboard, and then she locks the room.'

'And the keys?' Scapinelli asked.

'She keeps them. Otherwise we've got to figure out someone for her to give them to every day.' Just as it looked as if his cousin was going to protest, he added, 'And we'd have to pay him.' His cousin's words were left unsaid.

Dottor Moretti looked around at them all. 'It sounds sensible to me. Does anyone object?' Then, at their silence, directly to Caterina, 'Do you, Dottoressa?'

'No.'

Roseanna held up the keys and looked in turn at the three men. She then walked to the desk and placed the three keys to the storeroom, the single key to the stairs and the key to the Director's office on the reading table. Caterina nodded polite thanks.

Dottor Moretti took the opportunity of the ensuing silence to say, 'Since we have no idea what *is* inside these trunks, whether papers or objects and of what kind, and since I suppose we are all curious, to one degree or another, to have a look, I propose we ask Dottoressa Pellegrini to open them so that we can see, and then we leave her to her work.'

This time, Caterina did not wait. 'That sounds eminently sensible,' she said and approached the smaller trunk. She went down on one knee, grabbed the lid on both sides, and pulled it up until it was suspended by her left hand. Holding it upright, she looked inside and saw the reason for its lightness: it was only half full; the string-tied packets of papers on the top layer looked as though they had been shifting about for centuries, as no doubt they had. But because they were tied in the same manner as the trunks, with separate pieces of waxed string running perpendicularly and horizontally, the piles had remained intact.

She lowered the lid and heard noises of protest. *'Un momento,'* she said and went back to her bag. From it, she took a pair of white cotton gloves, slipped them on, and returned to open the trunk again.

Caterina reached in and pulled out the top packet on the left side. She carried it to the desk and placed it upside down, then returned to the trunk to take a more careful look at the remaining papers. She had heard the others move closer and now she felt their presence around her. Methodically, she began removing the papers from the left hand stack and moving them to the table, where she turned each packet upside down on top of the others. That done, she started on the other pile and repeated the process. When the trunk was empty, the cousins leaned over and peered into it to assure themselves that it was.

Signor Scapinelli gave Caterina a sideways glance, as if intending to check her sleeves, but glanced away when she looked at him.

When the cousins appeared to have seen enough, Caterina, again methodically, replaced the papers in the same order in which she had found them, leaving only the first packet she had removed, which she placed beside the keys.

Scapinelli looked at his watch, and Caterina could all but hear him thinking that it would soon be time to invite them to lunch. Hurriedly, she repeated the process of removing all of the papers in the second trunk. When it was evident that there was nothing but papers in this trunk, either, she replaced them and stepped back from the trunk. Dottor Moretti helped Stievani replace it at the back of the closet. Then they shifted the first one back into place in front of it.

Leaving the doors open, Caterina returned to the desk. She picked up the packet of papers and placed it on the other side of the desk, directly in front of the ex-Director's chair. Thus prepared for work, she turned her attention to the three men in the room. She moved the three keys together on the table. 'Thank you for your help, gentlemen,' she said to Dottor Moretti and Signor Stievani.

'And now?' asked Scapinelli, looking again at his watch, no doubt driven to it by the thought of the prices on the menus of nearby restaurants.

'I'm going home to have lunch,' Roseanna said.

'I have to meet a client,' Moretti said.

Signor Scapinelli said, 'My son is waiting for me in his shop.'

And his cousin added, 'I have to get a train.'

So strong was the temptation to sing, *'Io men vado in un ritiro a finir la vita mia'* that Caterina had to press her fingernails into her palms to stop herself from doing it. When she recovered some semblance of calm, she pulled out the chair and said, 'Then I think I'll go to work.'

9

When they were gone, Caterina sat down. Her job was beginning now, she told herself, conscious that, even as the trunks were being opened and the first papers removed, none of the people there had seen fit to mention Steffani's name, though all of them knew it. The idea that either of the cousins could have an interest in Baroque music was absurd, and she knew nothing about Dottor Moretti beyond the elegance of his speech and dress. By her own admission, Roseanna was interested in a general sense in the music and the musicians of the period, but wisdom had kept her almost entirely silent during the meeting and the opening of the trunks. Thus, in all of this, Caterina was the only person who took a real interest in Steffani, at least as he was represented by his music. And what else mattered, really, after all this time?

He had been a priest. She recalled that he had also been mixed up in politics at the courts where he worked as a musician, but when were priests not mixed up in politics? He might well, then, have left the whole lot to the Church. Maybe the documents would tell, but why then would Propaganda Fide have sent them back?

She tipped her chair back and latched her hands behind her head, feeling no urge to look at the papers just yet. She wanted to think about the Big Things at work here. If she did find some sort of 'testamentary disposition', it would have little legal weight, after three hundred years. Dottor Moretti must know this. '*Tanto fumo. Poco arrosto*,' she whispered aloud. There had indeed been a great deal of smoke: the suggestion that there had been other applicants for the job, the employment of a lawyer of Dottor Moretti's apparent calibre, the many restrictions surrounding the work. What, then, would the roast be? Or what did they expect it to be?

Caterina looked around the room and wondered why Roseanna had not appropriated it: after all, it was unlikely that the Foundation would ever have another Director.

'Pity you couldn't be a singer,' she told herself aloud, as if having had the courage to choose that career would have led to something more exciting than this room and the weeks of reading that no doubt lay ahead of her. Rigorous honesty intervened here and warned her that her vocal talent would have taken her, with luck, as far as the chorus of the opera house of Treviso.

She let the front legs of the chair hit the floor and pulled the packet towards her, worked at the knot in the string that held it together until it came free, wrapped it into a neat oval around her fingers, and placed it on the corner of the desk. Almost three hundred years, and it was still unbroken and strong enough to be reused. The paper on the top was a letter written in Italian in a strongly Italianate hand. It bore the date 4 January 1710 and was addressed to *Il mio fratello in Cristo Agostino*. She lifted the letter by the top corners and held it to the light. She didn't recognize the watermark, but the paper felt and looked right to justify the date.

Caterina had some trouble with the script, though none with the language or meaning. The letter made opening reference to the opera *Tassilone*, which the sender had had the immeasurable pleasure of seeing the previous year in Düsseldorf. Only now did the writer dare to break in upon the creative genius of the composer, whose time he dared not waste, by sending his humble praise of a work in which were displayed both the highest moral principles and the most sublime manifestation of musical creativity.

She glanced up from the letter and tried to dig into the musical memories lodged in her scholar's skull to get some sense of whether this was lickspittle flattery or honest praise. Steffani, she had once read, had introduced French fashions into Italian opera, a novelty imitated by that great borrower – to avoid using a different word – Handel.

The writer continued in this vein for another three paragraphs, detailing the 'countless excellencies' of the work, the 'sublime perfection' in the musical phrasing, and the 'convincing moral principles' maintained by the text.

Below this paragraph, a few bars of music were quoted: she read the first line: *'Deh, non far colle tue lagrime'*, hearing the exceptionally beautiful largo as she mouthed the words. Suddenly there appeared the voice of a solo oboe, and Caterina's voice was stilled by the enduring spell of its sound.

The page ended, and when she turned to the second, she was disappointed to see that prose had replaced beauty. Two more paragraphs carried her to the last, in which the writer, proclaiming his own unworthiness, asked the 'Most Worthy Abbé' to intercede with the Bishop of Celle in aid of the appointment of his nephew, Marco, to the post of choirmaster at the church of St Ludwig. The signature was illegible, as in the manner of signatures of those times.

Below this, in a different, backward-slanting hand, was written, 'Good man. See if this can happen.' Nothing more.

She reached into her bag and pulled out a notebook and pen. '1. Letter of request for position as choirmaster.

Favourable comment in different hand on bottom. 4/1/1710.' Perhaps Marco would show up again; perhaps another letter would thank the 'Most Worthy Abbé' for his help in winning the position for the young man.

The next paper was a letter dated 21 June 1700, addressed to *Mio caro Agostino*, the familiarity of which salutation brought the scholar in her to the equivalent of a hunting dog's freezing at point. There was general talk of work and travel, mutual friends, the problem with servants. Then things turned to gossip, and the writer told his friend Agostino about Duke N. H.'s public behaviour with his brother's wife at the last ball of Carnevale. The third son of G. R. had died of bronchial trouble, to his parents' utmost grief, in which the writer joined them: he was a good boy and barely eight years old. And then the writer told his friend that he had overheard Baron (it looked like 'Bastlar' but might just as easily have been 'Botslar') speaking slightingly of Steffani and making fun of him for singing along with his operas while attending them in the audience. The writer thought his friend should know of this, should he receive compliments or promises from the Baron. Then, with affectionate wishes for Agostino's continued good health, the writer placed his illegible signature at the bottom.

Caterina made notes of the contents and made no comment, though she felt something close to outrage that a mere baron would make fun of a musician.

She set the letter aside and picked up the next document. Her heart stopped. It was entirely involuntary: the shock of seeing it grabbed her heart and tightened her throat. On top of the pile now lay a sheet of music, the notes doing their visual dance across the lines from left to right. Making no sound that could be heard by anyone, she began to sing the music line by line, heard the bass line and the violins. When she turned to the second page, she saw the words and knew she was no longer giving voice to the instruments but was singing an aria.

She turned back to the first page and let her mind play through the music again. Oh, how perfect it was, that figure in the introduction, only to be repeated in the high register, right from the start of the aria. She looked at the words and saw the predictable, '*Morirò tra strazi, e scempi.*' And who had churned out that sentiment, she wondered? 'I'll die between pain and havoc.' If she could find a time machine, she'd go back and pick up most of the men who wrote libretti and bring them back to the present, though she'd drop them off in Brazil, where they could all get jobs writing the scripts for *telenovelas*.

A glance at the opening words for the second line, '*E dirassi ingiusti dei*', confirmed her in her temporal and geographical desires. She read through to the end of the aria, concentrating on the music, not the words. 'Well, well, well,' she said out loud and then turned off the music by looking away from the paper. 'Wasn't he a clever devil?'

She wished now that she had paid more attention to his music while at university and had seen more than the single performance of the wonderful *Niobe* in London. The genius manifest in this aria proved him to be a composer with a far greater gift than she had before thought him to possess. She paused: could it be that it had been sent to him by a colleague or a musician or even a student? She re-examined the manuscript, but there was no attribution and no signature, only the same back-slanting handwriting she had seen in the note on the bottom of the first letter.

Identification could be made in the archives of the Marciana: all she had to do was go there and have a look at one of Steffani's autograph scores, even find a book with a reproduction of a few pages of a score in his hand. She had a good visual memory and could take a clear image of the aria with her. But how much easier to stay here and read on: sooner or later, she was bound to come upon a signed score. She cheated by paging ahead to the bottom of the packet: no more music.

The beauty of the music drew her eyes back to the aria. She made a note of the probable title of the aria, then turned it face down to uncover yet another document in ecclesiastical Latin, this a letter from 1719, addressed to him as Bishop and attempting to explain the delay in forwarding him his benefice from the dioceses of Spiga, wherever that might be.

After making a note of the contents of this letter,

Caterina looked at her watch and saw that it was after two. Almost as if the sight of the time had released her from the spell of her own curiosity, she realized how hungry she was. She opened her bag and pulled out her wallet. She opened flaps and slots until she found her reader's card for the Biblioteca Marciana. It had expired two years before. In a normal country, in a normal city, one would go and renew the card, but that was to be certain that a clear, prompt process for doing so existed or functioned. Though Caterina had not lived in Italy for a number of years, she had no reason to believe that things had changed, and so her first thought was to find a way to get what she wanted without having to waste time with a system that, if memory served and if things had remained the same, exulted in creating ways to block people from having what they deserved or desired.

She ran her memory through the gossip and news of the last decade: who worked where, who had married, who had inserted themselves into the mechanism that kept the city going. And she recalled Ezio, dear Ezio, who had gone to school with her sister Clara and who had been in love with her for three years, from the time they were twelve until they were fifteen, and who had then fallen in love with someone else and subsequently married her, retaining Clara as best friend.

Ezio, by common agreement, was as clever as he was lazy and had never wanted success or a career: only to marry and have lots of children. He had them now, four, she thought, but he also had – and this is why Ezio came to mind – a job as librarian at the Biblioteca Marciana.

Caterina replaced the papers in the packet, but did not bother to tie it closed. She went to the storeroom and put it into the smaller trunk, then closed the door and locked it, using all three keys.

Only then did she go back to her bag and pull out her *telefonino*. The number, not used for a long time, was still in the memory. She dialled it and, after he answered, said, *'Ciao, Ezio, sono la Caterina. Volevo chiederti un favore.'*

10

Caterina felt no regret at so peremptorily having left Manchester, but she did regret having had to leave her books in storage, an act that made her entirely dependent upon the internet and public collections of books. Ezio had told her to come to the library at four, so after she stopped for a *panino* and a glass of water, standing at the bar as she had done as a student, she did another studentesque thing and went into an internet café. It would take her too long to go home and use her own computer to do the basic research, and all she wanted was to have the basic chronology of Steffani's life fresh in her memory when she went to the library.

Her grandmother had been famous in the family

for keeping her memory all her life, and Caterina was the grandchild said most to resemble her. As she read about Steffani's life, she justified family tradition, for most of the information was coming back to her: born in Castelfranco in 1654, he was early seen to be a talented singer and musician, choirboy at the Basilica del Santo in Padova from the age of ten. A nobleman from Munich was seduced by the beauty of Steffani's voice and took him home with him, where he had tremendous success as a musician and a composer. After two decades, he moved to Hanover, where he had more of the same. He seemed to drift away from music while he devoted himself to politics, working for the Catholic cause in a country whose rulers had decided to turn it Protestant.

'Ernst August,' she said out loud as she came upon a reference to the Duke of Hanover: yes, she remembered him. Here the writer of the article opened a parenthesis (and explained that Ernst August's people built him the most sumptuous opera house in Germany, not to delight him, but to attempt to keep him from taking his yearly, and ruinously expensive, trips to the Carnevale in Venice). His son, Georg Ludwig, was to become George I of England. Like most people trained in research, Caterina willingly gave in to its intoxication and sent Google running off after Georg Ludwig: wasn't there some scandal about his wife? Soon enough, there she was, the beautiful Sophie Dorothea, the greatest beauty and most desirable marital catch of the era; married at sixteen to Georg Ludwig (another parenthesis explained that they were first cousins) before being caught in adultery, divorced, and imprisoned for more than thirty years until her death. It all made fascinating reading, but it didn't tell her much about Steffani.

She went back to the original window and continued to read about his life after his virtual abandonment of music; he shuttled about endlessly on diplomatic missions here and there. He spent six years in Düsseldorf, chiefly concerned with political and ecclesiastical matters, producing his last three operas there. He appeared to have prevented a war between the Pope and the Holy Roman Emperor, both of them embroiled in the War of the Spanish Succession, and who remembered what that was all about? He had spent a good deal of his non-musical life attempting to persuade various North German rulers to return to the arms of Holy Mother Church. Caterina looked up from the computer and let her eyes trail to the façade of the church of Santa Maria della Fava. Suddenly her soul was enwrapped by Vivaldi, an aria for *Juditha Triumphans*, what were the words? '*Transit aetas/Volant anni/Nostri damni/ Causa sumus.*' How gloriously simple the score was: mandolin and pizzicato violin, and a single voice warning us that time passes, the years fly by, and we are the cause of our own destruction. What better message to give to the leaders of those empty churches? We are the cause of our own destruction.

'Would you like another half-hour, Signora?' the

young Tamil at the cash register called to her. 'Time's up in five minutes, but you can stay online for another half-hour for two Euros.'

'No, that's fine. Thank you for asking, though,' she said and resisted the urge to look for the aria on YouTube. Steffani moved back to Hanover in 1709, but there was no further mention of his music, only travel and political involvement. Almost no more music. Was genius painful? she wondered. Did it, at some point, simply cost too much for the spirit to continue to create? As she watched, the screen went blank, taking with it Steffani, his music, the Church he served, and all of his desires to restore that Church to her former power. She picked up her bag, thanked the young man at the desk, and started towards the library.

It took her no more than ten minutes to get there; to pass in front of the two caryatids and into the lobby of the Marciana was to move from the constant crowding of the Piazza into the calm tranquillity that thoughts and the books that contained them were meant to give. She stood for a moment, as if she were a diver waiting to decompress, and then she approached the guard and mentioned Ezio's name. He smiled and waved her through an apparently deactivated metal detector and into the foyer of the library.

One of the guards must have phoned him, for by the time Caterina got to the head of the stairs, Ezio was there, coming towards her with outstretched hands.

There were lines around his eyes, and he seemed both thinner and shorter than he had been the last time she saw him, almost a decade ago. But the brightness and the smile were the same. He wrapped her in a tight hug, pushed her free of him, kissed her on both cheeks, and then they took turns saying all of those sweet things that old friends say after not meeting for years. All of her sisters were fine, his kids were growing, and what was it she wanted him to do?

She explained the need to find information about a Baroque composer for a research project she was doing for the Foundation, of which he had heard, though vaguely. There was no need to explain any more. He said she was welcome to use the stacks as much as she liked, then excused himself and said he'd go and organize a reading card for her as a visiting scholar.

'No,' he said, turning back to her. 'Let me take you up to the stacks. You can get an idea of what's there.' When she began to protest, he refused to listen, saying, 'You're a friend of mine, so don't worry about the rules. Once I get you the card, you have access to almost everything.' He set off to the right and led her into the long gallery she recalled from her student days. The marble floor might have served as a chessboard for two opposing tribes of giants: there were far more than sixty-four squares, and a giant could stand on each of them. The glass viewing cases displayed manuscripts, but they passed through so quickly she could distinguish nothing more than the even lines of script and the large illuminated letter on some pages. The enormous globes of the Earth appeared to be the same, as did the outrageous vaulted ceiling without an inch of empty space. Why were we Venetians so excessive? Caterina asked herself. Why did there always have to be so much of everything, and all of it beautiful? She glanced out the windows and had a momentary sensation that the Piazza was hurrying past her stationary self.

She followed him from the gallery, like Theseus on his way to slay the Minotaur, thinking that she, too, should leave a trail of string behind. Turn and turn and turn about, and soon she had no idea where they were. These were inner rooms, so she could not orient herself by looking out and seeing the Basilica or the *bacino*.

At long last, they entered a room that had a row of windows, and beyond them she could see the long expanse of windows on the Palazzo Ducale across the Piazza. 'How do you find anything?' she asked when Ezio pointed to a wall of shelves.

'Do you mean a room or a book?' he asked.

'Both. I'd never find my way out of here. And how do I know what's here?' she asked, looking around for the computer terminals.

Smiling a broad smile, Ezio led her over to a shoulder-high wooden cabinet the front of which was entirely filled with small drawers. 'Do you remember?' he asked, patting the top of the cabinet. 'I saved it,' he said, obviously boasting.

'*Oddio*,' she exclaimed, 'It's a card catalogue.' When had she last seen one? And where? She approached it as a true believer would approach a relic. She reached out and touched it, ran her hand along the top and side, slid her finger under a flange and pulled a drawer out a few centimetres, then slid it silently back into place. 'It's been a decade. More.' In a conspiratorial voice, she said, 'I love them. They're so full of information.' Then, lower still, 'What did you do?'

In the voice of an actor in a war film suffering from shell shock, he said, 'They were going to destroy all of the cards. My superior told me: it was a direct order.' He paused and took in two very melodramatic breaths. 'First I threatened to quit if they removed it.'

She covered her mouth with her hands, though it was insufficient evidence of her horror. Then she said, 'You're here, so you didn't quit. What happened?'

'I threatened to tell his wife he was having an affair with one of my colleagues.'

Instead of laughing, which would have been her normal response, she asked, 'Would you have done it?'

Ezio shook his head. 'I don't know, really. Maybe.'

'But he gave in?'

'Yes. He said we could keep them, but we weren't to let anyone use them. The bulletin he sent said that the catalogue was to be fully computerized and the only access to the collection was to be via the computer.' Ezio made a gesture that looked suspiciously like spitting on the floor. 'He told us to do it, and then he cut our funding. So there's no money.'

'And the computer catalogue?'

He paused, smiled, changed roles and became any diplomat when asked a direct question. 'It's being worked on.'

'And your superior?' she inquired.

Again, the gesture. 'He's been reassigned to a provincial library.' Before she could ask, Ezio explained: 'It seems three of the last people he hired were relatives of his wife.'

'Where is he working now?'

'Quarto d'Altino.' He smiled. 'It's rather a small library.'

As so often happened when Caterina heard the tales told by friends or colleagues who had remained to work in Italy, she didn't know whether to laugh or cry.

She set her bag on one of the tables at the centre of the room and opened it to take out notebook and pencil. Ezio said, 'I'll get you your entrance card.' He indicated an empty carrel that stood between two of the windows. 'You can use that one if you want. Leave the books there while you're using them. When you're finished, put them on the desk near the door over there,' he said, pointing to the desk, 'and they'll be reshelved.'

She nodded her thanks. Ezio said, 'This might take some time,' and left.

Caterina went over to the window and looked down at the Piazza. People passed to and fro, few bothering to look to the sides of the Piazza: everyone was intent on the façade of the Basilica, as Caterina thought they should be, and those leaving often turned around to have another glimpse of it from a distance, as if needing to assure themselves that it was not an illusion. To her right, the flags flapped in the freshness of springtime, and she relaxed into the ridiculous beauty of the place.

Turning from this, she went to the catalogue and found the drawer that ran from Sc to St. From Scarlatti to Strozzi, which would also contain Stradella and Steffani. Under 'Steffani' she found entries in many different handwritings and just as many spellings of his name. She also found a cross-reference to 'Gregorio Piva', which a feathery note on the card explained was the pseudonym he used for the musical compositions of his later years. She retrieved her notebook and wrote down the call numbers for the books that looked like biographies of Steffani or might be more concerned with his life than with his music, then went to the shelves and began to hunt for the volumes.

By the time Ezio came back, more than an hour later, Caterina was sitting in the carrel with about forty centimetres of books lined up on the shelf in front of her. She turned when she heard him come in, keeping her finger in the book she was reading. He placed the card on the open page, bent down to give her a kiss on the cheek and, saying nothing, left the room. Caterina put the card in the pocket of her jacket and went back to reading.

The habits of the scholar had dominated Caterina's selection. First check the publisher to see how serious the book was likely to be, and then a quick check: anything that appeared to be self-published or that lacked notes or bibliography, she left on the shelves. What scholars were thanked in the acknowledgements? The culling process had taken some time, leaving her delighted that so much had been written about Steffani.

She started to take notes. Same information about the family: humble but not poor. Early gift for music. At twelve, so beautiful was his voice that while still a choir student in Padova, he had been sent to sing some opera performances in Venice. Was it success that had made him outstay his leave by several weeks? Despite his curt letter of apology, no punishment was given when he returned to Padova.

The Elector of Bavaria heard him singing in Venice and invited him to Munich, where Steffani was appointed musician to the court. To perfect his art, he was sent to Rome for a time and no doubt began his ecclesiastical training while there. His upward rise continued, all fairly normal for an ambitious young man of his era.

His career took wing with his move to Germany. Soon he was an abbé, though Caterina could find no reference to his ever having said a mass or administered any of the sacraments. Was Abbé merely a title or did it entail clerical obligation as well as status?

She pulled her thoughts from speculation and returned to Munich and to Steffani's growing fame as a composer. He was in the employ of a Catholic Elector and much in his favour, but in 1688 he chose to leave when the position of kapellmeister, which he believed he deserved, was bestowed on Giuseppe Antonio Bernabei, the son of the composer who had been his teacher in Rome.

Luckily, he had been seen and heard in Munich by Ernst August, the Protestant Duke of Hanover, who headed a court thought by some to rival that of France. Invited there as a musician, Steffani accepted and was soon moving in the highest intellectual circles, a friend of philosophers – Leibniz for one – musicians, and aristocrats.

His talent apparently flourished, his reputation grew, and he turned out yearly operas to ever-greater success. But then in the early 1690s, when it seemed he could become no more famous than he was, he suspended it all to go on a delicate ambassadorial mission which two writers attributed to the need to 'convince other German states to look with favour on the accession of Ernst August to the title of Elector of Hanover'.

After the death of Ernst August, Steffani moved for a few years to the court of the Catholic Elector Palatine at Düsseldorf, where he worked as a privy councillor to the Elector and at the same time as President of the Spiritual Council – another mystery to Caterina. His social stature must have risen, because he used a pseudonym for the operas he still continued to write, no doubt to avoid popular suspicion should a high-ranking clergyman engage in behaviour as morally and socially compromising as the writing of operas. As for writing under his own name, there were only the chamber duets and the Stabat Mater, which he wrote towards the end of his life.

Grateful for all his services, the Elector Palatine interceded on Steffani's behalf with the Vatican. The Pope finally gave in and made him a bishop. When she read that this was, unfortunately, only titular and produced almost no income, Caterina muttered, 'The wily bastards.' Then, unexplained, Steffani abandoned the Catholic duchy and returned to Protestant Hanover, where he remained until his death.

The books contained two pictures of him, the more common a lithograph made a century after his death and said to be a copy of an original, though in the ensuing century someone had added a goatee to his chin, as unflattering and unconvincing as those added to the photos of unpopular politicians. The other was the contemporary portrait of him that she recalled, wearing his bishop's cap. In the first, he looked earnest and busy, with his bishop's mitre and crozier visible behind him. In the second, he was dressed in his ecclesiastical best. He looked reserved, but chiefly he looked well-fed.

If there was no mention that he had ever said mass or performed a marriage ceremony or buried the dead or heard a confession, then why was he pictured both times in the regalia of his clerical position? He had spent the bulk of his life as a singer, composer, and diplomat, yet neither author could find a visual record of any of these, and one claimed that such images did not exist.

More importantly, for her immediate purposes, how could such a man accumulate 'treasure', and what form would it take? And if he did have it, why then did most accounts state that he had died in debt and poverty after first selling off most of his possessions? Why should he sacrifice a passion for a duty and die poor as a result?

Caterina glanced at her watch and saw that it was after seven. She felt the sudden, irrational fear of being locked inside overnight and snapped the book closed. She took out her *telefonino* and dialled Ezio's number. It rang five times before he answered, saying, 'I'm on my way to get you, Caterina. Be there in three minutes.'

Pretending, even to herself, that she had known he was there and would come for her, she put the book back on the shelf, put her pencil and notebook in her bag, and had a more careful look around the room. She went to stand in front of the card catalogue filled with the names of the people who had given music to the world, herself filled with a pride that surprised her: we have done so much; we have made so much beauty. Subtract Italy, wipe it from history, perhaps even cancel the peninsula from the Continent, and what would Western culture be? Who would have painted their portraits, or built their churches, designed their clothing, given them the concept of law? Or taught them how to sing?

Ezio's entrance broke into these reflections, which she decided to keep to herself. 'Did you find what you wanted?' he asked.

'Too much,' she said. 'I found four biographies, endless histories of the music of the period, of the politics of the times.'

'Will it be enough to answer your questions?' He sounded very interested. She remembered that Ezio had a degree in history and had more or less learned about libraries as he worked in one.

'That depends on what I find in the documents,' she said. Then, on an impulse, she asked, 'Am I allowed to take books with me?'

'Which ones?' he asked.

Turning back to the shelf, she pulled out one book, then another, then replaced that with a different one. 'These,' she said, showing him the two books.

He studied them, examining the bindings and not the titles, as if there were some secret library code hidden in their call numbers, then said, 'No.'

'Oh, sorry,' she said, realizing she had asked too much and reaching for the books.

'But I can,' Ezio said, slipping them under his arm.

Caterina laughed, then the scholar in her said, 'But you have to log them out.'

Still smiling at his own joke, Ezio said, 'Don't worry about it. I've known you for so many years, I know you're not going to disappear with the books. Believe me, it's easier this way.' He took her arm.

'What happens when I try to bring them back?'

'You just carry them in and put them back on that table down there,' he said, turning to point towards the restacking table.

'But how can I bring them in if they haven't been checked out?'

Confusion was written across his face. 'Just keep them in your bag and show them your card.'

'Won't they register when I go through the metal detector?'

'Of course not,' he said. 'It registers only metal.'

'Ah,' she said. 'Of course, a *metal* detector.'

Then, perhaps to keep her from getting ideas she shouldn't, he said, 'The machines at the public exit register chips in the bindings, so you can't take books out.'

Of course, she thought: who'd sneak a book into a library?

She stopped. They had come again to the front of the building, and there, ahead of them and off to the left, was the façade of the Basilica. 'What an absurd building that is,' she said. 'Look at it: all those domes and the arcs and the pillars all different from one another. Who'd build a thing like that?' she asked.

'We're in Italy, *cara mia*. Anything is possible.' He handed her the books.

11

They went into Florian's, to the bar at the back, and each ordered a spritz. The barman recognized Ezio and, smiling at Caterina, put a dish of cashews in front of them.

Taking one, she asked, 'Is this your reward for being an habitué? The most I ever get is peanuts.'

He laughed and took a drink. 'No. He's an old friend. We went to school together, so he always gives them to me.'

'It doesn't end, does it?' she asked, a remark that confused him.

'What doesn't end?'

'The advantages of having been born here,' she explained. Then, more soberly 'I saw in the paper this morning that there are now fewer than fifty-nine thousand of us.'

Ezio shrugged. 'I don't see what we can do. Old people die. Young people get jobs in other places. There's no work here.' Tilting his glass in her direction, he said, 'You're the lucky exception. You got called home to take a job.' Before she could respond, he asked, 'Are you staying with your family?'

'No,' she said. 'An apartment came with the job.'

'What?'

'An apartment. It's not much, and it's down in Castello, but it has three rooms and it's on the top floor.'

'Are you making this up?' he asked.

'No, not at all. It's just on the other side of Via Garibaldi, so it's easy enough to get to work.'

'How'd that happen?'

Here Caterina gave him an edited version of the facts, saying that the Foundation had an apartment it offered to visiting scholars. This was not true, and the apartment belonged to Scapinelli, who had agreed that she could stay in it while she did the research. It was usually rented out to tourists and was decorated – though Caterina thought that word an exaggeration – in the style that Venetians thought tasteful.

'Lucky you,' he said. 'Job and apartment.'

'Both temporary,' she reminded him.

He ate a few cashews and asked, 'You have any idea how long it might last?'

She shook her head. 'God knows.' She reached towards the books he had set on the counter. 'May I?'

'Oh, sure, sure,' Ezio said, handing them to her.

'The more I read, the sooner it will be done.'

'And then?'

She shrugged, then slipped the books into her bag. 'No idea. I've got job applications out all over the place: in four countries.'

'Where?' he asked, interested enough to set his glass down.

She counted them out on her fingers. 'Here, though I might as well forget about that. It's only teaching; no time for research.' Seeing how real his curiosity was, she went on, 'Germany, Austria, and the United States.'

'You'd go?' he asked, astonished.

This time, she waved the question away with her hand. 'If the job is interesting, yes. I'd go.'

'Well, good for you,' he said, meaning it. 'You've got the advantage of the language, haven't you?'

If the remark had come from another person, Caterina might have heard it as criticism of the advantage she had, but from Ezio it was admiration.

It came to her to say that she had the advantage of more than one language, but it would have sounded like boasting, and she didn't want to do that, so she contented herself with nodding in agreement.

He finished his drink. Half of the cashews were still in the glass bowl, but neither of them wanted any more. Caterina finished her drink and pulled out a ten Euro note. She placed it on the bar and caught the waiter's eye.

The waiter shook his head and made no move to approach them.

To Ezio, she said, 'Please let me pay. It's the least I can do.'

'No,' he said, pulling out his wallet. 'That would be close to taking a bribe, and you know how unthinkable such a thing is in our society.' He went on, and she remembered the clowning that had so charmed them all for years, 'I could not live with myself were I to believe, even for an instant, that I had somehow profited from my professional situation or shown favouritism in any way to someone who is a member of my family or a friend.' He pulled out a note and placed it on the counter, then looked at her, raised his hands as if to push away the approach of the Devil himself, and said, 'It would shame my ancestors.'

She gave him a soft punch in the arm and said, 'I'd forgotten that about you.'

'What?'

'How ridiculous you are.'

He heard the praise in her voice and laughed.

It was almost nine when Caterina got back to the apartment. After the cashews, she wasn't very hungry, so she decided to read for a while.

She pulled the two books out of her bag and walked to the sofa: it was a pale thing covered in rough, oatmeal-coloured cloth that silently screamed 'Ikea,' as did the tables, bookcases, light fixtures, curtains, and chairs. It had the single grace of being comfortable, so long as she put herself lengthwise, propped against the equally drab cushions.

She looked at the cover of the first book for a long time, studied the portrait of Steffani in the robes of Suffragan Bishop of Münster, whatever a suffragan bishop was. Plump of face and probably of body – the robes made that hard to distinguish – Steffani had a look of almost unbearable sadness. Thick-nosed and double-chinned, this man who was no longer composing music stared directly at the viewer, his long-fingered hand suspending the bejewelled cross he wore on a thick chain. His bald pate disappeared under his cap, leaving only puffs of hair on either side. It was a badly painted thing: were she to see it in a museum, she'd walk past it without bothering to find out the name of the subject or the painter; were she to see it in a gallery or shop, she wouldn't give it a second glance. It was interesting only because she knew the subject and hoped to decipher the painting.

She opened the book and started to read. Family background nothing special, a repetition of what she'd already read about his musical beginnings in Padova and Venice. Same story about overstaying his leave in Venice, although this time she learned that he claimed the delay resulted from an invitation to sing for a very important person, perhaps in private.

Not only was Caterina considered to be the intelligent daughter; she was also deemed the hard-nosed cynic of the family, though this was not a difficult title to earn in a family of decent, optimistic people. Thus the fact that an adolescent boy had chosen to remain behind in Venice to sing at the expressed desire of an older man who might have been an aristocrat and who was, at least, *un soggetto riguardevole* opened to her a possibility that the average person perhaps might not have contemplated at the combination of a young boy and an important man. She turned back to the cover. Almost fifty years had passed between the time of Steffani's prolonged stay in Venice and the painting of the portrait. It was hard to imagine this puffy-faced cleric ever having been a young boy with a beautiful voice.

She read on. Transferred to Munich at the invitation of the Elector of Bavaria, Ferdinand Maria, who had heard him sing, the young Steffani joined the court at the age of thirteen. Caterina began to nod as she read the names and titles of the people he met there, the musicians with whom he worked. Maybe it was time for dinner, for a coffee, for a glass of wine? The list of names and places continued, and then she found a passage from a letter Steffani had written late in life, describing his meeting with the Elector, who, according to Steffani, 'was attracted by something he must have seen in me – to what end I do not know – and, having taken me immediately to

Munich with him, placed me in the care of Count Tattenbach, his master of horse.'

'I beg your pardon,' Caterina heard herself say aloud in English, repeating the language of the book. She went back and read the passage again: 'was attracted by something he must have seen in me – to what end I do not know.'

She set the book down and got to her feet, went into the small kitchen and opened the refrigerator. She pulled out a bottle of white wine and poured herself a glass. She raised it in a toast, either to the air or to Steffani, or perhaps to her own perfervid imagination, and took a sip.

The kitchen had one small window that looked across the *calle* to the house on the other side, directly into the kitchen of the family that lived there. She leaned back into the living room and switched off the light, leaving herself in the darkness, glass in hand, looking out and now invisible from beyond the window.

There they were: Mamma Bear, and Papa Bear, and the two Baby Bears, a boy about eight and a younger sister. They sat around the table, still eating; they all looked relaxed and happy. Occasionally, one of them would say something, and one or two of the others would react with a change of expression or a smile, often a gesture. The boy finished whatever it was he was eating, and the mother cut him another piece of what Caterina now saw was a cake. Tall, light in colour, with darker-chunks that, this time of year, were likely to be apples or pears; perhaps both. It looked good enough to remind her of how hungry she was. But, while they were still there and still eating, she did not want to turn on the light and become as visible to them as they were to her. The boy suddenly reached his fork across the table and speared a piece of cake from his sister's portion. He held it up on the end of his fork and waved it in front of her, then brought it, in narrowing circles, towards his mouth.

Caterina heard nothing, but she saw the father lower his own fork and glance aside at his son. Instantly the circling stopped, and the boy leaned across the table and replaced the morsel on his sister's plate. The father turned towards him again. The boy bowed his head and finished his own piece of cake, then got down from his chair and left the room.

She left them to finish their meal and took her wine back to the sofa. She set the glass down and picked up the book, continued reading at the place where she had left off.

There was no record of Steffani at the court the first year he was in Munich, neither as a salaried musician nor as a member of the orchestra. When he did begin to appear in the voluminous records, he was being given organ lessons by the Kapellmeister, Johann Kerll, who received a significant sum beyond his normal salary to teach him. By 1671, Steffani was being pampered with 'a daily ration of one and a half measures of wine and two loaves of bread'.

Further, he had advanced to the position of '*Hof und Cammer Musico*'.

'*Oddio*,' she said out loud and set the book aside. There it was, the thing she had only suspected while at the same time reproving herself for thinking such a thing. She picked up her glass and finished the wine; then, turning the light on and not giving a thought to the three people who were still at the table in the house across the *calle*, she went into the kitchen and poured herself another glass.

'*Musico. Musico*,' she said aloud. She remembered a patter aria from a riotously funny production of *Orlando Paladino* she had seen in Paris that spring in which the word was also used. Even after the era of their greatness was finished, Haydn had still used the code to make fun of them. She'd read the word in scores and letters: when certain Baroque singers were described by contemporary writers or listeners as *musico*, they had always been castrati.

'*Oddio*,' she repeated, thinking of the man in the portrait, with his pudgy, beardless face, and his look of patient, unbearable sadness.

12

She woke at nine the following morning. After finding that word, *musico*, the previous evening, all she had been able to do was make herself some pasta, finish the bottle of wine, and go to bed with the second of the books she had taken from the library. But by the time she got under the covers, she was too tired, or too sodden, to be able to follow much of what she read, and she fell asleep, only to wake in the night, close the book and put it on the floor, turn off the light, and go back to sleep.

There was no sign of the Bear family when she went into the kitchen to make coffee the next morning, and their kitchen looked as clean as her own did not. 'I think it's time you started having a life, Caterina,' she said to herself as the coffee began to bubble up in the pot.

'Or a job with a future,' her more sensible, pragmatic self added.

She wondered if this is what happened to unemployed musicologists: they ended up in rented apartments filled with Ikea furniture, looking into the windows of their neighbours for reminders of human life? In order to give herself a sense of purpose, she did the dishes from the night before and put the empty wine bottle – telling herself it had been less than half full – into the plastic container meant to hold glass and plastic garbage. That was one positive change in the city since she had moved away: differentiated garbage collection. The thought depressed her, not that the city had such a thing but that she would measure progress in these terms. No new ideas, no new politics, no influx of young people with houses and jobs: only paper on Monday, Wednesday, and Friday, and plastic on Tuesday, Thursday, and Saturday. On Sunday, God and the garbage men rested. It would make a stone weep; so would the fact that most of her friends believed that it all ended up in the same place, anyway, and the whole thing was merely a scam to enable the company that did the collecting to raise the price. She abandoned these thoughts and went to take a shower.

Half an hour later, having stopped for a brioche and another coffee, she walked out on to Riva dei Sette Martiri, having decided to take advantage of the sun and bask in beauty on her way to work. The golden angel seemed to dance in the breeze from his post on top of the bell tower of San Giorgio. The sight of it lifted her spirits to such a degree that she wanted to wave at him and ask him how things were up there.

She remembered something the Romanian, in one of his rare moments of sobriety, had asked her once: how was it that angels got dressed? In response to her astonished look, he had insisted he was quite serious, and she was the only person he could ask. 'I see how their wings come out when they get undressed – that's easy: the cloth passes the right way over the feathers – but wouldn't it disturb their feathers to have to push them through their sleeves when they put them on?' It was evident that this lack of certainty troubled him. 'Do they have buttons?' he asked.

Her visual memory had summoned up Fra Angelico's *Annunciation* in Florence, the angel kneeling, star-struck, before the baffled Virgin. His multi-coloured striped wings stuck out behind him: of course the girl looked puzzled. The Romanian, she had to admit, had a point: a careful angel could probably fold them up and unbutton his side vents when he put his robe on, but slipping them through would still snag a lot of the feathers. Slipping them off would be easier, for the cloth would run along the feathers easily, as the Romanian had pointed out. Maybe they never, being angels, needed to change their clothes?

Illumination came and she had smiled at him with an all-knowing expression. 'Velcro.'

'Ah,' had escaped his parted lips, and he bent to kiss her hand. 'You people in the West know so many things.'

She turned in just before the church of the Pietà and worked her way back past the church of the Greci until she arrived at the Foundation. She let herself in, stopped in Roseanna's office, but there was no sign of her. She opened the door to the stairs and went up to the Director's office, let herself in, and set her bag on the table. She unlocked the storeroom and took out the packet of papers she had left in the smaller trunk. Leaving the doors open, she went back to the table, put down the folder, and took out her notebook. Whispering the word *'musico'*, she resumed reading the papers where she had left off the day before.

There was an affectionate letter from a priest in Padova, apparently a childhood friend, who told his 'Dear friend and brother in Christ, Agostino,' that the various members of his own family were all well and, with the help of God, would so remain. He sent his wishes and prayers that the same would remain true for his friend Agostino's family. In the absence of substance, all she could do was note the date of the letter.

The next was a document from October 1723, containing a list of the candelabra, books, relics, and paintings left to the church of St Andreas in Düsseldorf by a certain Johann Grabel. The candelabra were in brass and silver, the books all on religious themes, the relics a series of desiccated extremities, including the big toe of Saint Jerome. 'Left or right?' Caterina asked aloud. The paintings were portraits of saints, with a heavy preponderance of martyrs. Below this list was written, in Italian, in that backward hand, 'To the Jesuits. Fool.' She made a note and passed the document to her left.

She continued for another two hours, finding a random sample of letters from the later part of Steffani's life and all addressed to him, that contained requests for help of one sort or another, praise, ecclesiastical news, and more than a few requests for payment for articles such as wine, books, and paper. The letters came in from all over Europe, but strangely enough none of them made any further reference to music nor to Steffani's work as a musician. For all the evidence found in these papers, he might have been a clergyman and only that for his entire life. By the time she got to the last of the papers in the packet, there had been just that single aria to give evidence of a life beyond the Church.

She pushed the papers away from her and rested her chin on her palms and found herself thinking about her family. They had been lucky in one thing: none of them had had to survive the death of a child. One of her aunts and two of her uncles had died relatively young, but not before their parents and not before having had children. Two of her sisters had children, whom they loved to distraction. And she still had time to have them. Here, her inner cynic broke in to observe that, in a decade, it would probably be normal for women in their fifties and sixties to have children, so there was no sense of urgency, was there?

What would it be like, though, to know you'd never have them and not through your own choice? Would it bother a man to the degree that it tormented women?

She had never been especially curious about the sex lives of the castrati, had not bothered to see the film about Farinelli some years ago. She had read, years ago, of the tens of thousands of boys to whom it was done, all in the hope of producing a star. The lurid novel lying on the shelf in the Foundation's library could lie there until doomsday for all she cared. She had never bothered to speculate about what they did or did not do, and knew she did not care. She wondered only what they lost in terms of the bonding that came with parenthood, and was that worse than knowing there would be no children, no one to pass things along to, no one to teach or tickle? Was that the message in that sad man's eyes?

She reached out abruptly, retrieved the string and rewrapped the packet, took it back to the closet. She placed it on the flat top of the higher trunk at the back and took another packet from the smaller one. Back at the desk, she untied the packet and pulled out the first sheet. It seemed to be more of the same, an invitation dated 1722 for 'Monsignore di Spiga' to present his written request directly to the Secretary for Appointments and Benefices of the Archbishop of Vienna. She looked beneath this letter, hoping to find a copy of Steffani's request. It was common for people of that epoch to keep copies of the letters they sent, and they often attached the copy to the letter they were answering. But, instead, she found another begging request for help in winning an appointment to office, this one dated 1711, addressed to Steffani as the 'Assistant at the Pontifical Throne'. He was back in Hanover by then, she recalled, still working to bring Catholicism back to North Germany.

The next paper was a list of what looked like titles and clerical positions. Although it was written in German, the hand was Italianate and the document bore no date. She remembered then that one of the things she had wanted – and failed – to do in the Marciana was find an autograph score and check the handwriting against what she had found in these papers. Memory did tell her, however, that it very strongly resembled the writing in a letter of his reproduced in one of the books she had at home.

Because she had sat still too long, Caterina got up and went back to the cupboard, where she retrieved the first packet of papers. She untied it, opened it, and paged through until she found the aria. She took it back to the table and placed the first page next to the list of titles. She studied the papers for some time. Both of them had unusual d's and e's, each letter with a tendency to circle over itself back towards the left, as though the writer had tried to draw a circle but had grown tired of it and stopped a quarter of the way round. She had no idea if this was enough to prove that they were written in Steffani's hand, but she decided to believe that they were and see where that led.

She returned to the list of offices and titles that were lined up neatly beneath one another: Privy Councillor and President of the Spiritual Council; General President of the Palatine government and council; Monsignore di Spiga; Apostolic Prothonotary; Rector of Heidelberg University; Provost of Seltz; Envoy of the Palatinate in Rome; Apostolic Vicar of North Germany; Assistant to the Pontifical Throne; Temporary Suffragan of Münster; Member and President of the Academy of Ancient Music.

Below them, in what she believed was the same hand, was a row of question marks running from one side of the page to the other. She felt the hair on the back of her neck rise. Caterina was not a woman much given to reading scripture nor, for that matter, paying much attention to it, but her mother was a religious woman and was fond of quoting it. 'If I know all mysteries and all knowledge, and I have a faith that can move mountains, but have not love, I am nothing.' Provost of Seltz. What was that? Apostolic Vicar of North Germany? What was that worth to a man condemned to be childless for ever?

These reflections were interrupted by a light knocking at her door. She got to her feet and went over to open it. It was Dottor Moretti, in a dark blue suit made of the same quality fabric as the dark grey one he had worn the day before. The tie was a bit less sober: in fact, the burgundy stripes on a dark blue field, worn by a man of Dottor Moretti's sartorial sobriety, seemed to Caterina little different from a red rubber nose and yellow clown wig.

'I'm not disturbing you, am I, Dottoressa?' he asked.

'No, not at all,' she said, stepping back from the door to allow him room to enter. 'Please,' she said, waving him over towards the table.

'I brought you the computer,' he said and smiled. 'As I said, it's nothing special, but our tech person said it should be enough for simple things.'

'All I need to do is make notes on my reading and send them to you by email,' she said.

'And read *La Gazzetta dello Sport* if you please,' he said. 'If you need distraction from the eighteenth century.'

For a moment, she didn't understand, and then she did. 'Don't tell me *La Gazzetta*'s online, too?'

'Of course it is.' Seeing her expression, he added, 'You seem surprised.'

Caught, she had to admit, 'I suppose I have certain ideas about the people who buy it.'

'That they wouldn't be computer literate?' he inquired.

'That they wouldn't be literate, full stop,' she said.

It took him a moment, and then he laughed along with her. 'I'll confess I was surprised to learn it, too. My brother reads it online.'

'He likes sports?' she asked.

'Hunting and fishing and tramping around in wet fields all day with his pals,' Dottor Moretti continued, shrugged, and smiled.

'I have a sister who's a nun,' she said to suggest he was not the only one with odd siblings.

'Is she happy?' he asked.

'I think so.'

'Can you see her?'

Caterina smiled. 'She's not locked up, you know. She wears jeans and teaches at a university in Germany.'

'My brother's a surgeon,' he said, holding up his hands. 'Don't even think about asking. I don't understand anything.'

'Is he a good surgeon?'

'Yes. And your sister?'

'Head of the department.'

'In Germany,' he observed in the tone of respect Italians used when speaking of German universities. He looked down at the bag he was holding and placed it on the table. Unzipping it, he pulled out a laptop and its electric lead. He looked around to find a socket and had to carry the computer down to the other end of the table to plug it in.

He lifted the lid, pushed a button, and took a step

back from it, as though not at all certain what was going to happen and perhaps fearful there would be a loud noise or an explosion. The machine hummed and clicked, although in a very small, discreet voice. When the various lights stopped blinking, he bent over the computer and opened a program, then another. He stared at the screen, turned to Caterina, and asked, 'The thing for the Wi-Fi is down at the bottom, I think.'

'The thing?' Caterina asked herself. This was the lawyer in intellectual properties speaking, and he referred to it as 'the thing for the Wi-Fi'?

He touched the pad and moved the cursor to the bottom, tapped once, waited, tapped twice, and gave her a triumphant grin when Google appeared.

'See,' he said, 'you can send emails.' Then, looking stricken, he asked her, 'You won't mind using your own address, will you?' Before she could answer, he explained. 'Our tech man,' he said, speaking with unwonted awkwardness. 'He asked if the Foundation had an email address, and when I said I didn't know, he suggested I ask you to use your own.' Then, in a much lower voice, he continued, 'He did say I could give you an address at the office, but when he told me what had to be done to arrange that, I said I'd ask you if you'd be willing to use your own.'

When Caterina did not answer, he went on hurriedly, 'It's all right. I can have him set you up with an account at the office if you like.'

She smiled, glad to be able to relieve him of this

concern. 'It's fine. I can easily use my own.' She considered the work ahead of her and said, 'Besides, I don't know how much there will be to report at the beginning.'

He indicated the papers on the desk. 'Nothing?'

'So far, all I've found are documents about his career as a musician and a bishop and one aria that I think he wrote.'

'Aria?' he asked, quite as if he knew nothing about musical notation.

'I don't know where it's from, but it's an opera aria, not one of his chamber duets.' She saw that this distinction was not one he understood and so glossed over that by adding, 'I think it's in his hand. There's a copy of one of his scores in a book I'm reading, and the handwriting looks the same.' She pointed to the paper that lay on the table.

When Dottor Moretti made no comment, she said, 'It's probably his, but I'm not qualified to authenticate it.'

'You know what the first question from the cousins will be?' he asked.

'Of course: How much is it worth?'

Moretti said, 'I imagine it's at the whim of supply and demand, though you wouldn't think it would be like that for art, would you?'

'It's not art,' she said. 'It's just pieces of paper.'

'What? I'm not sure I understand.'

'The art is in the sound: the music, the singing. The score is just the way it's passed on.'

'But if it was written down by the composer? Mozart? Handel? Bach?' He sounded astonished and made no attempt to hide it. This was her profession, after all; she should know this sort of thing.

'If you don't know how to read musical notation, what good is the paper? If you're blind but you can still hear, what good is the paper? Unless you can *hear* it, what good is it?' She saw that he was stumbling after her, trying to understand but perhaps not managing to.

'Would you try to tell someone what a painting looks like? Or say that a perfume smells like a mixture of lavender and roses? Or tell the plot of a poem?' she asked. He looked at her with complete attention, and she realized he was following all of these examples. 'If you can't hear it, what is it?' she asked.

After a long time, Dottor Moretti smiled and said, 'I never thought of it like that.'

'Most people don't.'

13

After that, Caterina was silent for a long time, feeling strangely exposed by having so forcefully expressed her opinion. In situations like this, in which she found herself defending a position she knew that others would find extreme, she often tried to pour unguent on what she had said, but this time she didn't want to. She believed this: the art was the sound; the beauty was in the singing or the playing. To want to own the notes written down on paper, to place a greater value on the paper if it bore the signature of the composer, seemed to her an impure desire. She remembered something from her school catechism classes, about the sin of worshipping 'graven images'. Or maybe it was the sale of indulgences she was thinking of. Or perhaps she wasn't thinking at all and didn't need a comparison: it was creepy and it was wrong to think that the written music was the real music.

The lawyer smiled. 'I understand your position, really I do. But unless someone can write it down for the singer or the musician, they don't know what to do.'

'But that's not what I'm talking about,' she said. 'I'm talking about turning a piece of paper or an object into a fetish. Like a letter by Goldoni or Garibaldi's belt buckle. Goldoni's important because he's a great writer, and Garibaldi's famous because he banged heads and made this into a country. But his belt buckle's nothing. It's not him. And a letter from Goldoni has only the value someone is willing to put on it.'

'Isn't that true for music?' he asked. 'I mean, a performance. If everyone thinks it was lousy and howls at the singer, then how good was the performance?'

She smiled. 'Unfortunately, there isn't enough howling.'

'I beg your pardon?'

Caterina smiled again, pulled out her chair and sat down, waving to Dottor Moretti to take the chair opposite her. 'I mean that audiences are too polite. I've heard playing and singing in theatres that was disgraceful, and people applauded as if they'd just heard something wonderful. I think what's gone wrong isn't that bad performances are howled at, but that performances that should be howled at, aren't.'

'And the musicians? What about their feelings?'

This was a lawyer talking? 'I thought you lawyers were supposed to be hard-nosed and coolly analytical.'

He had the grace to smile. 'When I'm working, I'm as hard-nosed as they come and coolly analytical: it's part of the package.'

'But?' she prodded.

'But now I'm expressing some fellow feeling with musicians.' When she didn't answer, he said, 'I've had bad days in court, when I haven't presented things as well as I could have.'

'And?'

'And my client suffered the consequences.'

'And your point?'

'That people have good days and bad days, and it's . . .' he sought the proper word '. . . it's unkind to cause them embarrassment for what they do.'

'You ever take a malpractice case?' she asked.

'No. Why?'

'It's the same thing, isn't it? You get hired to do one thing, and you do it so badly that someone is hurt. Most people think it's right that you should be punished for that.'

'Bad singing hurts people?' he asked.

'It hurts some people in the audience directly,' she said, smiling and pointing at her ear. 'But it hurts everyone more generally because it lets the entire audience think – at least if no one boos – that *this* is what the music is supposed to sound like, and that does everyone a disservice: the composer, the other singers, and finally the people in the audience because it might stop them from learning what good singing can sound like.' She stopped abruptly, embarrassed to hear her didactic tone.

Dottor Moretti was silent for a long time and finally began, 'I never thought of . . .' before he stopped himself with a laugh. He looked at his watch and said, 'It's almost two. Maybe we're both being so serious because we're hungry. Would you like to go to lunch?'

Without thinking, Caterina answered, 'It's strange, but after only this short time, I feel as though I've got some sort of legal obligation to invite the cousins to come along if I say yes.'

Moretti, with full legal thoughtfulness, said, 'Since they'd assume that they'd have to pay for their part of the meal, I think we can assume they wouldn't come.'

'That's a lawyer's judgement?'

'I'd stake my reputation on it,' he said, astonishing Caterina, who had come to think of him as a man who would never stake his reputation on anything and who would never, moreover, make jokes about his professional integrity. Could it be that Dottor Moretti was not the man he seemed to be?

They went to Remigio, where lunch was easy and relaxed: he even unbuttoned his jacket when they sat down at the table. Caterina didn't pay much attention to what they ate, so surprised was she by the discovery that Dottor Moretti – he asked her to call him Andrea, after which they slipped into using *tu* with one another – was a man of culture and broad reading. He said he had studied history before deciding to transfer to law but that it had remained his – he hesitated before using such an inflammatory phrase – secret passion.

Dottoressa Caterina Pellegrini was a woman in her thirties with a certain experience of life. To find herself sitting across from a man who confessed that his 'secret passion' was the reading of history was not an experience with which she was familiar.

'I didn't tell you one thing, though,' he said, glancing away as if feeling awkward. 'I never finished my degree before I decided to come back to study law.'

'Came back? From where?'

'Well, from Spain. My mother's Spanish, you see, so I was raised speaking both languages.' Caterina was so surprised to hear him sounding – was the right word 'apologetic'? – that she simply waited for him to continue his story.

'I didn't finish,' he said.

'What happened?'

He set his fork down and ran his right hand across his perfectly combed hair. 'My father got sick, and someone had to come back to be here. He was a lawyer, my father, so one of us had to be ready to take over his practice. Both of my brothers are older than I, so they already had their professions.' He paused to look at her, as if to see if she were still sufficiently Italian, after all her years abroad, to understand the compelling necessity of his return.

Caterina said, 'Of course.' Then, 'But you were a historian, not a lawyer.'

He took another sip of his water, smiled, and said, 'Not a historian: a young man who had spent two years reading history. They're not the same thing.' He paused but Caterina waited for him to tell her all of this in his own way and at his own speed.

'I'd had two years of doing what I loved, so perhaps it was time to . . . to come home and grow up.' Leaning forward, and in a deeper and more sinister voice, he added, 'Slaves to their families, these Italians.'

In ordinary circumstances, she would have laughed, but something stopped her from giving more than a grin and a nod.

'Law was . . . different,' he went on.

'Easier?'

He shrugged. 'Different. Less complicated. I did the courses in three years, passed the exams, then the state exams, and here I am, two decades later and none the worse for it.'

She wondered about that but merely smiled and poured water into both their glasses. After some time had passed and she had returned to her pasta, he asked, 'What is it about music that attracts you?'

Without thinking, she said, 'It's so beautiful. It's the most beautiful thing we've done.'

'We, as in humans?' he asked.

'Yes,' she said. 'I believe that.' Surprised to hear herself sounding so uncharacteristically absolute, she added, 'Or maybe it's just that music is the one art that most thrills me. More than poetry and more than painting.'

'And why this Baroque music? Why not something closer to us in time?' he asked, sounding honestly curious.

'But it is modern,' she answered without thinking. 'It's got strong rhythms and catchy tunes, and the singers are free to invent their own music.' Seeing the question appear on his face, she went on, 'When they come close to the end of an aria, they can sing variations on what's gone before. The conductor writes them, or they find a score with variations in it, or they can write their own.' Involuntarily, she raised her hand and drew a series of arabesques in the air with one finger.

He smiled. 'No copyright infringement?' He smiled to show he was joking.

This nudged her towards confession. 'I'm a musicologist, so I shouldn't admit this sort of thing, but I love the spectacle of it, too: dragons, people and monsters flying through the air, witches, magic all over the place.'

'Sounds like fantasy movies.'

He meant it as a joke, but she gave a serious answer.

'That's what a lot of the operas were like. It was popular entertainment, and the producers put on a show. The singers were the Madonnas and Mick Jaggers of their times. They delivered the hit tunes. I think that's why the music is becoming popular again.' She saw his scepticism and added, 'All right, all right, not mass popularity. But most opera houses do a Baroque opera every season.' She thought about this for a moment, realizing that she had never been asked these questions by an attractive man, perhaps by any man. 'Or maybe it's only that singing's so close to us. We do it with our bodies.'

'Isn't dance the same?' he asked, reminding her that he was a lawyer.

She grinned. 'Yes. But I can't dance, and I once thought I could sing, or wanted to sing.'

'What happened?' he asked, setting down his fork.

'I don't have the talent,' she answered simply, as though he had asked the time. 'I had the will and the desire, and I think I have the love of it, but I didn't – and don't – have the vocal talent.' She rested her fork on the side of her plate and took a drink of water.

'That's very dispassionate,' he observed.

With something less than a smile, she said, 'It wasn't at the time.'

'Was it difficult?'

'If you've ever been in love, and the person turns and walks away from you, saying that you aren't the right one, well, that's what it's like.'

He looked down at his plate, picked up his fork, set it down again, looked back at her, and said, 'I'm sorry.'

Caterina smiled, this time a real smile. 'It was a long time ago, and at least the training helps me now. It's easier to understand the music, at least vocal music, if you think of it in terms of music you'll have to sing or want to sing.'

'Will you excuse my ignorance if I say I believe you without really understanding you?'

'Of course,' she said, and then to lighten the mood, she added, 'Besides, it gives a person the chance to see how very strange people can be.'

'Musicians?' he asked.

'And the people around them who aren't musicians.'

'Could you give me an example?'

She allowed stories to run through her memory, and then said, 'There's a story about King George the First – but before he went to England – having a conversation with Steffani and saying he wanted to change places with him. This went on until the King actually tried to run an opera company – and this is why I'm sure this story is apocryphal. After three days, he gave up and told Steffani it would be easier to command an army of fifty thousand men than to manage a group of opera singers.'

Moretti laughed and said, 'I've always admired people who can do that.'

'What?'

'Think of giving up.'

'You think the King was serious?' she asked, amazed that he could be so literal minded.

'No, of course not. But that he could think of it, want to do it.' He stopped for a moment, then added, 'I envy him.'

She didn't want to talk about this any more, so she asked, 'Did you have a century? Or a country?' Then, after a moment's thought, 'Or a person?' When he looked confused at the sudden change of subject, she added, 'As a historian?'

He smiled and the mood lifted again. 'I did.' Seeing that he had captured her attention, he added, 'And I have a confession.'

This stumped her. 'About what?'

'Monarchy.'

Caterina waved her hand in front of his face. 'Are you going to tell me you're the lost son of Anastasia, and you're really the Czar of all the Russias?'

He laughed out loud, put his head back and laughed so loud that people at other tables shot glances at them. The laugh changed to snorts, a word Caterina would never have thought usable in connection with Dottor Moretti, though perhaps it did fit with Andrea.

When these subsided, she said, 'Wrong guess, eh?'

'At least you didn't ask if I'm the son of King Zog of Albania.' That set him off again, and he ended up removing his glasses and wiping his eyes with his napkin.

Caterina waited. She uncovered a scallop from beneath her spaghetti and ate it, then a piece of courgette, and then she set her fork down and asked, 'What are you confessing about?'

'The Spanish Habsburgs,' he said.

'Is that a rock group?' she asked mildly.

This time she seemed only to confuse him. Quickly, she corrected herself. 'Sorry. It was a joke.'

He looked serious for a moment, then amused. Finally he said, 'It's because of a *fidanzata* I had there.' Then, to prevent any question she might have asked, he added, 'We took some classes together.' She said nothing, thinking silence would prod him more than a question.

So it proved to be. 'She was an aristocrat. The daughter of a duke, and distantly a Habsburg.' He shook his head, as if to ask how it was that a man who had once known the daughter of a duke could end up in a trattoria in Venice talking about her to a musicologist.

'She always went on about her father's right to the Spanish throne. After a while, I guess I got tired of listening to it.' Then, with a quick glance at her, 'Probably because I got tired of listening to her. But I didn't know that then: I was too young. I never met her father, but I disliked everything she said about him and her everlasting insistence that he was meant to be the King of Spain.' Then, as if he'd just heard himself saying all this, he added, 'And as I began to dislike more and more what she said about him, I realized I disliked her, too. But boys don't realize that when they're eighteen.' He smiled at the boy he had once been, and she joined him.

He broke off to thread tagliatelle around his fork, but he set it on the edge of his plate, untasted, and went on. 'So I started reading about kings – not only the one her father insisted had stolen the throne from him – and their ancestors and where they came from, and how they got to be kings, and what they did while they were. And then I found myself fascinated by the way so much of their behaviour led to such misery. Wonderful art, but endless human misery.' He looked across at her and smiled. 'But I was eighteen, as I said, so what did I know?'

She raised her water glass, though she knew it was improper to do so in anything other than wine, and toasted him. A man who so deeply regretted human misery deserved at least that much.

14

They laughed a great deal through the rest of the
lunch. The only disagreement came when Andrea
insisted on paying the bill, something he persuaded
her to accept when he promised he would pass the
expense on to his clients. It was perfectly legitimate,
he explained, because they had talked about music
and manuscripts during the meal. Indeed they had,
she agreed, delighted that the bill would be paid by
the two cousins and not at all troubled by questions
of legitimacy.

They were back at the Foundation in a matter of
minutes; Caterina found herself wishing it had been
further away. At the door, Andrea looked at his watch
– she noticed that it was gold and thin as a coin, which

would certainly have interested Signor Scapinelli. 'I've got to get back,' he said. 'I look forward to hearing from you.'

Caterina had been studying his watch when she heard these last words. As she raised her head to smile at him, he reached into his pocket to pull out his wallet. He took a white card from it and handed it to her. 'My email is there, so if you'll send me the results of your research, I'll forward it to the cousins.' Pleased as she was by his having adopted her habit of referring to Signori Stievani and Scapinelli as 'the cousins', she was disappointed – she admitted it – that his eagerness to hear from her seemed prompted by the documents.

'Yes,' she said, with what she thought was an easy, relaxed smile. 'I'll get back to it and send you a summary by the end of the day.'

'Good,' he said, extending his hand. She shook it, slipped his card into the pocket of her jacket, and let herself into the Foundation. As she started down the corridor, Roseanna came out of her office.

'Oh, there you are,' Caterina said, smiling. She was uncertain whether, now that they had almost become friends, she should greet Roseanna with a kiss, but she left it to the older woman to decide.

As Caterina got closer, she saw there was to be no kiss. In fact, Roseanna looked decidedly unfriendly.

'Where were you?' Roseanna asked by way of greeting.

'At lunch,' Caterina said, not specifying where or with whom.

'The office was open.'

'I thought I closed the door,' Caterina said without thinking.

'Yes, the door was closed, but it wasn't locked.' Roseanna waited, but Caterina's silence led her to continue. 'The documents were on your desk, and the storeroom was open.' Caterina listened to the tone: the words, as well as the facts, left her with no defence. Her delight at Andrea's suggestion had led her out of the room and she had given not a thought to the papers or her responsibility for them, a lack of attention in which Andrea had joined her.

'I'm sorry,' was the best she could say. 'I forgot.' She reached into her pocket for the keys to the door at the foot of the stairs, and her fingers found Andrea's card. 'I won't do it again.'

Roseanna unfroze a bit but still said, briskly, 'I hope not. We don't have any clear idea of the value of what's there.'

Again, Caterina heeded the tone far more than the words, for Roseanna's disguised question hinted that she had obtained information about the value of those papers, wanted to be asked about it and to be praised for having found it.

'What did you find out?' Caterina said, moving a few steps closer to her.

Roseanna went back into her office, leaving the door open, an invitation Caterina took. When they were seated on either side of her desk, Roseanna pushed a sheet of paper across the table. Caterina recognized the letterhead of an auction house in London; below it were listed three manuscripts and the sums paid.

Qui la dea cieca (1713?) 9,040 Euro
Notte amica (first page) (1714) 4,320 Euro
Padre, se colpa in lui (fragment) (1712) 1,250 Euro

Caterina looked up from the paper and gave a broad smile. 'Well, who's been doing her homework?' She glanced at the paper again and asked, 'How on earth did you persuade them to give you this information?' She tapped the three sums with the tip of her finger and said, '*Complimenti.*'

Roseanna smiled even more broadly and said, all anger or reproach fled from her voice, 'I sent them an email, saying I was the Acting Director of the Foundation and telling them that, in consequence of a large donation to our Acquisitions Fund, we were interested in any available manuscripts by Agostino Steffani and curious about recent purchase prices.' Nodding at the paper, she added, 'They sent me this.'

Caterina's open-mouthed admiration was entirely spontaneous. 'Acquisitions Fund?' she asked.

Roseanna waved her hand, dismissing the possibility that such a thing existed. 'I assumed they'd answer a request if it was something that might make them money.'

'Ah, Roseanna,' she said, 'you have a real call to work in the music business.'

Caterina picked up the paper. 'So this is what his work is sold for,' she mused. 'It would help if we knew when these sales took place.'

'Yes,' Roseanna agreed. 'You could call and ask, couldn't you? Or write to them.'

'What language did you use?'

'Italian,' Roseanna said. 'It's the only one I know.'

Caterina let the page drop back on to Roseanna's desk. 'It might be enough just to know this: that a presumably complete aria is worth at least nine thousand Euros.'

Both of them sat and considered this fact until finally Roseanna reached forward and put her finger on the highest sum. 'I hope the cousins don't think of doing the same thing I did and find this out.'

Caterina smiled at her. 'They'd start sleeping in front of the door, wouldn't they?'

'With a gun,' Roseanna added.

Peace restored, Caterina went back upstairs, telling herself not to be such a fool because of an invitation to lunch. 'Lock the papers up, lock the door,' she muttered to herself as she went back into the room. Even though she knew she had to be methodical and take the papers in the order in which she found them in the packet, she paged through the remaining documents – about six centimetres of them – looking for musical scores. Near the bottom, she unearthed a sheet of paper half of which was filled with bars of music, neatly written in a very small script, obviously not by the person with the back-leaning hand. Below were two paragraphs and then the signature: 'Your brother in Christ, Donato Battipaglia, Abbé di Modena.'

She set the paper down and looked across at the wall, feeling alert or alarmed but unable to tell the cause. She looked at the signature again. Battipaglia was a new name: this was the first letter from him she had seen, and she could not recall any previous reference to him. Still standing, she turned her attention back to the letter. It began with a description of a concert – not Steffani's, the writer hastened to clarify – which had sounded like 'the scraping of a badly-oiled carriage'. In the excessively complimentary style of the period, the writer praised Steffani's *Le rivali concordi*, a copy of which the writer had had the 'inestimable fortune' to see in the library of his patron, Rinaldo III, Duke of Modena. He praised the score in its entirety as well as the seriousness of the sentiments expressed in the text, and then turned his attention to an example of 'a singular mastery of musical invention'. The bars he quoted, he said, came from the duet, *'Timori ruine'*, which he found sublime. Caterina looked at the musical extract, which he provided in full, and fell into agreement with the sentiment of the Abbé. She hummed through it. Oh, he was good, this Steffani, she thought, with his fourteen operas, divertimenti, duets, and religious music and his glorious feel for what the voice wanted to do. Then she went back to staring at the wall, trying to nudge herself towards what it was in the letter that had caught her attention.

She looked again at the signature. Wasn't it said that people revealed themselves in the way they wrote their names? But the flourishes and squiggles were in no way unusual for their epoch. 'Donato Battipaglia, Abbé di Modena.'

'Abbé,' she said out loud. 'What the hell was an abbé?'

Liszt came to mind. He was an abbé, and if he had lived the life of a priest, Caterina was the heir to King Zog.

She switched to her email account and typed in Cristina's address at the university. It was a professional question she was asking, and Cristina was always sure to check that address rather than her personal one.

'*Ciao*, Tina-Lina,' she began, 'I hope this finds you overworked and happy. Look, I'm working at that job in Venice, examining the papers of the Baroque composer who worked and died in Germany and I need some information. He was an abbé. What's an abbé? Does he have to be a priest, or can he be something else and be called a priest? (a bit of deceit, of course, that your employer would never think of tolerating).' Old habits die hard, and

Caterina had spent more than twenty years of her life baiting Cristina for her decision to become a nun.

'Also, I've come to think this man might have been a castrato. I have it in my memory baggage that a castrato could not be a priest. Would making him an abbé be a way to get around this? (Not that your employer would . . .) Could you let me know about these things with something other than your usual glacial pace?

'*Mamma* and *Papà* are both very well and as happy as ever. Clara and Cinzia are fine; so are their kids. Claudia looks sensational and seems to be getting on better with Giorgio, though who knows how long that will last? Why didn't she get the same happy genes the rest of us seem to have inherited? I wish there were some way to . . . you know what I mean, but I don't know what to do. I'm fine, the work looks interesting, and . . .' she paused, wondering if she should mention Avvocato Moretti, but her good sense prevailed. They had gone to lunch together, for heaven's sake, that's all. '. . . it's sure to keep me here for some time, and by then one of those other jobs might well have come in. I hope this finds you happy and busy and giving Deep Thought to the Totally Erroneous Path You Have Chosen in Life. Love, Cati.'

Cristina, who had been the only other one in the family to opt for a professional life, had always been her favourite sister. The closeness explained Caterina's shock and, yes, horror at Cristina's decision to enter a convent, but it also permitted the irreverent tone which characterized her every communication with the *Professoressa Dottoressa Suora*.

She was about to put the computer to sleep when she remembered that Cristina had no background information at all. She started another email and added, 'His dates are 1654–1728, if that helps', and sent it after the other.

She closed the computer and slid it along the table until it was out of reach, then went back to reading.

After an hour and a half of taking notes about various ecclesiastical benefices granted, requested, or refused, Caterina got up and walked over to the windows. She opened a window and wrapped her hands around the bars; she pulled at them, and when they refused to move, did the same with the bars of the other window. Was this what it was like for Steffani, she wondered, trapped inside a body that had had physical limits placed on it? That's what prison was, wasn't it? Physical limitation, a restraint on what one was free to do. But prison was usually temporary, and the prisoner had, if nothing else, at least the hope of some day being free again.

That's the hope Cristina could have, were it not that Cristina did not see it in this light. If anything, she welcomed the limitation on her freedom, said it helped her concentrate on what was important in her life. Could Steffani possibly have come to think this way? But Cristina, for good or ill, had at least made the decision for herself. All right, she had made it at nineteen, but no one had made it for her, and no one had forced her into it. Quite the opposite – and she could always, if she wanted to, walk away. And if she did decide to leave, she'd keep her doctorate and her job, wouldn't she?

But Steffani? He couldn't walk away from what Caterina now believed him to be, nor could he have walked away from the Church that gave him definition and position and importance, even though that same Church had been complicit in making him a *musico*. Surely his genius would have brought him work and fame as a composer. Yet, the thought came to her, would it have provided him the respectability that the Church could give him? And would his genius have draped him in the crimson of a bishop and thus kept him hidden and safe from the jokes and contempt of men?

Whatever the reason, he had chosen to stay. Her thoughts went back to that duet in the letter: was it meant to be a hidden message from a man who had suffered and survived? She flipped the pages over and searched for the letter from Abbé Battipaglia.

Non durano l'ire	Angers don't last
E passa il martir	And suffering passes away
Amor sa ferire,	Love knows how to wound
Ma poi sa guarir.	But it also knows how to heal

Vera fortuna severa	Severe fortune
A'i nostri contenti	To our peace of mind
D'un alma che spera	To a spirit that hopes
Consola il desir	Please bring consolation

Once again, Caterina found herself quoting scripture. 'Jesus wept.'

15

The rest of the afternoon passed without event. She read, she made notes, she transcribed a few passages, all about Steffani's relatives: aside from Agostino, only a brother and a sister, also childless, survived to maturity. 'Cousin' frequently appeared as a form of address, both in letters to him and letters about him, but she was sufficiently Italian to realize that this was a term with an extra-legal meaning. As for testamentary instruction, she might as well have been looking for advertising jingles. She had so far found nothing written by or even containing the name Stievani or Scapinelli or any of the variant spellings of these names.

Among Steffani's friends and correspondents, the

person he seemed most attached to was Sophie Charlotte, the Electress of Brandenburg. Caterina found frequent reference to Sophie Charlotte in letters to Steffani from other people, in which she was referred to as, 'Your friend the Electress', 'The Electress to whom you so warmly refer', and 'Her Highness Sophie Charlotte, who so honours you with her friendship'. The letters that passed between them showed great warmth and even more openness than could be expected, given the difference in their status.

She wrote to tell him that she was studying counterpoint, the better to prepare herself to begin to compose music, hoping that her duets would be as natural and tender as the ones he wrote. He responded by joking that he hoped she would fail in her endeavour, for should she turn to composing, 'the poor Abbé will go forgotten'.

At five Caterina got up to turn on a light but resisted the desire to go out for a coffee, chiefly because she did not want to have to lock everything up and then go through the business of unlocking it and taking it all out again when she came back. At six she went to the storeroom and exchanged packets, pulling out an especially thick one that occupied most of the space on the left side of the trunk. The first letter showed promise, for it was sent by a certain Marc'Antonio Terzago and addressed Steffani as 'nephew'. He thanked Agostino for the help he had given in finding a place as a student at the seminary in Padova for a young nephew and for this proof that 'familial loyalty was not diminished by the immense distance between Hanover and Padova'.

She registered the man's name. Steffani's brother Ventura had been taken in by an uncle and had assumed his name, Terzago. So here was an entirely different family of 'cousins'. Could they have died out, or were they ancestors of Stievani or Scapinelli? Below it there was a letter in the less well formed hand of the boy himself, Paolo Terzago, thanking his 'dear cousin' for his efforts in finding him a place at the seminary, where he was 'very happy and warm'. The letter bore the date of February 1726. February in northern Italy: no wonder the boy commented on the temperature in the seminary.

At seven-thirty, feeling she had not progressed towards any understanding of Steffani as a man, and had gained little information about his relatives, she got to her feet, put the unread papers face down on top of the packet, tied it closed, and locked it in the cupboard.

Before she left, she thought she'd have a look to see if Cristina had overcome her legendary sloth and answered. And indeed the first thing she saw in her inbox was a mail from her sister's personal address.

'Cati Dearest,' she read, 'your Abbé Steffani does leave behind him a wake of uncertainty.' Though she knew she had not used his name, Caterina opened her Sent folder and reread her original email, and indeed, she had used only his title of abbé.

'I see you checking the Sent folder, dear, only to

confirm that all you gave me was his title. To spare your suffering or believing that my having crossed over to the Dark Side has endowed me with Dark Powers, I say only that you gave me his dates and the fact that he was a composer, probably Italian (he was a castrato, or so you suspect, and that's where they came from, alas), who died in Germany.

'You gave me these facts, and the training as a researcher given me at enormous expense by Holy Mother Church, which over the course of many years and countless thousands of hours has honed my mind to razor-like sharpness, gave me the sophisticated skills to put those three pieces of information into Google. Just one name comes up. Perhaps the Church could have saved all the money it spent on me and, as you so often suggest, given it to the poor?

'Indeed, "abbé" was, at the time of your composer's career, pretty much a courtesy title, and though the documentation is contradictory (I shall spare you the details) it is safe to say that to be an abbé is not necessarily to be a priest. Some were; many were not. There is a subset here of bishops who were not priests, either, and as your composer later became a bishop, I save time by telling you that wearing the mitre did not, in those times, require ordination. For more about this see his patron, Ernst August, who was also – though married, a father, and never ordained – the Prince-Bishop of Osnabrück. Of course Ernst August was a Protestant (hiss) but they seem to have had the same dodgy rules that allowed men (of course) to become bishops and even create/consecrate other bishops without themselves being ordained. It does make a person think of yoghurt, doesn't it, where all you have to do is add a little to make more.' Here, Caterina marvelled, not for the first time, at the lack of seriousness with which Cristina often spoke of the organization to which she had given her life and spirit.

'As to the injunction that a castrato could not and cannot be a priest, your memory is, as is so often the case, Cati dearest, correct. Canon Law 1041, #5 ° states clearly that anyone who has gravely and maliciously mutilated himself or another person or who has attempted suicide cannot be ordained. It is also a basic tenet that inadequacy for marriage renders a man similarly inadequate for the priesthood, no doubt an evasive way of speaking of castration or sexual dysfunction.

'Pope Sixtus V, on 27 June 1587 (you might not like us, dear, but you must admit we're very good at keeping records), made the Church's position very clear in his Breve *Cum frequenter*, by declaring that castrati are denied the right to marry.

'So there you have it, Baby Sister, and I can add no more until I have further information from two people I've asked about this, all of which will come to you in due course. Things here are fine. I'm working on another book, this one about Vatican foreign policy in the last century. It'll probably get me kicked out or sent to teach third grade in Sicily.

Or maybe you could hire me as a full-time researcher? Stay well, Kitty-Cati. Keep an eye on the family for me, please, especially poor sad Claudia, who should have married that nice electrician from Castello instead of that dreadful lawyer. I miss you all terribly. There are times when I want so much to be home that I could walk out the door and head south. Yes, that makes me remember the time we hitch-hiked to France and told *Mamma* and *Papà* that we were taking the train. Driving into Paris with that man – was he an accountant? I can't remember any more – was one of the most thrilling moments in my life. Getting a doctorate or being named full professor were nothing in comparison.

'I send my love to all of you and leave it to you to spread it around in direct proportion to how much anyone needs it. Love, Tina-Lina.'

As a researcher Caterina had been trained to read between the lines of texts. This was as much a habit for her as it was for a veterinarian to see mange on the skin of a friend's dog or a voice teacher to hear the first faint signs of excessive vibrato. Her sister's email left her uncomfortable, chiefly because of what it revealed about her mood but also because of her own initial self-satisfaction at reading it. 'ET, phone home,' she said in a soft voice.

She shifted from the mood of the email to its contents. What had begun as a wild surmise on her part was now confirmed as a distinct possibility; indeed, more than that. She thought of those long fingers, that beardless, puffy face, utterly devoid of the exciting angles and lines of the male face, even at the age of sixty, which Steffani had been when that portrait was painted.

She turned off the computer, picked up her bag, and went downstairs, but not before checking that the cupboard and the door to her office were locked. Roseanna had left. As she closed the outer door to the building, Caterina noticed a sign saying that the library was closed until the end of the month. The weather was fine, so there would be no suffering on the part of the people who used the reading room as a warm place to spend their time. But it was entirely possible that they also needed a place where they could pass the day.

Thinking about this and other things, she walked home; not the apartment where she was living, but her parents' house down near La Madonna dell'Orto, the area of the city that would ever be home for her.

She could have taken a vaporetto if she had walked back to the Celestia stop, but she didn't like that part of the city much, however well lit most of it was, so she chose to walk through Santa Maria Formosa, out to Strada Nuova, and home the same way she used to return from school.

So much taken with the thought of Steffani's life was she that, at first, she paid no attention to the man who appeared beside her, as if to pass her, and then fell into step with her. She glanced at him, but as it was not anyone she knew, she ignored him and slowed her steps. But he slowed his as well and kept pace with her. They came down into the *campo*, which was dark at this hour, its paving stones covered with a thin film of humidity that dissipated and reflected the lights. A few metres beyond the bridge, where light also came from the windows of the shops on her right, she stopped. She didn't bother to pretend she wanted to take something from her bag: she simply stood still, waiting to see if the man would move off. He did not.

The vegetable stand had already closed up and gone, but a number of people were crossing the *campo*, and three or four were within hailing distance, though she didn't know why she thought of it in those terms.

'Do you want something?' she asked, surprising herself but, apparently, not the man.

He turned and looked at her, and she didn't like him. Just like that: instinctive, visceral, utterly irrational, but the feeling was strong. Her instincts told her this was a bad man, and the fact that he stood and looked at her and said nothing was bad. She wasn't in the least afraid – they were in the middle of a *campo* and there were people around them. But she was uneasy, and the longer he didn't say anything, the more uneasy she grew. He was an entirely average looking man, about her age: short hair, no beard, normal nose, light eyes, nothing to remember.

'Do you want something?' she repeated. Again he didn't answer. He looked at her, studying her face, her shoulders, the rest of her body, and then again her face, as though memorizing everything he saw.

The desire to run or to strike out at him and then run came over Caterina, but she forced her body into obedience and remained standing still. A full minute passed. To her right, a church bell began to ring eight-thirty, and she was late for dinner.

She started walking towards the bridge on the other side of the *campo*. She did not look behind her but she listened. Her mind was humming, and she could no longer remember if his footsteps had been audible before. As she reached the bridge, the desire, the need, to turn and see if he was behind her became all but overwhelming, but she resisted it and continued up and down the bridge and then into one of the narrowest *calli* in the city. As she entered it, she prayed that someone would approach from the other end, but it was empty. She shook with the desire to turn around, but she kept walking until she was out of the *calle* and at the next bridge.

Up and down and into Campo Santa Marina, where she had to decide which way to go. Turn right and save a few minutes, but pass down Calle dei Miracoli, a narrow place with little foot traffic, or continue straight on and come out by San Giovanni Crisostomo and run into the heaviest foot traffic in the city as she headed for Strada Nuova and home. She continued straight ahead.

16

She made no mention of the man at dinner, not wanting to alarm either her parents or herself. He had done nothing to menace her, had not even spoken to her, yet he had unsettled her and, she admitted to herself while trying to pay attention to a story her mother was telling, had frightened her. The city was a safe island in a world that seemed to be going increasingly off its axis: to read the papers was to fear that some infection was abroad. She returned her attention to her mother's story, and to her food. Home-made polenta made from grain sent to her father by an old friend who still grew corn in Friuli. The rabbit came from Bisiol, where her mother had been buying rabbit for twenty years. The artichokes were from

Sant'Erasmo: her mother had recently joined a cooperative that delivered a basket of vegetables and fruit to the house twice a week. The purchaser had no choice about what was delivered: it was what was in season, and it was organic.

Her mother had complained about never having eaten so many apples in her life, but when Caterina ate one of them, cooked in red wine and covered with whipped cream, she would gladly have signed her mother up for another two months of apples. They talked of many things: her father's work, her mother's friends, her sisters' marriages, her nieces and nephews. If, one day, she had an estate to leave, Caterina wondered, would she be happy to leave it – in the event of her having no husband or children – to her nieces and nephews? They were only children now, but who knew what they would become as adults?

As she continued to half listen to her parents, she thought about Steffani. He had passed most of his life in Germany, going back to Italy only occasionally and usually for fairly short periods. How much had he seen of his relatives or their children? *Had* he seen them, known them, tossed them in the air and played with them and sung his songs to them? And the cousins, these men who descended from the children's children of his cousins, with what right did they stake a claim to his papers and estate, and where had the idea of a 'treasure' come from? No one had explained that to her. The only reference she'd found to his estate mentioned that, after his creditors had been paid, there remained '2,029 florins, some papers, some relics, medals, and music'. It was that 'and music' that hit her with force. Exclude that, and the man had lived seventy-four years: some papers, some money, some relics, and some medals. Treasure?

'Where did we all get the idea that your great-grandfather lost everything at the Casinò?' she surprised her father by asking. Both her parents stared at her, but neither asked her if she had been paying attention to what they were saying, so obvious was it that she had not.

Her father ran both hands through his still thick hair, something he did when he wanted time to think. Her mother, as she always did when things didn't go as she had planned, put more food on their plates. Everyone in the family except her mother and Cinzia ate like wolves and never changed weight by a gram. 'All I have to do is look at a carrot and I weigh a kilo more the next day,' was her mother's mantra.

'I don't know,' her father said, not about the carrot which played so frequent a role in his wife's conversation, but about the question Caterina had just asked him. 'It's family legend. People used to talk about it when we were kids, and I talked about it with your uncles Giustino and Rinaldo.'

'Did anyone ever check to see if it was true?' she asked.

Her mother gave Caterina a startled glance, but

her father smiled and said, 'No, I suppose we never thought about doing that.'

'Why?' Caterina asked.

He considered her question, then smiled again. 'Probably because it sounded so romantic and so Venetian – *palazzo* lost at cards, gambling away the family fortune.'

'What do you think really happened?'

He shrugged. 'I suppose what usually happens. My great-grandfather wasn't good with money, wouldn't listen to his wife, and lost it all.'

Her mother broke in to say, 'It's how we like to think of ourselves.'

'We?' Caterina asked.

'*Veneziani. Gran signori,*' she said, quoting the tagline of a common saying that defined Venetians.

'But instead?' she asked.

'Cati,' her mother said, 'you haven't been away so long you've forgotten. We love to make a deal and beat someone else out of something.'

'But you don't and *Papà* doesn't,' she said, knowing this was true.

Neither of her parents said anything. Eventually Caterina put her spoon down and admitted, 'All right, all right. You don't, but most of us do.'

'Do you?' her mother asked, as if she had just shown some sympathy for child prostitution or the MOSE project.

'No, I don't think I do,' she answered.

Before things could grow more complicated, her

mother said, 'You've got twelve minutes to get the boat at San Marcuola, Cati.' She hadn't looked at her watch, hadn't asked the time: she simply *knew*.

Hurried kisses, promises to call the next day, and every day, her mother's insistence that it made no sense for her to live all the way down in Castello when she had a perfectly good home to stay in, and then she was out of the house and on her way to the boat stop.

Her feet knew the way: out the door and right along the canal, then left over the bridge, and stop thinking about it and let your feet do it for you, and nine minutes later she walked out in front of the church of San Marcuola, where, she reminded herself, Hasse's tomb was hard to find, and straight to the boat stop. She took out her imob and pressed it against the sensor, heard the blip of acceptance, then walked into the lighted *embarcadero*.

And there he was: the man who had followed her from the Foundation. He sat on the bench to the left hand side, his legs stretched out in front of him, feet crossed at the ankles. His arms were crossed over his chest, and he looked like any person sitting and waiting for the vaporetto. He glanced up at her and, though he noticed her, there was no sign of recognition on his part, just as there had been none when he had looked at her on the street some hours before.

She opened her bag and slipped her imob into the inside pocket, walked past him to the front of the dock, turned right, and looked up the Grand Canal.

The boat was a hundred metres away, clearly visible in the brightly lit canal. Its headlight approached. What did she do if he got on the boat with her? Ignore him and get off at Arsenale and then walk home? There were sure to be people on the street, but perhaps not on the small *calle* where the apartment was. She could call the police, but what if he didn't get off the boat when she did? The boat came and she got on, went into the cabin and took an aisle seat on the left side, where she could see who got on after her. The man did not.

As the sailor flipped the rope loose, she waited for the man to make a sudden move and jump on the departing boat at the last minute, but he didn't. The boat started forward. She turned to the left and saw him still sitting there, legs comfortably stretched out in front of him, arms folded. As she moved past him, he continued to look at her, expression unchanged.

She looked forward. She felt something sting her eye, and when she placed her hand on it she found that perspiration had run down her face and soaked her hair. It took almost half an hour to get to Arsenale, and Caterina was glad of it, for she had time to talk herself into a state of calm.

The boat pulled in; the sailor tossed the rope and wrapped it around the stanchion, and five or six people lined up to disembark. She put herself in the middle of them, matching her pace to theirs. Careful to stay behind an elderly couple who were walking slowly, she got off the boat and walked down Via Garibaldi until she came to the street where she was living, Calle Schiavona. She paused, but only minimally, at the corner. The key to the front door had been in her hand since the boat had begun to slow for the stop.

The house was along on the left. She reached the door, put the key in the lock and let herself in. She turned on the light, walked to the top floor, let herself into the apartment. She walked through it, turning on all of the lights one after the other. When she was sure she was alone – though she tried not to think of it in those terms – she went into the bathroom and was violently sick into the toilet. She washed her face and rinsed her mouth, then made herself a cup of chamomile tea and took it into the living room.

Sleep, she knew, was impossible. She sat on the sofa and picked up the second of the books about Steffani she had taken from the library.

The story recounted so captivated her that she soon forgot about feeling sick, drank the tea, went and made more, and returned to the book. She read a few more pages, went into the kitchen and ate a few dry crackers, drank more tea, then returned to the book.

In 1694, the movie-star handsome – she liked this anachronistic description – Count Philip Christoph Königsmarck disappeared overnight from the castle of Ernst August, Duke of Hanover and Steffani's patron. He disappeared, she read, 'into thin air'.

It was subsequently rumoured that he had been killed on someone's orders, and even though the official version always remained that he had simply gone missing, nothing could prevent it from becoming the greatest scandal of the times. There were a few candidates for the role of killer, or sender, first among whom was Duke Ernst August himself – who objected to the openness of Königsmarck's affair with his daughter-in-law, the beauty of the century, Princess Sophie Dorothea.

With the entrance of a second double-barrelled Sophie, Caterina was forced to flip back to the genealogical chart at the beginning of the book. The Sophie Charlotte whom Steffani corresponded with and of whose friendship he was so proud was the sister-in-law of this second Sophie. The betrayed husband was Georg Ludwig, the future George I of England; his adulterous wife, Sophie Dorothea, was also his first cousin. She had been a desirable catch because of her beauty and charm and, not incidentally, because of the hundred thousand thalers a year that came with her.

The nausea had passed, and Caterina found she was hungry. She went into the kitchen and put some rice on to boil. On the way back to the sofa, she paused in front of the mirror next to the front door and asked herself out loud, 'Have you been watching too much television?' Since Caterina had never owned or lived with a television and never watched it, the question was rhetorical: it was a way of commenting on the melodrama of the story she was reading.

It was not, to say the very least, a love-filled marriage. Truth to tell, Georg Ludwig and Sophie hated one another. The book recounted an incident when an argument between them had escalated until he literally had to be pulled off of her. Georg had a series of mistresses: in fact, when he subsequently went to England to become king, he packed up two of them – whom the English looked at and quickly nicknamed the Maypole and the Elephant – and took them along. Sophie Dorothea seemed to have limited herself to only one, and everything Caterina could find suggested that her error was not the affair but her failure to keep it secret.

Steffani, she reminded herself – if simply to justify her reading of this lurid stuff, like something straight out of a scandal magazine – was involved inasmuch as the two lovers, Sophie Dorothea and Count Philip, sent each other hundreds of love letters, in many of them attempting to disguise their passion by quoting the lyrics from Steffani's operas. To show his eagerness Königsmarck mentions the swift duet, '*Volate momenti*', where the lover begs both time and the sun to quicken their pace to thus shorten the time of the lovers' separation. If the things she had read in the Marciana were to be believed, these letters were being intercepted and read by Countess von Platen, believed to be the former lover of Königsmarck and certainly the former mistress of Ernst August, who was the father-in-law of Sophie Dorothea.

Caterina stared into space. 'Let me see if I've got

this straight,' she told herself aloud. 'These two fools sent love letters back and forth in opera lyrics, but a mistress Königsmarck had dumped – who just happened also to have been the mistress of the father-in-law of her ex-lover's current mistress – was reading them, and she blew the whistle on the lovers.' She resisted the urge to go over to the mirror again and check to see if she had grown a second head.

She smelled the rice and went into the kitchen to turn off the flame. She took off the top and spooned some of it into a bowl, added more salt, and took it back into the living room with her.

Things became more interesting. Almost immediately after Königsmarck's disappearance, a certain Nicolò Montalbano, a Venetian who had been hanging around the court of Hanover for almost twenty years writing the occasional opera libretto, was reported to have been paid the astonishing sum of 150,000 thalers by persons unknown, whereupon he too promptly disappeared.

Poor Sophie Dorothea was divorced by her creep of a husband, Georg Ludwig, on the trumped-up charge that she had abandoned the marriage bed, and then old Georgie sent her off to rot away in a castle for thirty years and wouldn't let her see her kids. The author quoted a lovely but unreliable legend that she delivered a deathbed curse on Georg, and sure enough, he dropped dead in less than a year. Even so, she was to have no satisfaction from her curse, for she died before Georg did and so never saw her son become King George II of England though, as Caterina remembered, he was little better than his father. Makes a person understand the current royal family, she thought.

She sat back in her chair, then got up and went over and stretched out on the sofa, the bowl on her stomach. She stirred the rice around, letting it cool. Ernst August had spent a fortune and worked diplomatic miracles to be chosen as an elector, some sort of big deal title that only a dozen or so aristocrats got to have, and they in turn elected the Holy Roman Emperor. Yes, a big deal. But he had to wait a couple of years before he could be crowned or anointed or whatever it was that happened to turn him into an elector. While he was waiting for this to happen, he'd have had to keep his nose clean, and he'd have had to see that his family didn't disgrace him and thus scotch his chance to become an elector.

'So there you are, Monsieur Poirot,' she said out loud, waving her fork at the stout figure who did not stand by the door, 'you have your first suspect.' Instantly she added, 'And his son, Georg Ludwig, is the second.' And Steffani: how much would he have known? He was court musician, diplomat; his libretti served as the language of love. The affair was an open secret. Surely he would have known of it.

Caterina ate the rice, chewing each mouthful a long time. At one point, she remembered the face of the man who had followed her, and her throat closed up for a moment. Again, out loud, she said, 'I will not allow this to happen to me.' She did not define what 'this' was, and after a time she finished the rice and went to bed and slept.

17

The next day dawned cloudless and bright, and the night's sleep had restored Caterina's usual energy and good spirits. She didn't think about the man who had followed her until she left the house and went into a bar for a coffee. The barman recognized her and offered her a brioche with her coffee even before she asked for it, and she recalled thinking, last night, that a possibility for safety would be to ask one of the men in this bar to walk her home. In the bright light of an April morning, the very idea seemed ludicrous.

She had slept late and had not bothered to read her emails before she left the apartment. When she got to the Foundation, she said good morning to

Roseanna, who said that she hoped the sign would keep people out as long as Caterina was working on the documents.

She went upstairs and turned on the computer. When she had lived in other countries, she had read the Italian press online every morning, but she had abandoned the habit in recent years. It was all time wasted, she feared. The frequency with which certain faces appeared on the front pages changed, but none of them ever disappeared. Only death swept away the men who had devoted themselves to politics. Theft, involvement with the Mafia, payments to transsexual prostitutes, corruption, missing millions – none of this removed them. Convict them of anything, and they were still there. Turn your back and they changed political party or reinvented themselves, changed their hairline, found Jesus, or wept on television while begging their wives for forgiveness, but they were still there. Only death removed them from the scene, though sometimes not even then, for many of them came back as newly renamed streets or piazzas.

Better to read her emails. There were three. The first one she opened was the one from Cristina.

'Dear Cati, Destroyer of My Work Routine, for you've gone and done just that, and not for the first time. There I was, happily busy with my chapter on Pope Pius XII (what the likes of you would call a Nasty Bit of Goods, I fear) (an opinion I am coming to share) (which I ought not to admit) (but do) and his various evasions and prevarications, when your request, like a dog that has found a very interesting bone, drags in Clement VIII and drops him at my feet, to make no mention of the question of castrati, the title of abbé, and the various deceptions to which men in power are prone. Just as a bit of history, you might be interested to learn that Pius X banned castrati from the Sistine Chapel. In 1903. You want deception, I give you deception, my dear.

'As you can see, I've been busy in your interests. I've found – not without difficulty – a *breve* from Clement VIII, declaring that castration was sanctioned for singing in "the honour of God". And I ask you here, Cati – and I'm not joking – please not to comment on this or try to provoke me about it: its existence is sufficient provocation.

'There is also the dispensation, which a pope can give for pretty much anything he chooses. So, as that American songwriter told us, "Anything goes."

'Yes, my tone is an indication of how tired I am of my current research; not of the research itself, which is fascinating, but of what it makes me think and feel. So I welcome the chance to jump back in time and read about these long-dead people. You've sent me into the archives and created a curiosity that has put me in touch with colleagues I've not contacted for years; to my surprise, they seem as lit up by this subject as I am and have been raining down information upon me. Or perhaps we are all tired of our own research?

'One old classmate of mine, a man who is now teaching at the University of Constance, suggested I tell you to take a closer look at the Königsmarck Affair: he says he has seen a manuscript that claims your musician was involved in it. He said he would send further information if you want, although my guess is that he'll send it to me, anyway, even if you don't want it, since there doesn't exist the scholar who doesn't love gossip, even if it's a couple of hundred years old. I know of the Affair only in the most superficial manner but would love to read what he says and will do so if it's addressed to me. Ah, how proud *Mamma* would be to learn that the taboo about privacy she fed us with her milk is alive and well in Tübingen. From which city I send you my love, dear Cati, as well as my offer to continue to look into all of this for you. It keeps me from my own work, and I want that. For now. Love, Tina-Lina.'

Oh my, oh my, oh my, Caterina thought: it sounds as if Tina is coming to the end of the line. It had always puzzled her that it was Cristina who had been bitten by the religion bug, not Cinzia or Clara or Claudia, who were not given to asking questions about the world they found themselves in. All of them were lukewarm where religion was concerned: Cinzia and Clara had their kids baptized and confirmed, even went to church once in a while, and told the kids that God loved them and it was wrong to lie or to hurt people. Cristina excepted, her sisters had little respect for priests, hated the Vatican as only

Italians could hate it, and thought the Church should not be allowed to comment on politics.

'Stop it,' she told herself out loud and read the other emails. One was from a classmate from Liceo, saying he'd just heard she was back in town and would she like to go to dinner? 'Not unless you bring your wife and kids, Renato,' she said and erased the mail.

The last was from Dottor Moretti, informing her that he had received phone calls from both cousins the day before, asking why she had not informed them of the progress of her researches. Nothing more.

She wrote back to him immediately, saying she was still reading through the documents in the first trunk and had not yet found anything worth reporting about the testamentary dispositions of the Abbé Steffani. She thus found it necessary to expand the focus of her research – if he could be formal in his mail, then she could be too – and would be obliged to consult other sources. She would, therefore, be absent from the office of the Foundation for the rest of the day while she pursued these researches.

'Take that, Dottor Moretti,' she said, as she punched the Send key, and off it went. Mention of the aria she had found could wait.

She flipped open her phone and saw that there was one message. She recognized the Romanian's voice instantly, the easy Italian, the occasionally fumbled word. She saw that it had come in at three-thirty in the morning, making her grateful that she had turned the phone off before she went to bed.

The Romanian, she was surprised – and then not, when she thought about what a brilliant teacher and researcher he was – had been offered the chairmanship of a department of musicology – he did not bother to say where – and was considering the offer, both depressed and inspired by her having had the courage to leave Manchester and abandon him to the 'misery of boredom'. His voice trailed off and ended in the middle of a sentence. She closed the phone and placed it on the desk.

Caterina was suddenly overcome by an attack of conscience. The cousins were paying her to find something in these papers, and the least she could do was have a look through them to see if anything referred to this Königsmarck thing. She opened the storeroom and removed the thick packet she had been reading the day before. Back at the table, she untied the string, again pausing to marvel at its survival all these centuries, and started to read the top sheet. Realizing it was a letter she had read, she chastised herself for not having followed her usual scholarly routine by placing the already-read documents face down on top of the pile before tying it closed.

Or had she? She tried to remember, but the events of the previous evening had wiped out any recollection she had of her routine actions before leaving the office. Caterina was unsettled by this lapse of memory. She paged down until she found a document she had not read and started there. By limiting herself to date, salutation, first two paragraphs, and signature, she speeded the process of reading; this way, she moved quickly through the remaining documents, finding nothing that appeared to be related to Steffani's family, his feelings for them, or his possessions and will.

She closed the packet and took it back to the storeroom, set it upside down on the top of the taller trunk, and pulled out another packet, almost as thick as the other. Underneath there was nothing except the wooden bottom of the trunk.

Opening this packet, she left the strings on the table beside it. As quickly as she could, she went through the papers, touching them with the care that comes to anyone who has spent time reading documents that are hundreds of years old. She always held them at the centre of the page on both sides and lifted them gently from the page below. At the first sign of resistance, she moved the sheet lightly on its axis: so far every page had quickly come free.

After the first ten sheets she accepted the fact that she was wasting time: the only way to guarantee that she understood everything was to read each document carefully from beginning to end.

That decided, she put the papers back in order, closed the packet, and took it back to the storeroom. She slipped them all back inside the trunk, then closed and locked the metal doors.

She connected to the internet, put in Cristina's

address and wrote: 'Dear Tina-Lina, Of course, it's all right for you to read whatever goes between me and this man in Constance, and of course I'm curious about anything he has to tell me about Steffani. I've read a bit about it myself, and it seems that they – the two lovers – used lines from his operas in their letters. You believe in the Holy Ghost, so you should have no trouble in adding that to the list of things to believe. At any rate, dear one, I have so far seen no other mention that Abbé Steffani was involved in the matter, and it's already risking exaggeration to consider this "involvement."

'Listen to me, Tina-Lina. We all love you and respect you and will love you and respect you whatever you do or whomever you do it with. I'm back to doing research, so I'm reading between the lines of texts, and that includes yours. Stay well, know that you are loved, eat your spinach and say your prayers. Love, Cati.'

She clicked Send.

She left the room, locked the doors carefully and went down to Roseanna's office, hoping that she would have heard all the noise of her industry and caution. But she had left.

She stopped in a bar for a *macchiatone*, ate a tuna *tramezzino*, and had a glass of water. Her reader's card got her into the Marciana without trouble and with no search, and she found her way – telling herself she must be using the same system as passenger pigeons, feeling the electromagnetic waves from the various places she passed near – to the second floor reading room with its view of the Palazzo Ducale. She set her bag down and took her notebook over to the card catalogue. Before pulling open the drawer marked K, she patted the cabinet on the top as though it were the dog or cat of an old friend. Not only did the catalogue have eleven books, in three different languages, for the Königsmarck Affair, but it contained a number of handwritten cards in a series of hands best described as 'spidery' that directed her to other books and collections in which further information was contained: in two cases these were held in the manuscript collection.

She jotted down the names, authors, and call numbers of these and took them down to the main desk, where the librarian gave her the forms that would summon them from their store cupboard. When she gave the completed forms to the librarian, the woman took them with an almost total lack of interest or enthusiasm, leaving Caterina to suspect that her grandchildren might some day see the tomes from the manuscript collection, whereupon she slipped into Veneziano and said she was a friend of Ezio's.

'Ah,' the librarian said with a smile, 'in that case I'll get them and bring them to you at your carrel.' She studied the numbers on the paper. 'Take about half an hour,' she said and smiled again.

Caterina thanked her and went back to her carrel, stopping to collect the books about Königsmarck.

One, she was surprised to see, was a nineteenth-century French novel. She shrugged and placed it unopened on the shelf in front of her.

Half an hour later, the librarian found her hunched over her desk, notebook open at her side, pages covered in pencilled notes. Caterina was as incapable of using a pen in a library as she was of punching a hole in a lifeboat. When the librarian set the two large manuscripts on the table, Caterina jumped, as if the woman had poked her with a stick. The librarian said she had logged the books out to Ezio, so Caterina could keep them there as long as she needed to.

When the woman was gone, Caterina lowered her face into her hands and rubbed at it, ran her fingers through her hair. She was suddenly hungry, ravenously, desperately hungry. She opened her bag and at the bottom found half a dusty Toblerone, which she'd been eating on a train to – how long ago it seemed – Manchester. She looked around guiltily and saw the backs of two men seated at the carrels at the other end of the room. She got to her feet, moved away from her carrel, and from the books and manuscripts, then tore free a dusty triangle. Slipping it into her mouth she let it melt, then chewed at the nougat, enjoying the way it clung to her teeth to prolong the sensation of eating.

Back at the carrel, she looked at her notes. Königsmarck had disappeared on the night of 1 July 1694, when he was seen to enter the palace and make his way towards Sophie Dorothea's apartment. It was generally accepted that he had been the victim of four courtiers, their names, at least according to the Danish Ambassador to Hanover, well known and spoken of at the time. His corpse was said to have been wrapped in a sack, weighted with stones, and tossed into the river Leine, never to be found.

In less than a month, the English envoy to Hanover, George Stepney, relayed to one of his colleagues that in the House of Hanover a political murder had taken place. 'Political murder,' Caterina muttered under her breath. Hearing it like that urged her to get to her feet and go over to study the façade of the Palazzo.

'Political murder', she said again, and then only 'Political'. Not a murder for honour and not a murder for love, though the second was always really the first. Political. The involvement of the Hanoverians in the murder would do more than weaken, perhaps destroy, their claim to the electorship. What of their claim to the throne of England, which they so desperately coveted? Surely even the English would baulk at inviting a murderer or the son of one to become king.

Although this was not her field, it was her century of study, and Caterina had a wealth of background information. Aristocrats were free to have lovers, so long as those women who did had already given their husband an heir and a spare and then were relatively discreet in their choice of lover. Don't endanger the bloodline; don't imperil the passing of the estate from father to son. Men could legitimize their bastards; women never.

Caterina remembered a conversation she had had with the Romanian, years ago, when she had first gone to Manchester. It was, in fact, the first time she had eaten dinner in Commons. Drunk, he had pulled out a chair beside her, asked if he could sit there, and sat down with only a glass and a bottle of red wine. He had said nothing while she ate her salad and then a piece of swordfish she remembered had been over-cooked and covered with a sauce that added to the unpleasantness of the meal.

'We never know who our children are,' he said, then turned and asked, 'Do we?'

'Who's we?' she asked, the first words she ever spoke to him.

'Men.'

'You never know?'

'No,' the Romanian said sadly, shaking his head and taking a long drink from his glass. He refilled it, shook his head again, and said, 'We think we know, we believe, but we never know. Do we?'

'If it looks like you?' she asked.

'Men have brothers. Men have uncles,' he said, this time sipping from the glass.

'But?' she asked, certain that this was a point he meant to lead somewhere.

'Women *know*,' he said with heavy emphasis. 'They *know*.'

Caterina thought it incorrect to mention DNA tests to a man the first time she spoke to him; furthermore, he was a colleague and not a native speaker of

English. Instead, she said, 'More proof of our superiority,' and sipped white wine from her own glass.

The Romanian smiled, took her hand and kissed it, then gathered up his bottle and glass, got to his feet, and started to walk away. When he had gone three steps, he turned back and said, 'There's no need of proof, my dear.'

18

The memory faded; Caterina returned to the book she had been reading. She dipped back into Steffani's life at the time he was working as a diplomat, first in Hanover and then in Düsseldorf, where he moved in 1703. He worked to facilitate the making of treaties and to arrange princely marriages, though with little apparent success. He failed to prevent his former patron Maximilian Emanuel from getting mixed up in a war against England and Germany he had no chance of winning, and he failed to arrange a marriage between Maximilian Emanuel and Sophie Charlotte, who turned him down, got an upgrade, and ended as Queen of Prussia. Poor woman, she held the title for only a few years before dying at the age of thirty-six, though in the few years she was queen she won the friendship of Leibniz. Caterina recalled the frequent references to her in the letters found in the trunk, the queen who 'had so honoured' Steffani with her friendship. Did Andrea Moretti feel himself so honoured by the friendship of Caterina Pellegrini?

She continued to read the account of the tangled history of the times in which Steffani had lived and worked, when Protestant and Catholic monarchs fought for the souls, and taxes, of whole nations. It seemed that Steffani was in the business of propaganda: her choice of word, she admitted. Politicians often used religious enthusiasm to disguise the lust for raw power, though it was possible that Steffani sincerely wanted to win souls back to the One True Church. So many One True Churches. Yet Steffani did almost no preaching; nor, for that matter, did he administer the sacraments, whether to large or small groups. The Abbé busied himself with the titled and powerful, attempting to return them to the embrace of Catholicism or to convert to it from their born religion of Protestantism. To the best of Caterina's understanding, all this missioneering had little to do with religion: these were political moves based on the chances of alliance or marriage. If power shifted away from a king or emperor, an elector or a count, one way to ensure survival was to bail out of the religion of the loser-to-be and sign up with the other side, then wait to see if reconversion would be necessary.

She thought of a classmate of hers from Alto Adige. Though his family had lived in the same house for centuries, his grandfather had been born in Italy, his father in Austria, and he in Italy, nationality changing as the border shifted back and forth according to political whim or the spoils of war.

She wondered what belief, today, held the same force for the majority of Europeans. One way to determine that would be to try to think of the things people would die for. Transubstantiation? The Trinity? Surely not. To save their family or the life of a person they loved? Yes. But beyond that, and perhaps the attempt to save their property, Caterina could think of nothing. At dinner parties, she had heard people – mostly in England and mostly men – assert that they would give their lives for the freedom to say or write what they wanted, but Caterina didn't believe that, just as she had never believed it for herself.

She thought of all those legends she had been taught in school, all those stories of heroic resistance and sacrifice: Giordano Bruno, Matteotti, Maria Goretti, the endless list of martyr saints. How long ago that was, and how different we are from them.

She had no idea what danger Steffani or his fellow Catholics might have been in during the years when he was attempting to change the course of history, but her sense of the times suggested it wasn't great. He might not have had to die for what he believed, but the more she read, the closer she came to the view that he had truly been willing to live for it. He seemed to have been conscientious about his job: he travelled tens of thousands of kilometres in Germany and Austria, Belgium and the Netherlands; went back and forth to Rome a number of times. Here she thought of the accounts she had read of what it was like to cross the Alps in the eighteenth century: carriage, horse, or foot, and the endless winding back and forth and up and down on impassable roads, through snow, avalanche, mud, never knowing when, or if, you would arrive. *That* was dedication.

If what she suspected was true, he had been castrated to prepare him to sing in a church choir. And yet, and yet, and yet he had remained faithful to the Church for his entire life, dedicated his energies to the propagation of that faith, had worked with full strength and conviction to convert or return rulers to that faith and thus bring into the flock the people they ruled, thus expanding the power of that Church.

She found some contemporary opinions of Steffani and read them eagerly, curious to know what people who had actually known him would have to say. 'The metamorphosis of a mere entertainer into a Bishop is as ludicrous as the scene in Lucian where a courtesan is changed into a philosopher.' Anger swept over her. He was far more than an entertainer, you supercilious bastard: she had heard the music and she knew. And then she read another one, commenting on Steffani's acceptance of praise for one of his operas: 'The haughty style seemed to me more to befit the theatre than ecclesiastical humility.' Why shouldn't he be proud of his music? And where'd this nonsense about 'ecclesiastical humility' come from? When had anyone ever seen any of *that*?

Caterina got up and went to the window, looked out, seeing nothing. Was that why Steffani so needed the Church: to give himself respectability and to protect himself against open affronts? These mean-spirited comments showed that he could never be free of them nor safe from them. They could criticize his vanity or make fun of his 'short black hair that is slightly mixed with grey and a satin cap, a large cross with brilliant diamonds and a large sapphire on his finger', but so long as the cross on his chest was a bishop's cross, they could never make fun of his masculinity.

She thought of what she had read of the apparent profligacy of his life: earning and spending great amounts of money, collecting books and relics and paintings, eating and drinking well, travelling often and always in style. Was all this meant to prove that he was one of the truly anointed? She thought of that round, sad face, turned back to her desk, and picked up the French novel about the Königsmarck Affair: at least lust, adultery, and jealousy made sense to her.

She opened the book, and her eye fell on an elaborate bookplate showing a nearly naked woman lying on a sofa, a book held open in one hand while the other lay on her rather-more-naked breast. Caterina's eye fell on the title of the book the woman was not reading: *La città morta.* Above the drawing appeared

Donna Leon

the name Gabriele d'Annunzio and below it *'Principe di Montenevoso'* and *'Presidente dell'Accademia Reale d'Italia'*. Left entirely without power to comment, even to herself, Caterina began to read.

'Little did the handsome and gallant Count Philip Königsmarck know what destiny held in store for him when, at the tender age of fifteen, he first set his gaze upon the beautiful Princess Sophie Dorothea. Destiny had chosen her to be his love, his joy, the star to the wandering bark of his passions, and, ultimately, the cause of the train wreck that was to carry him to death and her to a life of misery, pain, abandonment, and shame.'

The same destiny that had endowed the Count with these things had endowed Caterina with a sensitivity to truth and accuracy, and so she looked up from the opening paragraph and said, 'He was sixteen, and she wasn't a princess.' She drew a veil of unknowing between her mind and the metaphor of the train wreck and returned her eyes to the page. Although the book was written in French and she could read the language easily, she still didn't have the immediate knee-jerk response that a native speaker would have. It took a split second before the absurd vulgarity of the language caused her to giggle.

Within ten pages, Caterina was lost in a world of climactic intemperance, with 'gusts of sighs', 'floods of tears', 'tempestuous passion', and 'lightning flashes of rage'. Sophie Dorothea, she learned, was 'married to a brute', and was 'a loving mother', 'an injured wife', 'a delightful tease', and 'slow to anger'.

Königsmarck was 'a clever rake', 'ambitious and hard-working', 'one of the most brilliant swordsmen of his time', and 'unfaithful to all women until his heart was given – for life and for death – to the beautiful Sophie Dorothea'.

After forty minutes, hands still holding the book, she told herself to stop this, to stop reading. It might have been good enough for d'Annunzio, but it was not good enough for her. She realized only now what the good sisters had meant when they warned the ten-year-old Caterina and her classmates that a book could be an 'occasion of sin' though she was in some confusion as to the precise nature of the sin she was committing. What religion said it was a sin to waste other people's time or to be unwittingly ridiculous?

Again she walked to the window, where she opened her bag and took out an energy bar, the sort of thing people think is meant to be eaten during an assault on Everest. She glanced at the motionless backs of the two other researchers, who appeared not to have moved since last she looked at them, muffled the noise she made opening this wrapper, and ate it in four bites.

She had skimmed a hundred and fifty pages, and once back at the desk she flipped to the end to see the page number: there were just forty pages left. Life is never guilt-free, she reflected, and perhaps it was good enough for her, after all. 'Jealous wrath', 'violent rages', and 'unbearable torture' came at her, only to be countered by 'moments of bliss' and 'joy such as she had never known', which is not to overlook 'two spirits united as one'. The villains appeared – all wearing the requisite 'dark cloaks' – and the worst of them, Nicolò Montalbano, was the one to commit the 'vile deed'. Not from any interest in the prose or curiosity about the fate of the protagonists, but simply because she was growing progressively hungrier, Caterina speeded the pace of her reading, and within another fifteen minutes she was done with it. She snapped it closed and tossed it – something Caterina was not in the habit of doing with books – on to the desk.

How had it happened that the historical accounts, which were more or less locked to the reported facts, had fascinated her and aroused her sympathies for these two careless fools, while the fictional telling of the tale, which was meant to bare their souls and was free to attribute to them the most tempestuous emotions while playing with the reader's, only left her feeling relieved that these two selfish little geese had been removed from the scene?

The energy bar had not been enough. Hunger attacked her, and she gave in to it. She chose three of the books and put them in her bag, left the library unquestioned, crossed the Piazzetta and started back towards Castello, walking along by the water and happy to do so. At the bottom of the first bridge she turned left and down a *calle* running back from the

Bacino. Up on the right, her feet and stomach remembered, there was a ridiculously small bar that used to serve tiny pizzas topped with a single anchovy. And so it was, and the spritz was unchanged, and after three of the first and one of the second, Caterina was ready to go back to the Foundation and work her way through the remaining documents in the last packet in the trunk.

They dealt with the transfer to Steffani of a benefice and an estate in Seltz, which she learned was on the Rhine and belonged to the Palatinate. It was one of those cities that ping-ponged between Catholic and Protestant: the Reformation turned it Protestant, and the French turned it back to Catholicism. And then the Jesuits came on the scene, and Caterina, *una mangia-prete* of no indifferent conviction, had a presentiment that things would get worse for everyone involved, and there would be a lot of empty pockets. She remembered then that backward-slanting note added to the list of things that had been left to the Jesuits. 'Fool.'

The account she read was complicated, for it attempted to explain in historical and legal terms what was, to put it crassly, a case of people's fighting over money. The earnings from Steffani's appointment as Provost of Seltz were denied him because of the prior involvement and subsequent claims of the Jesuits, who insisted that the monies were theirs by right. The case rumbled through the ecclesiastical courts for years as the Pope dodged this way and that way to avoid making a decision about who was to sweep up the loot.

In 1713, Steffani, who insisted on his full right to the money, received just 713 thalers out of the total payments of 6,000. Appeals and people willing to defend Steffani's claim to the money went to and from Rome, but the matter continued to drag on without resolution. 'Jesuits,' she muttered under her breath, much as a person of lesser civility would utter an obscenity.

Some documents suggested that the missing money was a serious blow to Steffani's finances. Because the legal cases took place in the decade before his death, and since his claims repeatedly referred to his parlous financial condition, Caterina again wondered where all the money had gone. He was to retire soon after his unsuccessful attempt to collect the benefice of Seltz; some accounts claimed that he also had severe difficulty in collecting the money from his benefice in Carrara. Caterina remembered that the sale of indulgences was one of the grievances that Luther made public when he nailed up his theses on the door of the cathedral. Had the bargaining with benefices been another?

The dispute continued as Steffani's financial situation worsened. He repeatedly petitioned the Pope, the Jesuits, and various temporal rulers. What surprised Caterina were the names of the people to whom he felt comfortable enough to write to ask for help: the King of England, the Elector of Mainz, the English

Ambassador in The Hague, even the Emperor himself: 'I have asked the Emperor if he, as an act of charity or fondness, could buy the paintings from me so that I can survive a little while longer.' 'My lamentations can be matched only by those of Jeremiah. In the end I need to plead for alms. The King of England urges me to remain in Hanover more strongly than do the people in Rome. It is the world turned upside down.' At the same time that he was addressing these people, he was writing to others to tell them he was reduced to begging for alms. 'I now have nothing more to sell with which to maintain myself.' 'I have sold all of my possessions, even my small chalice, made of silver. Because of this, I can no longer provide myself with even those things people think are necessary.' All the letters implied that at this time in his life he was reduced to selling his possessions, which rendered the cousins' belief in a family 'treasure' even more ridiculous.

Caterina went back to the computer and to the archives holding material on Steffani: in Munich, Hanover, and Rome. She logged in to the Fondo Spiga in Rome, named after Steffani's benefice, and started scrolling down the papers that were posted. And found the cousins. No, not the cousins, but the men who must have been their ancestors and thus the direct heirs to Steffani's estate. In 1724, the Abbé wrote to Giacomo Antonio Stievani and to the arch-priest of Castelfranco, Antonio Scapinelli, inquiring about the deeds to some houses in the San Marcuola section of Venice which the three of them had jointly inherited but which had been somehow usurped by the Labia family. Steffani suggested that the men meet to arrive at an agreement on how the estate should be reclaimed and divided among them: the archive had no record of a response from them.

An heir writes to his cousins to ask how they might divide property they have inherited in common, and the others fail to respond to, or even acknowledge, the request, no doubt preventing any attempt to sell the property or divide and pay out the profits. Caterina remembered how much it used to annoy her, when she was younger, to hear her mother speak of her distrust of anyone who 'came of greedy people'. She had attempted to reason with her foolish mother, victim of her antiquated beliefs in hereditary family characteristics. Ah, those who have eyes and see not.

Reading randomly in the archives devoured the rest of Caterina's afternoon, and by the end of it, though she had found out more about the financial difficulties that afflicted Steffani near the end of his life, she had no firmer grasp of the man.

At seven, mindful of the cousins' eagerness and reluctant to have to listen to another admonition about having failed to do what she was being paid – they'd surely mention that if they dared – to do, she typed in Dottor Moretti's address and wrote, 'Dear Dottor Moretti, pursuant to our agreement, I am continuing with my reading of the documents: to make sense of them in the historical or personal

context, I find it necessary to conduct further background research, without which many references,
lacking context, will have little or no meaning. I
would not like the claim of either Signor Stievani or
Signor Scapinelli to be in any way weakened by my
failure to understand a reference which might favour
the case of either one of them, and thus it is necessary . . .' she backed up and deleted that word,
replacing it with 'imperative' '. . . that I pursue my
research at the Marciana, where I am currently
reading through books and documents in Italian,
French, German, English, and Latin' – take THAT,
cousins – 'some of which make reference to the family
situation and do create a context that suggests the
Abbé's assumption of familial responsibility and
mutual interests.'

Here she began a new paragraph to describe her
archival research and transcribed Steffani's letters to
his cousins, noting drily that the archives contained
no response from them.

'I am optimistic that wider familiarity with this
information will be of great service in my pursuit of
a clear understanding and interpretation of Abbé
Steffani's testamentary dispositions.' She closed with
a polite salutation and signed both her first and last
name, omitting her title. She was also pleased that
the letter avoided the use of any form of direct
address, either polite or familiar.

Send.

When she looked at the table and saw that she had,

in five hours, read only four documents, she thought of the weeping Francesca's words to Dante as she explained how she and her lover Paolo, standing at her side there in Hell and mingling his tears with hers, had spent their day reading until, 'That day we read no further.' Their reading had led them to lust, to sin, and finally to death and Hell: Caterina's was going to lead her to pasta with tomatoes, olives, and capers and half a bottle of Refosco. How much she would have preferred lust and sin.

19

She left the Foundation and, a slave to beauty, took the longest way to the *riva*. Once in sight of the water, she turned towards the Basilica to watch the light disappear behind its pale domes. As she turned away and started walking towards Castello, she noticed how the remaining light fell on the faces of the people walking towards her and brightened them in every sense. The tourist current was high with the approach of Easter, and sudden riptides had begun to sweep past the unwary natives or slack tides becalm them, permitting large chunks of flotsam to flow around them. Things had changed in the years she had been away, and the local population now had the freedom to move swiftly against the approaching current only a few months a year. But, Caterina observed, that was better odds than the salmon got.

She had slipped her *telefonino* into the outside pocket of her bag, telling herself why it was necessary to do this. Perhaps she'd decide to call a friend and suggest dinner; perhaps her mother would call; or another old classmate would learn she was back in town and suggest the cinema and a pizza. 'Or perhaps the heavens will catch fire, Caterina, and you'll have to call the firemen,' she told herself out loud. A short woman walking by with the aid of a cane gave Caterina a startled glance and looked around quickly, searching for a place to move away from the crazy woman.

Caterina ignored her, pulled out her phone, dropped it inside her bag, and zipped the bag shut. The phone did not ring, and so she had both the time and the sense to stop in the neighbourhood store and buy olives, capers, and tomatoes, go home, make the pasta, and drink the rest of the Refosco.

Only then did she turn on her own computer and look at her mail. Sure enough there was one from Tina.

'Dear Cati,' Cristina began, 'this is the email that my friend in Constance sent. To me. Addressed to me. So I read it. Let me send it along to you so you can read him before I say anything.'

"Dear Sister Cristina, I'm happy to give what information I can to your sister and hope it will be of help to her in her research. Even after that, I will still be in your debt for your generosity in helping me gain access to the Episcopal Library of Trent.

"Your sister is evidently familiar with the 'Affair', so I need waste no time outlining it. The manuscript, which I came upon while researching a book on Post-Reformation ecclesiastical taxation, is in the possession of the Schönborn family and appears to be the memoirs of the Countess von Platen, one of Count Philip Christoph Königsmarck's former lovers, reported by all to have been passionately jealous of him. She had also been the mistress of the Elector Ernst August, by whom she had two illegitimate children. (I've no idea of the proper form for putting a footnote in an email and so am forced to use this parenthesis. She, Clara Elisabeth von Platen, also tried to persuade her lover, Königsmarck, to marry her own illegitimate daughter by Ernst August, which fact you are free to use should a colleague ever attribute dissolute morals to the Italians. And to prevent your going off to discover the destiny of her daughter, be pleased to hear that she was said to be the mistress of Georg Ludwig – her half-brother and soon to be King George I of England, to which country she accompanied him, later becoming the Countess Darlington and dividing his favours with the Duchess of Kendal, Melusine von der Schulenburg.)

"How the manuscript could have ended up in the archives of a family that also has an important collection of musical manuscripts, among which are many by your sister's composer, is not within my competence to determine. Letters from Countess von Platen now held in the Graf von Schönborn'sche Hauptverwaltung in Würzburg confirm the handwriting.

"In this manuscript, which begins with the explanation that it is being written in the shadow of death, she claims a desire to tell the truth in God's ears before that event. I read manuscripts, not souls, so I have no idea if this is the truth or her invention. Her desire to make her peace before God is quickly forgotten, for she does not miss a chance to speak badly of most of the people she mentions, even those who had died decades before.

"Of Königsmarck's murder, after saying only that four men were involved and one of them gave the fatal blow, from behind, she says she hopes 'his spirit found peace', though she also says she is not surprised at the manner of his death, 'at the hands of those he injured', which presumably implicates the family of the Elector, although even the most cursory reading of the Count's brief history might extend that list.

"After a bit of moralizing about the 'justice meted out to this sinner and betrayer of womanhood', she writes, 'though it was the hand of God that struck him down, it was the Abbé who gained from the fatal blow that sent him to his Maker'.

"Then, as if someone had asked her for evidence, she writes, 'Did he not, Judas-like, make possible and profit from the crime? The blood money given to him bought the Jewels of Paradise, but nothing can buy him manhood and honour and beauty.'

"After that, at the beginning of the next line, as though the writer intended to continue with the text, there is the single word 'Philip', but nothing follows that word. The memoirs continue on the next page, but she has nothing further to say about Königsmarck."

There followed his hope that her sister could make use of this information, then some details of his own ongoing research, a polite closing, and an offer to facilitate access to the manuscript, should her sister so desire.

'And there you have it, my dear,' Cristina continued. 'I've no idea what the Countess means by all of this. She doesn't say she was there, she doesn't say she saw your Abbé kill him, only that he "made possible the crime". Like my friend, I don't read souls, only texts.

'Let me go back to the idea of reading souls for a minute, if I might and if you don't mind. Mine is very tired and because of that probably illegible. I keep working at the research, but the more I read, the more irrelevant it all seems. The Vatican's foreign policy during the twentieth century? What can any thinking person believe it was except manoeuvring in pursuit of power? On the wall in front of my desk, I've put an old photo of the Pope giving communion to Pinochet, and that's enough to make a person go out and join the Zoroastrians, isn't it? They, however, don't allow people to convert, and can you think of a more noble tenet for a religion to have?

'Yes, Kitty-Cati, I'm thinking of jumping ship, of telling them they can have their wimple back, not that I've ever worn one, or would. I'm deeply tired of it and of having to close an eye and then close the other one and then close a third one if I had it, so much do I read and see about what they've done and still do.

'They're drunk with power, the men at the top. Please don't tell me you told me so. It's not the basic faith that's troubling me. I still believe it all: that He lived and died so that we would be better and it – whatever "it" is – would be better. But not with these clowns in charge, these old fools who stopped thinking a hundred years ago (I'm in a generous mood and so left the other zero off that sum).

'Please don't say anything at home, and please don't be angry that I asked you that, as if I couldn't trust you to keep your mouth shut. I know they don't really believe it, but I don't want them to worry about me because they know I do and know how much it will cost me to walk away. Isn't it funny how it all shifts around at a certain age, and we start worrying about them and try to spare them from being hurt? You think that's what it means to be a grown-up?

'I'll probably wake up in the morning with a hangover for having said all this, but you're the only one I can say it to. Well, there's someone here, but he doesn't want to hear this sort of thing from me. Or, more accurately, he does; what he doesn't want is for me to go back and forth or agonize over it, just to

DO it. Yes, Kitty-Cati, it's really a "he", just to put your mind at rest after all these years. No, that's to do you an injustice. You wouldn't care one way or the other, would you? And he's nice and single and uncomplicated and very smart and leaves me alone when I want to be left alone and doesn't when I don't, and where does a girl find that sort of thing these days. Eh? It's still too soon to tell you more about him, but don't worry, please: he's a good man.

'All right, go back to your research, and I won't go back to mine. I just don't care about it any more, and I know myself well enough to know I won't ever care about it again. I find your Abbé and his doings far more interesting, probably because he is so far removed in time, so if you don't mind, I'll continue to work as your research assistant. That failing, you think Uncle Rinaldo would hire me as an apprentice plumber if I came back? Love, Tina-Lina.'

For the first time in her life, Caterina was hurled into a crisis of faith. So strong was Caterina's faith in her sister's faith that she had stopped arguing with her about it years ago and confined her comments to the odd flash of sarcasm. The zest of confrontation had gone out of it for Caterina in the face of what she believed was Tina's happiness at having found the place in the world where she belonged and where she could work at what she loved while believing that to do so somehow made a difference to the god she worshipped.

And now along comes Tina and pushes down the graven image that Caterina had built. She had no idea what happened to an ex-nun, or even how a nun went about becoming an ex. Did she have to ask permission of someone, or was it enough simply to pack her bag and walk out, a clerical Nora closing the door behind her?

So certain had Caterina's faith in her sister been that she had never seriously considered the possibility that she'd bolt. A marriage couldn't just be walked away from because it was, at base, a contract between two people, and the contract had to be dissolved before they could be free of one another. With whom did a nun make a contract: the order she joined or the god she joined it to serve? And who had God's power of attorney?

Caterina felt the pull of irony and the absurd, two tidal forces she found hard to resist. Their mother was forever giving the girls the advice that they should think one year ahead before trying to assess the importance of any situation, but Caterina had always found her life trapped in the instant. Tina's pain – for it had been pain animating her email – was now, not a year from now. If you discovered the man you had been married to for more than twenty years was not the man you believed him to be, that his virtue was a show, his honour a sham, what did you do?

Caterina closed the window and created a new mail: how strange that Windows should use that verb, rather than 'Write'. 'Tina-Lina, my dearest dear, you've got a job, a family that loves you beyond reason (I'm in there, as mindless as the others), your health is good, you have intelligence, grace, and wit. And you still have the Baby Jesus, asleep in His bed. If you do jump ship, you have a safe, warm berth to come to, though I'm sure they would keep you on there: you just switch from the Catholic side to the Protestant, and how clever of you to work for a university that is religiously ambidextrous.

'If you decide to come home, no one will care why, and *Mamma* will be delirious at the possibility of cooking for you again, and she'll love it even more if you bring your friend and give her another mouth to feed. You are such a hotshot in your profession that universities will fight to have you.

'I shouldn't say this, but I will: in the end, does it matter if your God exists or not? And isn't it pretentious and self-important of us to insist that we know how to describe or define him/Him? We can't figure out the value of pi, and yet we think we know something about God? As *Nonna* said, it would make the chickens laugh.

'To put an end to your worst existential uncertainty, I promise to call Uncle Rinaldo tomorrow and ask him if he wants an apprentice. Love, Kitty-Cati.'

20

Instead of sitting and contemplating the collapse of her favourite sister's life, Caterina chose to work. Spurred by the email from the professor in Constance, she began looking into Countess von Platen and learned of her semi-official position as the mistress of Ernst August.

Caterina was struck by how little things changed in this world of hers. Kings were once wont to make their mistresses the duchess of this or the countess of that, and now prime ministers gave them cabinet ministries or ambassadorships. And the world chugged on and nothing changed.

She checked the dates and, sure enough, the Countess had been in Hanover at the time

Königsmarck disappeared. There was a great deal of contemporary testimony stating that Königsmarck had been one of her lovers and that she was violently jealous of the younger man. Caterina also found an 1836 magazine article about Countess Platen's purported memoirs, in which the reviewer wrote that she claimed to have been a witness to the murder. The Countess was often named as the person who reported the affair between Königsmarck and Sophie Dorothea to the Elector Ernst August, though what Caterina had read made her suspect that the few people who might not have known about this affair were the deaf and the blind and perhaps the halt and lame.

'If only she'd played by the rules,' Caterina caught herself thinking. If only silly, besotted Sophie Dorothea had been a bit more discreet about her affair, things could have gone along without fuss: Georg would have his mistresses, she could have her lover, and she would have ended up Queen of England, instead of a prisoner in a castle, cut off from her children and the world and all visits save that of her mother, whom she did not particularly like.

Caterina had been reading all day and she was tired, but she told herself she didn't have to clock into the office at nine the next morning so could continue reading as late as she chose. Besides, she was intrigued by how much these people and their behaviour seemed familiar to her: change their clothing and hairstyles, teach them other languages, and they would feel completely at home in Rome or Milan or, in fact, London, where a number of the minor players had remained and prospered.

Adulterous behaviour among the Hanoverians was no news to Caterina nor to any person in Europe who knew where the Saxe-Coburg-Gothas and the Windsors came from. Not that, she reflected, their Continental relatives had distinguished themselves by the sobriety of their comportment.

She had been using the standard JSTOR site to access scholarly journals, but now, sated with the serious tone of what she had been reading, she switched to a more mainstream search. She was not troubled to find a Thai girl who was looking for a considerate husband – 'age and looks don't matter' – lurking at the side of the page, and she was so accustomed to seeing ads for cars, restaurants, mort-gages, and vitamins that she no longer saw them in any real sense. On the ninth page of articles available under Steffani's name, she found a listing for *Catholic Encyclopedia* and thought she'd have a peek, much in the way one tried to see what cards another poker player might have in his hand.

It was only towards the middle of the article that Steffani's clerical endeavours were mentioned, when it was noted that the Church had made him Prothonotary Apostolic – whatever that was – for North Germany, presumably in return for 'his services for the cause of Catholicism in Hanover'. 'Services?' The wording in the article was unclear; the closest date used in conjunction with his appointment to that post was 1680, when Steffani would have been twenty-six.

That ambiguity set her grazing through another source, where she found mention that he was an apostolic prothonotary by 1695. The year after Königsmarck's murder. 'Services?'

She heard a noise, a dull buzzing, and with no conscious thought, her mind turned to the man she had seen on the street and who had been sitting at her boat stop. A bolt of panic brought her to her feet and took her to the door, but as she moved away from the table, the sound grew dimmer. When she realized it was her *telefonino* ringing in her bag, Caterina felt her knees weaken and her face flush with heat. She walked back to the table, opened her bag, and pulled out the phone.

'*Pronto?*' she said, in a voice out of which she had forced every emotion save mild interest.

'Caterina?' a man asked.

Aware of how moist the hand that held the phone was, she transferred the phone to her other ear and wiped her hand on the back of her sweater. '*Sì.*' She was every busy woman who had ever been interrupted by a phone call, every person who had been disturbed at – she looked – nine-forty in the evening – and who certainly had better things to do with her time.

'*Ciao.* It's Andrea. I'm not bothering you, am I?'

She pulled out a chair and sat 'No, of course not.

I couldn't find the phone.' She laughed, then found the whole situation funny and laughed again.

'I'm glad you did,' he said. 'I wanted to tell you about the cousins.'

'Ah, yes. The cousins,' she said. 'They aren't happy?'

'They weren't happy,' he said, stressing the second word. 'In fact, Signor Scapinelli accused you of spending all of your time walking around the city and drinking coffee.'

'But?' she asked, repressing the impulse to observe that it was better than accusing her of walking around the city drinking grappa.

'But I used the same technique you did in the mail and explained that you were merely being conscientious and wanted to be sure you missed nothing that might make an attribution of the putative estate in favour of one claimant or the other.' Oh, my, she thought, how lawyerly he sounded.

'Thank you,' was the only thing she could say.

'There's nothing to thank me for. It's true. Unless you read whatever background information you can find, you won't understand the context of what you read in the documents. And then either you'll make the wrong decision, or you won't be able to make any decision at all.'

'It's possible,' she said with the mildness of the hardened researcher, but then she considered the second possibility and asked, 'What happens if I can't make a decision?'

'Ah,' he said, drawing out the sound. 'In that case,

any documents that have value would be sold, and they'd divide whatever they bring. So far, though, you haven't found anything that could be of great value, have you?'

'No, not to the best of my knowledge.'

'Then, as I said, they'll sell everything for whatever they can get and split the profits.'

'But?' she asked, responding to the underlying uncertainty in his voice.

'They've told me there's a legend, on both sides of the family, about the ancestor priest who left a hidden fortune.' The fact that Andrea could also tell this story, she thought, made it no more believable than when Roseanna had told it.

'There are lots of legends,' she said, then added drily, 'but there are few fortunes.'

'I know, I know, but the Stievani family insists he had it when he died. They have an ancestral aunt – this is in the nineteenth century – who supposedly had a paper from him where he said that he had left the Jewels of Paradise to his nephew Stievani – Giacomo Antonio – who was her great-grandfather.'

The use of the exact phrase Countess von Platen had used in her condemnation of Steffani shocked her. In a voice she tried to make dispassionate and lawyerly, she asked, 'And this paper?'

This time he laughed. 'If you ever get tired of music, you might consider the police force.'

Caterina laughed outright. 'I'm afraid I'm not cut out for that sort of thing.'

'You ask questions like a policewoman.'

'Like a researcher,' she corrected him.

'Could you explain the difference?'

Realizing how much she enjoyed sparring with him, Caterina said, 'Researchers can't arrest people and send them to jail.'

He laughed. 'That's true enough.'

Out of the blue, it came to her to ask him. 'Do you believe this story about the aunt?' He was their lawyer, for heaven's sake. What did she expect him to say?

He was silent for so long that she feared her question had offended him by its impertinence. Just as it occurred to her that he might have hung up, he said, 'It doesn't matter. It's legally worthless.'

'And if the paper had miraculously been preserved?' she asked, passing from impertinence to provocation.

'A piece of paper is a piece of paper,' he said.

'And a fragment of the True Cross is only a splinter of wood?' she asked.

There was a long pause before he asked, sounding falsely casual, 'Why do you say that?'

She thought the comparison ought to have been clear enough, but she decided to explain. 'If enough people choose to believe something is what other people say it is, then it becomes that to them.'

'Like what?' he asked amiably.

'The example I just gave you,' she said, 'Or the Book of Mormon or the Shroud of Turin, or a footprint in a stone where someone or other jumped up to Heaven. It's all the same.'

'It's interesting,' he said, not sounding persuaded.

'What is?'

'That all of your examples are religious.'

'I thought I'd use that because it's the area where they're all sure to be nonsense.'

'Sure to be?'

She had the grace to laugh. 'To the likes of me, at least.'

'And to the rest of us?'

'Then a piece of paper isn't only a piece of paper, I suppose,' she said. 'Depends on what you want to be true.'

He was silent for so long that she was sure she had gone too far and offended his beliefs or his sensibility and he was going to say good-night and hang up.

'Would you be free for dinner tomorrow evening?' he surprised her by asking.

When she and her friends had first started going out with boys, there had been general agreement that one should never accept the first offer: it was a bad tactical move, they had all decided, with the wisdom of teenagers.

Well, she was no longer a teenager, was she? 'Yes.'

21

When she finished the call, Caterina had the choice of going to bed or going to work. She returned to the article in the *Catholic Encyclopedia*. Near the end there was a remark that, in light of everything she had discovered about Steffani, deserved closer scrutiny. 'A delicate mission was entrusted to him at the various German courts in 1696, and in 1698 at the court in Brussels, for which office he was singularly fitted by his gentle and prudent manners.'

Could this 'delicate mission' at the German courts have been related to the Königsmarck murder? In everything she read about it, the murder was referred to, even in the indices, as the 'Königsmarck Affair', a triumph in rebranding if ever she had seen one.

Had that rebranding been the office for which Steffani was singularly fitted because of his gentle and prudent manners? Gentle and prudent men are not often believed to be in the employ of murderers or of men who commission murderers, are they? She switched away from the *Encyclopedia*, determined to consult more reliable sources.

Duke Ernst August had for years longed to add the title and power of 'Elector' to his string of titles, and it was finally granted to him by the Emperor in 1692. Soon after, his daughter-in-law's attention-getting lover disappeared, leaving not a trace save in the memoirs and gossip of members of his court and of the North German aristocracy. His disappearance was referred to as an 'Affair', and the man who stood most to profit from it remained unblemished by it.

She dived into the catalogue of the library of the University of Vienna, in whose waters she had been swimming for years, and quickly discovered the precise honours and powers that came along with the title 'Elector'. Besides electing the Holy Roman Emperor, an elector got to call himself Prince. 'Big deal,' Caterina muttered to herself, having picked up the phrase from an American friend. More interestingly, the electors had the monopoly of mineral wealth in their territories, in an age when currency was based on gold and silver. They could also tax Jews and mint money. Thus 'Elector', beyond being an honour that would satisfy the urgings of vanity, would satisfy those of greed, as well. Who could resist such a combination?

But if your fool of a daughter-in-law put your reputation at risk by her public carryings-on with a noted rake, how seriously would your position be treated by the gilded and titled, or even by the common people? And how likely was it that the other electors would vote you into the club, a prerequisite her reading had revealed to her? Caterina had but to think of the death, three centuries later, of another beautiful young princess believed to have taken a lover, even though she was no longer married to the heir to the throne. When she died a very public death along with her lover, the world had exploded in an orgy of wild surmise and gossip about the 'true' cause of their deaths. Would it have been any different if the death of Königsmarck had been a public event? Official information always moves with glacial majesty, while gossip travels at the speed of light. Softly, then, softly in the night: how much better a quiet disappearance that left behind only the 'Affair' than a corpse at the side of the road.

She opened the book about Steffani and had another look at the portrait, said to have been painted in 1714. Take away twenty years of fat, remove the double chin, give him back some of his hair, and he'd look as able as any man to stick a knife into another man's back. Many accounts spoke of the sweetness and peacefulness of Steffani's character. He was in Germany as a diplomat, a class of man not best known for breaking up pubs in drunken brawls while in pursuit of their goals. But still his mission was the reconversion of Germany to Catholicism, and who better to start with than the Protestant Duke of Hanover, and how better to win his favour than by doing him an enormous favour by eliminating an inconvenient relative who would make a mockery of his claim to the electorship? As Stalin was later to observe: 'No man, no problem.'

Steffani might have failed to reconvert North Germany to the true religion, but he did win religious toleration and a new church for the Catholics of Hanover, and his Vatican masters might well have calculated this as a fair exchange for the death of a man who was, after all, only a Protestant. Caterina came upon another reference to Nicolò Montalbano and the 150,000 thalers. She might have been a bit hazy about the exact value of a thaler in 1694, but she was in no confusion about the size of 150,000.

The next year, Steffani's opera, *I trionfi del fato*, presented the idea that humans are not entirely responsible for their emotions and thus not for their actions. What more anodyne sentiment with which to calm the gossip-bestirred waters of the electoral court? Was this part of Steffani's 'delicate mission'?

It was past midnight, and she decided she had had enough of speculation and wonder and moving around to see events from a perspective that might make them look different.

In the kitchen she drank a glass of water, then went

into the bathroom, washed her face and brushed her teeth. As she looked at herself in the mirror, she saw a woman in her mid-thirties with a straight nose and eyes that were green in this light. She put the toothbrush in the glass on the side of the sink, cupped some water in her hands and rinsed out her mouth. When she was upright, she looked at the woman again and told her, 'Your sister is a historian. She'd know how to find this Montalbano guy. Besides, she's living in Germany, and that's where all this happened.' Nodding at her own sagacity, she went back to the desk and turned on the computer again.

'Tina-Lina, I'm sorry to leave you in existential high water, but I want to ask you a favour. Hunt around and find me more about Nicolò Montalbano, a Venetian living at the court of Ernst August when Königsmarck was murdered and who came into a lot of money soon after his death. His name is already familiar to me, but I think it's familiar because of his involvement with music and not for murder and blackmail. I'd be very grateful if you would try to find him in other places. I also came across mention of him in a lurid novel about the euphemistically called "Affair", an exact reference to which I can send you, should you want to read it and learn. If Uncle Rinaldo can't take you on as an apprentice, perhaps you could give a thought to a literary life. Think of the use you could make of your years of historical study; think of the passionate scenes you could toss into novels about the Council of Worms or the War of the Spanish Succession, and I'm sure there's some neck-and-neck competition to be Bishop of Maienfeld that you could transform into the *Gone with the Wind* of our times.

'It's late, I'm tired, and I'm having dinner tomorrow night with a very attractive man I've met here. I almost hope nothing comes of it because he's a lawyer, and I'd hate to have to revise my opinion of them as blood-sucking opportunists.

'There's a spare room in this apartment they've given me, just in case you think about coming home and maybe don't want to stay with *Mamma* and *Papà*. Love, Cati.'

As soon as she sent the mail, she realized she should not have said that last, about coming home. That's the trouble with emails: you write them in haste and send them off, and that means there's never time to steam open the letter and read it through again to see if you should say it or not.

She turned off the computer and, leaving the open books where they were, went to bed.

The next day she awoke filled with an inordinate sense of expectation, and for the first few moments she could not locate the source of the feeling. But then she remembered her dinner date with the blood-sucking opportunist, laughed out loud, and got out of bed.

Andrea was to come by and pick her up at the Foundation at seven-thirty: this would give her the chance to stop there before going to the Marciana to spend the day in the library, and then return to the Foundation to send a report of the day's reading. She could not rid herself of conspiratorial glee at the thought that she would go to the Foundation to send her email to Dottor Moretti to send on to the cousins and then go out to dinner with him.

As soon as she stepped outside, she felt that the weather had changed and the spring had decided to become serious. She had spent time in Manchester, she reminded herself, and she had learned to mistrust the weather, but still she saw no need to go back up four flights of stairs to get a heavier jacket or a scarf. When she came out on to the *riva*, however, she was hit by the wind coming from off the water and hurried towards the Arsenale stop, deciding to take the vaporetto, even if it was only one stop. A Number One came from behind only a minute after that, but her automatic calculation told her there was no way to get it, even if she were to break into a run, which she refused to do. She watched it pass her by, and she kept on walking, cutting in at Bragora to get away from the wind.

She let herself into the building and went down to Roseanna's office. The door was open, and she looked in to see Roseanna at her desk, her *telefonino* at her ear. The other woman smiled and waved her inside, said a few polite words into the phone, then ended the conversation. She dropped the phone on her desk, and came around her desk to give Caterina two kisses. 'Any progress?' she asked, but with interest and not reproach.

'I've been doing background reading at the Marciana,' Caterina explained. Roseanna leaned back against her desk, her hands propped flat behind her, ready to listen.

'I found a letter he wrote to two men called Stievani and Scapinelli.'

'Really?' Roseanna's curiosity was splashed across her face.

'Yes. The original two cousins,' she said and was pleased to see Roseanna's answering smile.

'What did he tell them?'

'They – he and the two of them – were heirs to some houses near San Marcuola that had been taken over by the Labia family. He wanted to meet them to discuss what to do about getting possession of the houses and selling them. It sounds like he was short of money.'

When Roseanna didn't respond, she continued. 'They didn't answer him.'

'What happened?'

'I don't know. There was no answer from them in the archives.'

'What did he sound like?' Roseanna asked thoughtfully, as if she were speaking of a person Caterina had just met.

'Excuse me?'

'Steffani. What did he sound like in his letter?'

'Polite,' she said after a moment's reflection, not having given this conscious thought while she was reading the letter. 'And weak,' she added, surprising herself even more. 'He practically begged them to get in touch with him, and he kept insisting that his only motivation was the good of the family, almost as if he thought they'd have reason to doubt that.' She considered the letter a bit longer and added, 'It made me – I don't know – uncomfortable.'

'Why?'

'Because the tone was so humble. People then were more formal with one another than we are, and the language was more elaborate and full of all sorts of formulaic courtesies,' she conceded. 'But this was too humble, and I suppose it troubled me because it was so out of place in a man of his stature.'

'As a musician?'

'Yes. And he was a bishop, for heaven's sake. So to hear him use this tone with two cousins from a provincial place like Castelfranco, to try to convince them that they should help him get money . . . well, it was difficult to read.' It occurred to her that, if anyone knew for certain whether Agostino was a castrato, it would be members of his family; perhaps this explained his painful deference to them.

'Does that mean you've come to like him? Steffani?' What strange questions Roseanna asked: Caterina had never thought in terms of liking him or not. His life puzzled her, but she had persuaded herself that her main interest was in trying to find out enough about him to be able to do her job.

She raised a hand and made a see-sawing gesture. 'I don't know if I like him.'

She did like his industry, the fierce pace at which he drove himself, but those were qualities, not a complete person. 'I have to keep on looking,' she heard herself say.

'Upstairs?' Roseanna asked.

'No. In the Marciana. I've still got a few things to look at.'

'Good luck.'

Caterina smiled her thanks and, spirits suddenly uplifted, started for the Marciana.

She found her carrel as she had left it the day before. She had stopped on the way to replenish her supply of chocolate and energy bars, though her researcher's conscience did not rest easy about this. Before turning her attention to the books, she stood at the window and reviewed the last few days. What she had read, both in the documents at the Foundation and in the books in her carrel, had raised as many questions as they had answered.

She opened her notebook, pressed it flat, then opened a new book. This one separated its analysis into biography and music. She had started it two days before but been waylaid by the allure of the 'Affair'. Well, enough of that. Back to work.

Carefully she read over the by now familiar details of Steffani's early life, until he went to Hanover in 1688 as court composer. As ever, she was struck by how odd that combination now seemed.

Vivaldi was a priest as well as a musician, but he

had used his position in the Church as a means to further his music, the real centre of his life. He had lived and worked as a musician, and he had composed up until his death, probably in the arms of his life's companion, Anna Girò. Caterina knew precious little about his life, but she knew that things ecclesiastical, other than sacred music, played no part in it, nor did he ever aspire to any higher clerical position.

Yet benefices and titles rained upon Steffani. The shining purpose of his life, for which he apparently abandoned composing, was the return of North Germany to the Catholic Church, at which he proved a dismal failure. She found accounts of his endeavours in two histories of the Church in North Germany, written in Latin and German. Each praised his enterprise and dedication, describing his achievements in Hanover and Düsseldorf. The German text devoted a mere five pages to his work as a musician.

When she emerged from the second of these, hunger drove her from the library and to the nearest bar, where she had two sandwiches and a glass of water before returning – unquestioned and unexamined – to her place in the library.

The next book was a 1905 edition of the correspondence between Sophie Charlotte and Steffani, in French, which both of them wrote with ease and grace. One of his letters found him at a low ebb. 'The bitter grief I suffer because of the affairs of the world; the pain I suffer in seeing so many people whom I respect wishing to destroy themselves entirely.' He wrote of leading a life 'that is truly a burden' and of his 'unlimited hypochondria'. He described a life in which his only friend and source of safety was his harpsichord. It seemed to Caterina that, after saying all of this, he suddenly realized he had to try to joke his way out of the truth he had revealed, but the tone did not ring true to Caterina. What did ring true was the ease with which he addressed the recipient: she hoped the Queen had accepted this because of his musical gifts rather than his clerical position. Or was it the unspoken awareness that he was a castrato that rendered his liberties harmless?

She continued reading the letters, trying to think of them as the performance of a person whom fate had moved up the social ladder but who remained aware, no matter how high he rose, of just how precarious his position was. Seen in this light, a new tone became audible in his prose. She noted the excessive gratitude he poured upon Sophie Charlotte for the simplest favour, the flattery that sometimes became overwhelming: 'since you have power over all'; 'the graces that your Majesty deigned to bestow upon me'; 'the letter with which your Majesty honoured me'; 'Your Majesty cannot do anything that is not at the peak of perfection'; 'I have the pleasure of serving your Majesty.'

At this point, Caterina told herself to bear in mind that Steffani was corresponding with the Queen of Prussia, a woman renowned throughout Europe for the depth and breadth of her learning. Caterina remembered the palace in Berlin named for her and the enormous, passionate support she gave to countless musicians. This thought was enough to dispel her last opposition to Steffani's deference. 'Narrow-minded liberal,' she whispered in self-accusation.

But still . . . but still, she was filled with the desire to take Steffani and shake him by the dangling ends of his alb and tell him that, three hundred years later, Sophie Charlotte had been remaindered to footnotes in histories of Prussia read by a few hundred people, while his music was still performed and admired. 'Narrow-minded snob,' she whispered to herself this time.

22

'The troubles of this century no longer cause me much pain because they are making you again turn your hand to music. Throw yourself in headlong, I implore you. Music is a friend who will not abandon or betray you, nor will she be cruel to you. You have drawn from her all the delight and beauties of the heavens, whereas friends are tepid and cunning and mistresses are without gratitude.' This was the answer Steffani received from the Queen in response to his troubled letter. Her words rose above the usual courtly language and revealed her heart. Caterina felt her own heart warm to find that he should have had this gracious, generous support from a woman he admired so fully.

Nevertheless, within months, the correspondence was dead. Steffani, in response to a request from a Medici cardinal, implored the Queen to change her decision not to allow her favourite court musician to return to his monastery in Italy. And she, in queenly fashion, was not amused. The correspondence ended, but not before Leibniz, that most savvy of philosophers, remarked to a friend that he understood Her Majesty's anger. 'After all, if a Duke had only one hunter, and someone requested him to give it up, how else would he expect the Duke to respond than by anger?'

Well, Caterina thought, old Leibniz certainly had no illusions about describing the pecking order in a royal court, did he? And he'd certainly hung around enough of them to have learned a thing or two about the position of musicians, and let's forget all the flowery praise. Steffani's bishopric hadn't protected him one whit, not when he stepped over that invisible line. You're a genius and I am enthralled by the beauty of your music, but just remember to stay in your proper place, and don't think for an instant that you can question the decisions of the Queen of Prussia.

Looking at her watch, Caterina saw that it was after six, which gave her just barely enough time to get back to the Foundation and write a report to Dottor Moretti. Because she was going to be out to dinner that evening, she left the books where they were, planning to return the next day to continue reading the background material.

She got to the office before seven but found no sign of Roseanna. She went up to what had become her office, but did not open the storeroom. Instead, she turned on the computer. There were three emails, but before so much as glancing at the names of the senders, she opened a blank mail, addressed it to Andrea but, addressing the cousins by their surnames, gave a hurried account of the results of her research that day. Without bothering to read it over, she sent it off and returned to her inbox.

The first mail was from a bank she had never heard of and inquired if she wanted to take out a loan. Delete.

The second came from a young Russian woman, twenty-four, with a doctorate in electrical engineering, hoping to begin a meaningful correspondence with a well-educated and well-bred Italian man. Resisting the temptation to forward it to Avvocato Moretti, she deleted it.

The last was from Cristina, sent early that afternoon. 'You studied law, Cati, and it wasn't so very long ago, so surely you remember what those legal people call a statute of limitations on wills. Any unclaimed bequest Steffani might have made lapsed centuries ago: if there turns out to be something of value among those papers, it in no way belongs to the egregious cousins but, alas, to our even more egregious State.

'I don't have any idea of what sort of people you're mixed up with. The non-heirs sound unpleasant, at least to someone who has been out of the city for as long as I have. Surely their lawyer must know this basic legal fact, which makes me wonder what he's up to. I don't want to say anything unpleasant about him in case he's the lawyer you're going out to dinner with, but if it is he, he should have known.

'If you have no luck with him, and if you can tell me exactly where the trunks were in Rome – that is, what bureau or office had them – I might be able to do a bit of trekking through the muck for you and find out how they were released. I still have a number of friends there who believe that the discovery of truth begins with an accurate account of verifiable events and is not an elaborate progress towards some predetermined truth. Besides, I'm curious.

'Thanks for your offer of hospitality. If I decide to bolt, it's the first place I'd go, believe me. Love, Tina-Lina.'

The clock at the bottom of the computer told her it was seven-fifteen and so, without planning what to say, Caterina hit Respond.

'Dear Tina,

'The trunks were in the care/possession of the Propaganda Fide, as sinister a name as your lot could come up with short of KGB or CIA. I was told that someone who was doing an inventory found the trunks. His research probably found the names of the original cousins too and he looked for people with the same surnames in the area about Castelfranco and got in touch with them. That's certainly what I or any other researcher would do, but it's only a guess.

'When I opened them, it looked as though no one had done so since the time they were first sealed, but I'm sure breaking and entering and leaving no traces is the least of the Black Arts practised by the PF.

'Yes, tonight's lawyer is the cousins' lawyer. I'll ply him with wine and grappa and try to get him to explain how they got their hands on the trunks. That failing, I might be forced to tempt him with the possibility of my charms, and where's the grown man who could prove resistant to those?

'Thanks for the information about the statute of limitations, and I'm ashamed I never thought of it. Of course I knew it, but I'm afraid Avvocato Moretti quite drove all memory of the study of the law, to make no mention of good sense, out of my head. Or maybe I simply wanted to keep this job because it's interesting and lets me be at home. Love, Cati.'

Ten minutes after she sent the mail, her *telefonino* rang. Her first thought was her parents, calling to see if she was free for dinner, ever ready to feed their last-born and save her from a night of solitude.

She answered with her name.

'*Ciao*, Caterina,' Andrea said. 'I'm out in the street. Come down when you're finished.'

'Don't you have a key?' she blurted.

'Yes, but I'm off duty tonight,' he said with a laugh.

'Listen, there's a bar out on Via Garibaldi, first on the left. I'll be in there, all right?'

For a moment, she was taken aback, then said, 'I'll be two minutes. Order me a spritz, all right? With Aperol.'

'*Sarà fatto*,' he said and was gone.

The tactic of playing hard to get had never appealed to Caterina, not because it was not effective – her friends had used it with great success – but because it was so obvious. Above all, she hated being kept waiting, and few things could embarrass her as much as keeping another person waiting unnecessarily. She turned off the computer, put her *telefonino* in her bag, then locked up and went downstairs.

Andrea was there, standing at the bar, that day's *Gazzettino* spread open beside him as he sipped at a glass of white wine. A spritz of the proper orange stood on the counter to the left of the newspaper.

He heard her come in, looked up, and smiled. Closing the paper, he set it to the side of the counter. 'I didn't take you away from anything, did I?' he asked. For a moment, Caterina was puzzled by the change in him. Face and height the same, wire-rimmed glasses and carefully polished shoes. But he was wearing a light tweed jacket. A tie, of course, and a white shirt, but he was not wearing a suit. Was this an honour or an insult?

'No, not at all. I was sending an email.' She nodded towards the paper. 'Anything there? I haven't read the papers for days.'

'Same old things. Jealous husband kills wife, North Korea threatens the South, politician caught taking a bribe from a builder, woman gives birth at sixty-two.'

Andrea, obviously judging this the wrong way to begin their evening, handed her the spritz, tapped his glass against hers, and said, '*Cin cin.*'

'Sounds like I'm wiser to stay in the eighteenth century, then,' she said and took a sip. It was perfect, sharp and sweet at the same time, and today was one of the first days of the year when a person might want to drink something cold.

'Still digging?' he asked, but idly, as if he were only being polite.

'I've stopped digging,' she said. His expression of more than mild surprise led her to add, 'That is, digging into things that don't concern me.'

He gave her a long, appraising glance, as if weighing her answer, and then said, 'That's the first time I've ever heard a woman say that.' His smile and the glance that preceded it took any sting out of the remark.

'Ha, ha,' she said in the manner of a cartoon character and then allowed herself to laugh, managing thus to disapprove of the remark while still being amused by it.

'What is it you're not digging into?' he asked and took another sip of his drink. He signalled the barman and asked for some peanuts. 'I didn't have lunch today,' he said by way of explanation.

Caterina started to ask why, but he said only, 'Meeting,' then, 'Tell me about your not digging.'

He sounded curious, so she told him the background to the Königsmarck Affair. His lawyer's mind, accustomed to hearing many names dragged into a story, seemed to keep them all straight. When she moved on to the account contained in Countess von Platen's memoirs, he stopped her to ask if this was Königsmarck's ex-mistress, impressing Caterina with both his memory and his concentration.

'She's an unreliable witness,' he said. He watched her expression, then added, 'I mean in legal terms, theoretical terms.'

'Why?' she asked, though it was evident. She wanted to know if he had some other, lawyerly reason so to judge her.

'The obvious one is that she had reason to dislike him, especially if he ended the affair. That means she'd be unlikely to speak in his favour.'

'To say the minimum,' she agreed. 'Why else?'

'It means, as well, that she might attempt to hide the real killer.'

'For ending a love affair?' Caterina asked, unable to stifle her astonishment.

'Your surprise does you credit, Dottoressa,' he said, raising his glass to her and finishing his wine. He set it on the counter and went on, 'And, yes, for ending the affair.' Before she could protest, he said, 'I don't practise criminal law, but I have colleagues who do, and they tell me things that would make your hair stand on end.'

He saw that he had her complete attention. 'You've

probably read the phrase in the paper: *motivi futili.* My friends have told me about a lot of trivial motives that cost people their lives: a car parked in someone else's space, the refusal to give a cigarette, a radio too loud, or a television, or a minor car accident.' He raised his hand to the barman, signalling for the bill.

'So keeping quiet about the murder of someone who said he wasn't in love with you any more, especially if he wasn't graceful about it . . . it makes complete sense to me. So does saying something that might protect the murderer.'

'So you doubt her account? That she saw Steffani kill him?'

'Is that what she says? That she saw him do it?'

Caterina had to think back over the precise wording in Tina's friend's email. 'Something about his having received blood money,' she said.

'I'm not sure that's the same thing as saying she saw him commit the murder,' Andrea said and then, just as she was about to make the same suggestion, added, 'Maybe we could talk about something else?'

What a relief his suggestion was. He paid the bill and moved over to the door to hold it open for her.

He led them to a small trattoria behind the Pietà, a place that held no more than half a dozen tables, the stout-legged sort Caterina remembered from her youth, with surfaces scarred and carved and edges hollowed out by countless forgotten cigarettes. Bottles stood on mirrored shelves behind the zinc-covered bar; a rectangular space with a sliding door opened into the kitchen.

Two of the tables were already taken. The waiter recognized Moretti and showed them to a table in the far corner. He handed them menus and disappeared through a pair of swinging doors.

'I hope you don't mind eating in a simple place,' he said.

'I'd rather,' she said. 'My parents keep telling me how hard it's become to find a place where the food's good and you don't have to take out a mortgage to pay the bill.'

'That's not the case here,' he said, then laughed and said, 'I mean, the food's good, not that it's cheap.' Then he added, 'That's the reason I come – that is, because the food's good.' Hearing what a pass he had talked himself into, he shrugged and opened his menu.

Conversation was general: families, school, travel, reading, music. Much of Moretti's life was completely at one with the persona he presented: father a lawyer, mother a housewife; two brothers, the surgeon he had already mentioned and the other a notary; school, university, first job, partnership. But then came the odd bits: a case of encephalitis seven years ago that had left him in bed for six months, during which he had read the Fathers of the Church, in Latin. When these facts were spread on the picture Caterina was attempting to form of the man, everything went out of focus for a moment. A brush with death: she knew little about encephalitis save that it was bad, quite often fatal, and just as often left people gaga. Perhaps that last explained six months reading the Fathers of the Church, her cynical self remarked, but her better self limited her to asking, 'Encephalitis?'

He bit into a shrimp and said, 'I went for a hike in the mountains above Belluno. Two days later I found a tick on the back of my knee, and a week later I was in the hospital with a temperature of forty.'

'Near Belluno?' It was only two hours from Venice, a beautiful city where nothing happened.

'It's common. There are more and more cases every year,' he said, then smiled and added, 'More evidence of the wisdom of living in cities.'

She decided not to ask about the Fathers of the Church. The evening continued, and conversation remained general and friendly. The absence of reference to Steffani or Königsmarck came as a great relief to Caterina. How pleasant to spend a few hours in this century, in this city, and, she added to herself, in this company.

They shared a branzino baked in salt, drank most of a bottle of Ribolla Gialla, and both turned down dessert. When the coffee came, Andrea grew suddenly serious and said, with no preparation at all, 'I'm afraid I have to confess I haven't told you the complete truth.'

There being nothing she could think of to say, Caterina remained silent.

'About the cousins.'

Better than about himself, she thought, but said nothing to him, certainly not this. If he was confessing he had lied, she had no obligation to make it easy for him. To appear to be doing something, she poured sugar into her coffee and stirred it round.

'The story of how the trunks got here,' he said, then drew one hand into a fist and placed it on the table.

'Ah,' she permitted herself to say.

'They didn't track them down. The trunks turned up during an inventory, and the researcher did find Steffani's name on them, and he did do the research and locate the descendants.'

He paused and gave her a quizzical glance, but Caterina kept her face impassive. 'Descendants,' he had said. Not 'heirs'.

She stifled her curiosity and drank her coffee. He must have realized she was not going to be cooperatively inquisitive, so he said, his voice a mixture of the pedantic and the apologetic, 'They have no claim to ownership. You studied law, so you probably know that it reverts to the state.'

Caterina kept her eyes on her coffee cup, even lifted the spoon and ran it around the empty bottom a few times. Then she carefully spooned up the mixture of melted sugar and froth from the bottom and licked the spoon before replacing it on the saucer.

She raised her eyes and looked across the table at him, in his lovely, expensive jacket and his moderate tie. He met her eyes with his own steady glance and said, 'I apologize.'

'Why did you tell me a different story?' she asked, consciously avoiding the use of the word 'lie'.

'They asked me to.'

'Why?'

He looked down at his own empty coffee cup and said, 'They said they didn't want to have to explain how the trunks got here. The real way, I mean. Or so I presume.' Even in his explanation, she noticed, he still strove for clarity.

Making herself sound the very voice of moderation, she asked, 'Why wouldn't they want anyone to know?'

He tried to shrug but abandoned the gesture, with one shoulder higher than the other. 'My guess is that they bribed someone to have the trunks sent here.' When her gaze remained level on his, he actually blushed and said, 'In fact, it's the only way it could have happened.'

'The researcher?' she asked, knowing this was impossible. He would have no power over where the trunks went.

Andrea smiled at her question and said, 'Not likely.'

'Then who?' she asked, doing her best to look very confused.

'It would have to be someone at the Propaganda Fide, I'd guess. Or at the warehouse.'

'Then why me?'

'What do you mean?'

'Why me? Why spend money on a researcher when they could just get the trunks here, open them up, and have a look themselves?'

'They needed a researcher,' he said, holding up his thumb to count the first reason. 'He was a cleric and worked in Germany, so they needed someone who could read different languages.' He held up his forefinger. 'And that person would also have to have some understanding of the historical – perhaps even the musical – background.' Another finger shot up.

'That's absurd,' Caterina snapped, finally losing patience with the role she had decided to play. 'I just told you: all they had to do was open them, take out any musical scores that might be inside, do a minimum of research on what Steffani's autograph scores are worth, and sell them. Split the money and hire someone at the university to read through the other papers. Sooner or later, they'd know whether there was a treasure hidden somewhere or not.'

Andrea tried to smile, reached a hand halfway across the table, as if to place it on her arm, but pulled it back when he saw her expression.

He picked up his coffee cup, but it was still empty, so he set it back in the saucer. 'There was a . . . a falling out, I suppose you could say.'

'Of thieves?'

Her directness obviously distressed him. He had to think of a response before he said, 'Yes, you might describe it that way. Once they had the trunks here, they realized how little they trusted each other.'

'And I suppose they began to add up the sums,' she said angrily.

'I don't understand.' Though she thought perhaps he did.

'They'd have to pay by the page or by the hour if they hired a freelance translator, and they didn't know what was in the trunks or what the papers – if there were papers – would say. Or what they would be worth.' As she spoke, Caterina remembered an old folk tale about three thieves who discovered some sort of treasure. One went off to town to get enough food and drink to keep them going while the three of them decided what it was worth and how to divide it up. While he was gone, the two who remained behind planned his murder, and when he came back, they killed him. They ate and drank to celebrate their victory, but the dead man had poisoned the wine he brought back, so they too paid the price of the Jewels of Paradise.

She looked across at Moretti, her face neutral, waiting for him to speak.

'Neither of them trusted the other not to cheat,' he finally said. 'Even though they had no idea what was in the trunks, each still believed the other would be clever enough to cheat him out of his share. Or to see that the division wasn't equal.' He saw that he had her interest and went on. 'Nothing can shake them loose from their belief in a treasure.'

'Have you tried?'

'Yes.' He shook his head to show the hopelessness of that endeavour.

'So they agreed to pay my salary?'

This question made him visibly uncomfortable.

'What is it?' she asked.

'For the first month, yes,' he said.

'What?'

'It was in the contract.' She thought it embarrassed him to say this, and that surprised her. She suppressed her own embarrassment at not having bothered to read the contract.

'You told me my position was secure until I'd read through all of the papers,' she said in a cool, firm voice. 'I left my job to come here.'

'I know,' he said, his eyes on his plate. Could it be that he was ashamed of the part he had played? She had no doubt that he had played it.

She said nothing.

Forced to continue, Moretti finally said, 'I thought at the beginning that they'd continue to pay you until you had a definite answer to give them: yes there is a treasure or no there is not.' He made that half move with his hand across the table, but again he stopped. 'I thought they were serious. That's why I worked to convince them you could do the research in the library.' She thought it best not to tell him she'd realized the futility of that research.

'They've changed their minds, I assume?'

'Stievani called me this afternoon. One month. That's

all. If they don't have an answer by the end of one month, they'll figure out a way to do it by themselves.'

'Good luck to them, the fools,' she couldn't stop herself from saying.

'I agree.' Then, in a calmer tone, he said, 'If you want, I can try to persuade them.'

She smiled. 'That's kind of you, Andrea. I'd appreciate it if you could try.' Suddenly, she opened her mouth in an enormous yawn. 'Sorry,' she said, looking at her watch.

He imitated her gesture and said, 'It's after eleven.'

From the way he said it, she wondered if he had to be home before midnight. He signalled the waiter with a writing gesture. In a very short time, he was there, with a real receipt. 'You always do that?' she asked, pointing to the bill as he set a few notes on top of it.

'Pay the bill when I invite a woman to dinner?' he asked, but with a grin.

'No. Ask for a *ricevuta fiscale* in a restaurant where you come often.'

'You mean because of the taxes they'll have to pay?' he asked.

'Yes.'

'We all have to pay taxes.'

'Does that mean you pay yours? All of them?'

'Yes,' he said simply.

She believed him.

They got to their feet. He opened the door for her and they walked together, talking of things other than Agostino Steffani and the cousins, towards the apartment where she was staying. At her door, he kissed her on both cheeks, said good-night, and turned away.

Caterina went up the stairs to her apartment, unlocked the door, and let herself in.

Again she looked at her watch: it was almost midnight. Cristina did not have a *telefonino*, so she could not leave her an SMS and ask her to call if she was awake. There was a phone in the apartment, with a meter: it would be much cheaper to call Germany on that.

She took her *telefonino* from her pocket and dialled Cristina's number. It rang six times before a groggy voice answered with '*Ja?*'

'*Ciao*, Tina,' she said. 'Sorry to wake you up.'

After a long pause, Tina said, 'It's OK, I was reading.'

'Lying's still a sin, dear.'

'Not really, if it's in a good cause.'

'You rewriting the Commandments now?'

'I'm awake, so tell me what's wrong – I can hear it in your voice – and I'll leave the rewriting of the others till tomorrow morning.'

'You know that lawyer I told you about?'

'Yes.'

'He's a cold-hearted bastard like the others.'

'Why do you say that?' Tina said, sounding sad.

'Because he's been reading my emails.'

23

'Which emails?' Cristina demanded, her voice fully awake.

'The ones I've been writing on the computer he so generously gave me to use in the office. He said his company wasn't using it, so he had one of his tech people work on it . . .' Here she had to stop and take a few deep breaths before going on. 'And he took it there, and I've been using it ever since.' Two more deep breaths. Her knees were shaking; she sat down on the sofa.

'How do you know he's reading them, Cati?'

'At dinner tonight, he told me I'd understand something because I'd studied law.'

'Well, you did. Two years, if I remember correctly.'

'I never told him.'

'Then maybe he read it on your CV.'

'It's not there,' Caterina said with fierce energy. 'I never talk about it, and I did not include it in the CV.'

'But how do you cover over a gap of two years?'

'I added a year to the things I did before and after. I figured they wouldn't check: no one ever does. And if it wasn't in the CV, and I never said anything to him about it, then the only way he knows is from your mail.'

'How can you be sure?'

'I just told you, Tina,' she said. Hearing the anger in her voice, she moderated her tone. 'He knew I studied law, and the only way he could have known that was from reading your email, where you mentioned it.' How many times would the sleep-sodden Cristina have to hear this before she understood?

'But why should he say that to you?'

'He was telling me that things revert to the state after a certain period if no heir makes a claim, and I suppose he meant to be complimentary or inclusive, make me feel like one of the pack, and said I should know that because I studied law.'

'Did you react?'

'I hope not. I acted as if it didn't register with me. He probably thinks he read it in my CV. After all, who wouldn't mention something like that?'

'You, apparently,' Tina broke in to suggest. Her laugh restored the usual warmth of their conversation.

'What's he up to?' Caterina asked, aware of a vague sense that the documents in the storeroom had been moved or tampered with.

'That's not the question to ask.'

'What is, then?'

'What to do? If he didn't realize you know he's reading them, then you and I can just continue to write back and forth. We have to. If we suddenly stopped, he'd suspect something.'

'What is this – James Bond?' Caterina asked.

'Only if you want it to be, Cati,' Cristina said calmly. 'If not, then you continue to do your job, read the papers and tell the cousins what they say, let them find their treasure or not, and then you take the money and run.'

'That's very worldly advice.'

Tina said nothing, which probably meant she didn't want to begin a discussion like this, not at this hour.

Thinking out loud, Cristina said, 'I wonder if the cousins put him up to it?'

'Who else would he be doing it for?' Tina asked.

It certainly sounded like something the cousins would do to be sure she didn't try to cheat them. Her only question was whether Dottor Moretti – Andrea – would be party to such a thing. The fact that she believed he might saddened her immeasurably.

For a long time, neither of the sisters spoke. Caterina ran through the jumbled memories of her conversations with Avvocato Moretti. For a moment, she thought of encephalitis and its effect on the brain, but she dismissed that. 'He spent six months recovering from encephalitis by reading the Fathers of the Church in Latin,' she said aloud. Then she asked, 'Is your computer on?'

'Like the love of the Holy Spirit, my computer is always on.'

'Put in his name and see what comes up.'

'Should I call you back?'

'No, just do it,' Caterina said briskly.

She heard the footsteps, the sound of a chair scraping the floor, and then a long silence.

'What's his full name?' Cristina asked.

'Andrea Moretti.'

'How old?'

'About forty-five.'

'Born in Venice?'

'I think so.'

There was a long, silent pause, during which Caterina stood first on one foot and then the other, an exercise someone had once told her would help her keep her balance in old age. '*Ach du Lieber Gott*,' she heard her sister say, speaking in German and shocking Caterina by doing so.

'What?'

'Do you want to guess where he studied?'

'I know I'm not going to like this, so you better just tell me,' Caterina said.

'The University of Navarra,' Cristina told her.

'Novara?' Caterina asked, wondering what he was doing in Piemonte.

'Navarra,' Cristina said, pronouncing it as though it had four R's.

'*Vade retro, satana*,' Caterina whispered, then added, 'Founded by that lunatic who started Opus Dei,' too late to consider that this was perhaps not the way to refer to a colleague of a woman who had taken final vows.

'They run the place. Their graduates are everywhere,' Cristina chimed in, suggesting that she might not have been offended by the remark.

'I never would have thought . . .' Caterina began but let the thought wander off, unfinished. 'That means I can't believe anything he's told me.' She'd said it.

'Probably.'

Leaving her reflections on Avvocato Moretti's motivation to some later time, Caterina asked, 'Then what's he after?'

'With them, power's always a safe guess,' Tina said, causing Caterina, who had the same suspicion, to wonder if they'd both fallen victim to paranoia of the worst sort.

Caterina couldn't stand it any more. 'If you can think that, Tina, why do you stay with it?' There was such a long silence that she finally said, 'Sorry. None of my business.'

'That's all right,' Cristina said in a very sober voice.

'Really sorry, Tina-Lina.'

Again Cristina was silent, this time for so long that Caterina began to wonder if she had gone too far.

She waited and something like a prayer formed in her mind that she had not asked the wrong question of her favourite sister.

'Right,' Cristina said decisively. 'So we go on corresponding naturally, and I'll pass on any information I find or anyone sends me.'

'Good,' Caterina agreed. 'But . . .'

'I know, I know, if I learn anything that he shouldn't know about, I should send it to . . . to where?'

Caterina floundered, trying to think of someone she could trust to pass on information. She didn't want to involve her family. Her email account at the university in Manchester had been cancelled when she left. That gave her the idea. 'Look, you can send it to the address of a friend. He almost never reads his emails, and I have his password. I can go into an internet café to check.' When Cristina agreed, Caterina carefully spelled out the Romanian's email address.

After that, they both started to laugh, though neither of them knew why. Feeling better, Caterina said good-night, hung up, and went to bed.

The first thing she did the next morning was send two emails to Dottor Moretti, just as if they had not had dinner together the previous evening. The first was formal and described in some detail Steffani's correspondence with Sophie Charlotte and explained that the ease of his connection with her would have given him added social status and, directly or indirectly, aided him in his pursuit of work as a composer.

Declaring that she was sensitive to her employers' understandable desire to see her research come to a conclusion, she announced her intention to suspend her library reading for a few days and continue with the papers in the trunk.

In the second, to 'Andrea', she used the familiar form of address and thanked him for the pleasant time she had had with him the previous evening, both the conversation and the discovery of a good restaurant.

She gave considerable thought to how to close the email and decided on *'Cari saluti*, Caterina,' which, while being informal, was nothing more than that but certainly suggested continuing good will.

That done, she took a shower, stopped and had a coffee, and walked to the Foundation, arriving soon after nine. She went up to the office, unlocked the cupboard, and took the pile she had last been reading. She sat at the desk and started to do the job she was being paid to do, at least until the end of the month.

There were three documents in German, all of them reports from Catholic priests about the success of their mission in various parts of Germany governed by Protestant rulers. To one degree or another, they spoke of the deep faith of their own parishioners and the need to remain strong in the face of political opposition. All asked Steffani to intercede with Rome for more money to aid them in their labours, a phrase two of the writers used.

There were a few letters from women with German

surnames, none of whom Caterina managed to find in any of the articles or records she consulted online, praising Steffani for his music. One asked if he would favour her with a copy of one of his chamber duets. There were no copies of answers to any of these letters.

Had Steffani, then, gone through his papers in the years immediately preceding his death and chosen to keep those he thought important, or had everything simply been bundled up by the people sent to sort out his possessions? Try as she might, she could find no common thread, even common threads, among these papers. Save for the musical score, nothing seemed more important than anything else.

She retied the stack and took it to the storeroom. Now there remained only one more parcel in the first trunk. Back at the desk, she untied it and began to read.

After more than an hour of close reading, she had got through only one of two tightly written pages, front and back, and had decided that this was bottom-feeding. These were accounts of the events and conversations, kept in a hand other than the one she had verified to be Steffani's, – did he have a secretary? – leading to the conversion or reconversion to Catholicism of various German aristocrats and dignitaries. Because no identification was provided beyond their names, Caterina could not measure the political importance of their religious change of stance. She was diligent with the first page, searching through the usual historical directories and sites for their names and managing to identify most of them. But what was the importance of the conversion of Henriette Christine and Countess Augusta Dorothea of Schwarzburg-Arnstadt, even if they were the daughters of Anton Ulrich of Braunschweig-Wolfenbüttel?

It was two and she was hungry and she was bored to the point of pain, something that had rarely happened during past research. It was all so futile, trying to find some indication of where Steffani might have left treasure, only so his greedy descendants could fight over it. Better to go out and find more novels like the one owned by d'Annunzio and sit reading them until the end of the month, producing inventive reports and translations of the papers she did not read: perhaps she could use the plots of the novels as sources for her summaries of the unread papers? Perhaps she could go and get something to eat?

She carefully locked the papers away and locked up as usual. Then she went down to Roseanna's office and found the door open: it had been closed when she came in and had remained so when she knocked on it. So Roseanna had been in and had not come up to check on her. Good or bad?

She left the building and locked the door. During the time she had been inside, the day had turned to glory. The sun beat down, and she was quickly warm, and then so hot she had to remove her jacket. She decided to walk to the Piazza, if only to have the chance to look across at San Giorgio and up the Grand Canal. As to lunch, God would surely provide.

She cut out to the *riva*, turned right and walked towards the Piazza, eyes always drawn to her left by the excess on display. There were more boats moored to the side of San Giorgio than she remembered, but everything else was the same. Remove the vaporetti and the other motor-driven boats, and it would look much the same as it had centuries ago. As it had in Steffani's day, she told herself and liked the thought.

At the Piazza, she stopped and looked around: Basilica, tower, Marciana, columns, flags, clock. The ridiculous beauty of it all moved her close to tears. This was normal for her; this was one of her childhood playgrounds; this was home. She crossed in front of the Basilica, thinking she'd go back towards Rialto, but the crowds coming towards her down the Merceria frightened her, and she turned right past the *leoncini* and headed back, feeling abandoned by God, towards San Zaccaria.

Halfway to the end of the Basilica, she glanced into one of the numerous glass shops to the left and saw, sitting in a chair behind the cash register, reading a newspaper on the counter in front of him, the young man who had followed her the other night. She missed a step but kept moving forward and regained her balance. There had been no doubt about it, no hesitation before she recognized him: it was the same man. She continued walking; it was only when she was long past the window that she turned back and noted the name of the shop.

It provided scant comfort to know he was not a paid killer; seeing him had still been a shock. She might not know who he was, but finding out would not be difficult. She could ask Clara or Cinzia to help: they could take one of their kids, to make themselves even more innocent, and start talking to him in Veneziano. Clara would be better: her radiant happiness would drag secrets from anyone. Caterina's thoughts turned to Clara's husband Sergio, who weighed just short of a hundred kilos and stood almost two metres tall. He was a far better choice of visitor.

Immeasurably cheered, she continued down towards San Filippo e Giacomo and turned off to go and have three of the small pizzas, two for lunch, and one to celebrate her discovery of the man who had followed her.

24

She returned to the Foundation and found Roseanna in her office, sitting at her desk, reading, and looking quite the Acting Director of the Fondazione Musicale Italo-Tedesca. So fond of her had Caterina become in these days and so accustomed to seeing her that her hairstyle now seemed carefully executed and eye-catching.

'What are you reading?' Caterina asked as she came in.

Roseanna looked up and smiled in greeting. 'A book about psychoactive medicine.'

'I beg your pardon,' Caterina said. 'Why that?' Few subjects could seem farther from the business of the Foundation.

'My best friend's been diagnosed with depression, and her doctor wants her to start taking these things.' From the harsh tone Roseanna used, Caterina was left in no doubt about her thoughts on the subject.

'And you disagree?'

Roseanna set the book face down on the desk. 'It's not my place to agree or disagree, Caterina. I don't have any medical or pharmacological training, so some of what I read I don't even understand.'

'And the book?' Caterina asked.

Shrug and smile. 'We've been friends since school, best friends, and she asked me what I thought she should do. So I decided to read about it, both sides, and see if I could make any sense of it.'

'Have you learned anything?'

'Not to trust statistics or numbers or the published results of experiments,' Roseanna said instantly, then added, 'not that I ever did; well, not much.'

'Why?'

'Because the people who make drugs don't have to publish the bad results, only the good ones, and medicines are usually tested against a placebo, not against another medicine.' She patted the back of the book affectionately. 'This writer makes the observation that it's not hard to make a medicine that is more effective than a sugar pill.' Her eyes went into half focus for a moment, and then she said, 'I've never smoked, but I've seen how my friends who are smokers seem to relax as soon as they light a cigarette. So you could run a test and show that smoking a cigarette is an excellent way to reduce stress.'

'Better than a sugar pill?' Caterina asked.

'I'd say so.' Then, as if suddenly aware of how far afield this conversation was from their common interest, she asked, 'I thought you had gone to the Marciana.'

Caterina shook the suggestion away. 'No, I'm going to read through the papers, at least those in the first trunk, before I go to the library again.' She paused and then added, 'I can't make up my mind about him.'

'Because he was a priest?'

'No, not that. It's because I don't have any idea what he wanted. Usually we can tell that – what a person most wants – if we've been around him for a while or read about him. But, with Steffani, I just don't know. Did he so desperately need to be accepted as an equal by the people he worked for? Did he really want to save the Church? He writes about his music and the pleasure he takes in it, but there's no compelling desire to be famous for it, to be thought a great composer. It's obvious that he loved it and loved composing it, but . . . but he gave it up so easily. If it were his compelling passion, he couldn't have done that: just stop.'

Caterina saw no reason why she shouldn't tell Roseanna what she had discovered, or thought she had discovered, so she added, 'He might have been a castrato.' She tried to say it neutrally, but she wasn't sure she succeeded. It was not a remark that lent itself to neutrality.

'Oh, the poor man,' Roseanna said, pressing one hand to her face. 'The poor man.'

'I'm not absolutely sure he was,' Caterina said immediately. 'But he's described somewhere as *un musico*, and that's the word that was used for them.'

'To fill the choirs to sing the glory of God,' Roseanna said calmly, as if there did not exist sarcasm sufficient for the words.

'There's only the one reference,' Caterina said, choosing not to mention the Haydn libretto.

Neither of them found anything further to add. 'I'll go back upstairs,' Caterina said. She headed towards the door, and was almost there when Roseanna said, 'I'm glad they hired you.'

Without turning back, Caterina acknowledged the remark by raising her right hand in the air. 'Me, too,' she said and pulled her keys out of her pocket.

Upstairs, she sat at the desk and pulled her *telefonino* from her purse. On the way back, she'd considered what to do about the man who had followed her. Before she made the call, she wanted to be sure what to say. She had no proof that her research was related to the fact that he followed her, and then waited for her, but no other explanation made sense of it. Any of the many odd men in the city might have followed her; in fact, it had happened to her once, years ago. But he knew which vaporetto stop she would take, which meant he knew where her parents lived and where she did. Or else blind chance had . . . she dismissed this possibility even before it was fully formulated.

She tried to tell herself he hadn't done anything more than cause her some emotion between surprise and unease, but then she remembered kneeling in front of the toilet and vomiting, and admitted that he had terrified her. Accepting that, she punched in the number of Clara's husband, Sergio, who owned and managed a factory on the mainland in Marcon that made metal sheeting.

Sergio had been left an orphan at the age of eleven; part of his joy in marrying Clara was that she gave him back a family. She had four sisters, and two of those had children, so, with glee, he had taken on the whole lot of them, becoming the big brother none of them had had and acquiring not only a wife, but the endless set of obligations and responsibilities he had pined after for years.

'*Ciao*, Caterina,' he answered.

'Sergio,' she began, deciding to waste no time. 'I have a problem, and I thought you would be the person to help me solve it.' By presenting it this way to Sergio, she knew, she was pandering to his desire to be loved by the family and his need to believe himself a useful part of it.

'Tell me,' he said.

'A few nights ago, a man followed me from where I'm working to Campo Santa Maria Formosa. I was on the way to *Mamma* and *Papà*'s,' she said, conscious of using those names to reel him in, 'and then he was waiting at the vaporetto stop when I went home.'

'The same man?' Sergio asked.

'Yes.'

'You know him?'

'No. But I know where he works. I walked past a shop, near the Basilica, and he was sitting behind the counter.' She started to describe the man and was astonished to realize that all she remembered was light hair, cut very short.

'What do you want me to do?'

That was the essential Sergio: no time wasted asking if she was sure or if she had considered the consequences of getting him mixed up in this. Blood was thicker than water. Had he asked this question while she was being sick into the toilet, she probably would have told him to rip the man's head off, but time had passed and the menace had been let out of the situation, as air could be let out of a balloon.

'Maybe you could stop by and ask him what he wanted?'

'You want to come?'

Caterina remembered a time, decades ago, when she had come home from school after hearing the expression, 'Vengeance is a dish that is best eaten cold', and told her mother how clever she thought it was, forgetting that her generation had been brought up in a different epoch. Caterina had been surprised by her mother's failure to laugh, then more surprised when she said, 'It doesn't matter, darling, if it's hot or it's cold: vengeance still destroys your soul, either way,' and had asked her youngest daughter if she'd like a piece of chocolate cake.

For a moment, Caterina toyed with the thought of the man's expression when she walked into his shop with Sergio looming at her side. 'No, he didn't hurt me. He scared me, but it was just the one time, and I haven't seen him since. Except in his shop.'

'All right. Tell me where he is and I'll talk to him.' Then he asked, 'Is there any hurry?'

She was about to say that there was, but good sense intervened and she said, 'No, not really.'

'Then I'll go past it on my way home. Not today and not tomorrow. I'm sorry, I can't, really. But I will, I promise.'

Caterina had no doubt of that and reassured him that there was no hurry, none at all. She described the location of the shop and did not remind Sergio that he had a factory to run and shouldn't spend his time coming into the city in the middle of the day. She wanted an explanation, and if Sergio could provide it for her, all the better. To suggest that she had no sense of urgency whatsoever, she spent a few minutes asking about the children, all possessed of genius and beauty beyond that usually bestowed upon even the most gifted children. Then a voice called Sergio's name and he said he'd call her after he'd spoken to the man.

Caterina returned to the documents and read through the three remaining sides of paper listing the names of the people Steffani successfully brought to or back to the Church. She forced herself to do the basic historical research and was rewarded by identifying all but six of them. Even if the result turned up nothing meaningful about Steffani, the professors who had taught her how to do research could still be proud that they had taught her so well.

She plodded on, all but aching for anything that would save her from the tedium of these letters.

As if to wish for it were to make it materialize, the next paper was the manuscript of a *recitativo*, '*Dell' alma stanca*'. Caterina had perhaps spent too long a day reading through papers of a certain banality, and so to come upon this title pushed her, if only for an instant, beyond the limits of her scholarly patience, and she said out loud, 'This *alma* is certainly very *stanca*.'

Recovering from that moment of truth-telling, she took a closer look at the score and recognized both the music and the handwriting. She sang her way through the soprano part, remembering that it was scored for – wonder of wonders – four viole da gamba. She joined her voice to the silver shimmer of the instruments and heard how well it worked and then heard how sublime it sounded. As often happened, the quality of the music far outclassed the libretto, and she felt a moment's sympathy for Steffani for having had to use these threadbare sentiments over and over. She remembered the performance of *Niobe* she had seen, where in the following aria, strings and flutes had joined the viols. She realized that the score must have been printed and thus the sale of this page would not condemn it to some private archive, never to be heard. Smiling, she made a note of the document, listing the packet number and counting through the sheets to get the right page number. This way, either the victorious cousin or the two of them together could easily find one of the saleable documents and do with it as they pleased.

The next paper was a letter from Ortensio Mauro, whose name she recognized as that of Steffani's best friend and librettist. Dated 1707, it must have been sent to Steffani in Düsseldorf and seemed to describe events in Hanover, which he had left four years before. She read a few paragraphs of gossip and then found this: 'Here there is singing and playing every evening . . . You are the innocent cause of this. This music has more charm than Sympathy itself, and all that are here feel the sweet ties that stir and exhilarate their souls. You might issue a blessing, confirm or consecrate, excommunicate, whatever you like; neither your blessing nor your curse will ever have such force or charm, such power or pathos, as your agreeable notes. There is no end here of admiring and listening to them.' She ran her hand across the surface of the page, as if to caress the spirit of the man who had been generous enough to write that.

Another two hours passed as she read her way through more of the documents left behind by a busy and active life. Some of them could be there only because of a random gathering up of documents. There was a series of land transfer papers from a farm in the town of Vedelago: the names Stievani and Scapinelli appeared on all of them as sellers. A quick look at a map showed her Vedelago was about ten kilometres to the east of Castelfranco, the town where Steffani was born. Then there were more about the sale of another farm in the same town, these too bearing the names of the ancestors of the cousins. A letter dated 19 August 1725, from Scapinelli, said that, of course, their cousin Agostino would be sent his share of the money received from the sale of the houses, but he must understand that these things took time. There was only the one letter. And then there were no more documents: she had read through all of the papers in the first chest and had found nothing that in any way expressed a 'testamentary disposition' on the part of Abbé Agostino Steffani, though she had found tantalizing mention of the two families.

She put the papers back in order, tied up the bundle, and took it back to the open storeroom. She put the papers, all read and tallied, back inside the trunk, closed the trunk, flirted with the idea of beginning with the papers in the other, but decided her time might be better spent considering her immediate future.

25

Caterina was in no way a greedy person. She had little interest in the accumulation of wealth and spent most of what she earned on leading what she considered a decent life. Part of this might have resulted from the security that comes with happiness. She had always been loved and cared for by her family, so she assumed that being loved and cared for were things that would continue throughout her life, regardless of her salary or wealth. Many people were strongly motivated by the desire to accumulate money, she knew, but she found it difficult to muster the energy for the attempt.

Caterina did, however, have a sense of fair play. She had been promised a job and had left the relative security of Manchester to return to Venice in order to begin that job, she told herself, ignoring the fact that she had been eager to leave Manchester and would have jumped at any offer, as well as the fact that she had overlooked the time limitation stated in the contract she had been so eager to sign. She had, she admitted, been told that the position was temporary, but she had chosen to believe it might last several months. Now she heard that it would last only one month, even though she had no idea how long it would take her to read the remaining documents.

She turned on the computer and checked her emails. There was an offer for unlimited local calls and high speed internet for only eighteen Euros a month, the offer of a smartphone for next to nothing, and an email from Tina. She deleted the first two and opened the third, curious to learn how their conversation of the night before and the revelations prompting it would have affected Tina's style.

'Dear Cati, As you might have expected, the interest of my friends has waned in the absence of new information or questions about Steffani. Even my friend in Constance has gone mute, so I guess you are on your own. I've been reminded of a deadline and so have to get back to my more recent events, but please understand that I'll always abandon them to help, if you give me some idea of what to look for. You don't even have to tell me why.

'Maybe the Marciana has some of those compilations of documents and letters to do with musicians from the period. It's the librarian's equivalent of what the rest of us do with oddly matched socks: just throw them all in a drawer and forget about them. I'm sure the librarians could tell you if they have such things.

'Other than that, I have no advice to pass on to you and can hope only that you will discover more dark revelations about lust, adultery, and murder, so very much more interesting than my own tedious analysis of Vatican foreign policy. Love, Tina-Lina.'

It was a very limp attempt to sound limp, so perhaps it would convince whoever else was reading her emails to believe that Caterina and her sister were both bored with the research and everything surrounding it.

Caterina opened a new mail and answered, 'Dear Tina, Yes, once we got beyond the thrills of the Königsmarck Affair, things have indeed become a bit dull. Blame it on the even tenor of Steffani's life, I fear.

'I did, however, come on papers today that have him, as well as members of the Stievani and Scapinelli families, involved in the transfer of ownership of some farms near Castelfranco, and I'm going to try to see if I can find more about it tomorrow. Right now, I'm too tired after almost an entire day of reading handwritten documents in Latin and German and Italian to see straight or even think. I'd like nothing better than to lie on the sofa and watch reruns of something uplifting like, for example, *Visitors*. Remember how we adored it? Good Lord, it must be twenty-five years ago, and I still remember those giant reptiles gobbling humans down as if they were large mice. How I'd love to watch it tonight, pretend I was a Visitor, and gobble down dozens of people.' She read over what she had written and cancelled the last sentence. Though Caterina had no idea why, she wanted Dottor Moretti to read and believe that she was tired and bored with her research.

She continued the email: 'You think they stole the idea from Dante? I've always wondered about that.

'On that note of unresolved attribution, I'll go home – to an apartment where there is no television and thus no possibility of *Visitors* – have some dinner and get in bed with *l'Espresso*, which this week promises me revelations about garbage in Naples and the dangers of breast implants. Or maybe I'll take the biography of Steffani – who had to worry about neither of those things – and finally finish reading it. Love, Cati.'

She switched to the site of Manchester University and opened the Romanian's mail, whispering a silent apology to him for invading his privacy, his life; perhaps his secrets. When she noticed that there were one hundred and twelve unread emails, she smiled and retracted the prayer. She put the senders in alphabetical order and, seeing that there was nothing from Cristina, put them back in the order of arrival and left the site without having glanced at the names of any of the senders, very proud of her own force of will.

After that, she wrote to Dottor Moretti, saying that she was following the trail of land transfers near Castelfranco that involved both Steffani and his two cousins. These papers, she told him, might display some preference for one side or the other of the family and thus be useful in her research.

She pushed the Send key, thinking that a person could get to enjoy this James Bond stuff, locked up everything, and went home.

The search for records of the land transfers took her two days. She worked in the Foundation office because she did not want to turn herself into a recluse in the apartment. She did not so much as open the door to the storage place where the trunks were kept. First she accessed the records of the Ufficio Catasto of Castelfranco, the city closest to the village where both parcels of land were located and where the titles were registered; then she searched in Treviso, the provincial capital. The online information from the first office stated that what records they had from the eighteenth century had been put online, though when she phoned to point out the impossibility of finding these records, no one she spoke to seemed able to tell her just where online they had been put. When she was forced to call the office in Treviso to ask for the same explanation of their files, the woman she spoke to gave her the appropriate file numbers but could not tell her to which general file the numbers referred.

At last, doing what she should have done in the first place, she entered the three names into the records of land transfers currently online in the province of Treviso. When a flood of documents from the last few years began to arrive, she moderated her search to the last twenty years of Steffani's life, which reduced it to a trickle.

Caterina waded through these for the rest of the first day and most of the second and found that some years had not been entered into the online records but that, during the years for which there were records, the two families inherited, sold, bought, borrowed money again, and lost countless lots of property. She extrapolated some familial relationships when inheritances were left to 'my beloved son Leonardo', or 'the husband of my much loved sister Maria Grazia's second daughter'. Steffani inherited three pieces of land during this time, then two of them were sold, but from none of the documents could she infer any preference on his part for either side of his family: pieces of earth passed into and out of his ownership, and that was that.

Caterina was diligent and sent a daily email to Dottor Moretti to report on her findings and was careful to list every reference to either cousin's ancestors. His responses were always pleasant, although he explained that he was sending them from Brescia, where he was working on a complicated case, and looked forward to seeing her when he got back to the city. The first day she went to lunch with Roseanna, but the second day the other woman did not appear in the offices.

On the morning of the third day – aware that she did it because she wanted to enjoy the long morning walk along the *riva* – Caterina returned to the Marciana and entered by means of her by-now-standard invisibility. Her carrel was just as she had left it: even the wrappers from her chocolate and power bars were still in the wastepaper basket.

Following a suggestion from Cristina, she decided to take a look at the two outsized volumes of manuscripts the librarian had delivered to her days before and which had remained there untouched. To open them on the small space, she first had to move the other books to the shelf above.

She slid the two large volumes to the centre of the desk and opened the first. She read quickly through the opening pages and discovered just what Tina had said: this was the sock drawer, and there was little matching that could be done. There was a marriage contract between a 'Marco Scarpa, *musicista*' and 'Elisabetta Pianon, *serva*'. She found a bill from a 'supplier of wood' to the 'Scuola della Pietà', though in the absence of anything other than price, Caterina had no idea if the wood was for burning or for making musical instruments.

There was a contract between someone listed as 'Giovanni of Castello, *tiorbista*' and 'Sor Lorenzo Loredan', setting a price to be paid for the playing of a series of three concerts during the wedding ceremonies of '*mia figlia*, Bianca Loredan'. The next document was a letter addressed to Abbé Nicolò Montalbano. Caterina's hands tightened into fists and she sat up straight. She looked at the name again.

In the references she had found to Montalbano, the title 'Abbé' had never been attributed to him. Though known chiefly as a librettist, Montalbano had remained, for the researchers she had read, a figure of shades and shadows. The Countess von Platen had referred to him as the person 'who gained from the fatal blow and who had made it possible'; it was Montalbano who had received the 150,000 thalers soon after Königsmarck's disappearance.

The letter, the letter, the letter, she told herself: read the letter that is lying there under your eyes. It was dated January 1678, and was a list of criticisms of Montalbano's adaptation of the libretto of *Orontea*, the first opera to be presented in Hanover. She knew the music had been written by Cesti, the composer of *Il pomo d'oro*. The writer, whose name was indecipherable, was harsh in his criticism of Montalbano's text and said that he much preferred the original libretto of Giacinto Cicognini.

The next page in the collection was a list of the singers in the first Venice performance of Cesti's *Il Tito*. She continued reading through the documents but found no further reference to Montalbano, though she did find many more cast lists and letters from men who seemed to be impresarios and musicians trying to organize performances of operas in different cities and countries. They wrote to ask if a harpsichord would be provided by the theatre or, if not, could one be rented from a local family and, in that case, who would guarantee the quality of the instrument? Was it true that Signora Laura, the current mistress of Signor Marcello and said to be with child by him, was still going to sing the role of Alceste?

Caterina read through to the end of the first volume, filled with a sense that the real life of music and opera was contained in these papers and not in the dry things her colleagues spent their lives writing and reading.

The second volume interested, and then disappointed, her by containing the libretto of an opera entitled *Il Coraggio di Temistocle*, which, judging by what she could make out from the Prologue and the list of characters, extolled the virtues of the leaders of the Greek forces at the Battle of Marathon but was not the libretto of Metastasio. Caterina held out against the thumping and thudding of the verse for eleven pages before giving in and giving up.

The libretto took up the entire volume. She closed it and set it on top of the other, then carried them both over and stacked them where they would be taken off to be refiled. She resisted the impulse to take another look at the libretto for fear it would become worse. If this was an example of what had eventually led to the death of *opera seria*, Caterina had no uncertainty about the justice of its demise.

Now, standing at the window and looking across

at the windows on the opposite side of the Piazzetta, she throbbed with uncertainties about the demise of Count Philip von Königsmarck and the identity of the Abbé whose fatal blow had sent him to his maker.

Her mind wandered from this and turned to the fate of the woman involved in the search, and then it passed involuntarily to the strange loneliness of her life. She was in her home town, with relatives and friends all over the city, yet she was living the life of a recluse, going from work to home to bed to work to home to work. Most of her school friends were married, with children, and no longer had time for their single friends or their single pursuits. She blamed her failure to contact old friends on the urgency with which she had invested her research. She might as well have been one of those miners British novelists were always writing about, who never saw the light of day save on Sunday, when they had to go to church in the rain and dark and cold, and who were probably happier in the mine, where at least they could spit on the floor. She was in the Work Pit, her link to the outer world her cyber contact with Tina, a few apparently friendly conversations with a man who was betraying her, occasional phone calls to her parents, and precious little else.

Her link to the outer world rang and she answered it gladly.

26

'Cati,' said a voice she recognized as Sergio's. 'I have to talk to you.'

'News?' she asked brightly before the sound of his voice registered. A second too late, she asked, 'What's wrong?'

Instead of answering her, he said, 'Tell me where you are.'

'I'm in the Marciana.'

'I'm down at the Museo Navale. I can be there in ten minutes. Where can we meet?'

'Florian's. In the back.'

'Good,' he said and broke the connection.

Sergio had sounded tense and worried, something she had never heard before, and she began to castigate herself: her rash request that giant Sergio go and menace the man in the shop had refused to factor in Sergio's sweetness of character. What was to stop the man who had been so successful in terrifying her from turning his attentions, and his menaces, on Sergio? As she walked towards Florian's, she thought about the possible consequences: it would be easy enough for this unknown man, whom she assumed was Venetian, to use the same spiderweb of connection and information to identify Sergio, and from there it would be simplicity itself to find his factory, his home, his wife, his children. His sister-in-law.

She had set it all in motion, had hidden behind a man and his muscles and his size in hopes of intimidating another man who had used the same weapons against her. And all she'd managed to do was put at risk the people she most loved. So preoccupied was she with these thoughts that she failed to notice the elaborate gilded mirrors or the silk-covered chairs and sofas when she reached the café, nor did she respond to the smiles and greetings of the waiters. She went to the bar at the back, distracted by bitter regret and self-castigation. 'Fight your own battles,' she whispered to herself as she sat on the tall stool at the bar.

'*Scusi*, Signorina?' the waiter said with a smile. '*Non ho capito.*' She gave him a startled glance. No, no one would understand what she had done and what it might lead to.

'*Un caffè,*' she said. She didn't want coffee, but the

thought of adding alcohol of any sort to her fear repelled her. The coffee came quickly, one of the advantages of sitting back here. She tore open an envelope of sugar and spilled it slowly into the cup, stirred it around, set the spoon on the edge of the saucer, and turned to one side, more to avoid her reflection in the mirror than to be able to see Sergio arrive.

Waiters came to the bar and spoke their orders, carried trays to the people sitting at the tables in the café. She had noticed some courageous souls sitting at tables in the Piazza, shivering in their jackets and scarves in the thin spring sun as part of the full price of the Venetian experience.

She glanced at the coffee, realizing it would be cold by now and even less appealing. When she looked up again, Sergio was there: tall, thick-bodied, safe. She slid from the stool and wrapped her arms around him, put her face into his neck and said, 'I'm sorry, Sergio. I'm sorry. I'm sorry.'

When she pulled away from him, she saw surprise spread across his face, and when she glanced at the waiter, she saw it mirrored on his, mixed with open curiosity.

'What's wrong?' Sergio asked. 'What's happened?'

'That man. What did he do?'

Sergio held her by the arm and moved her back to the stool and didn't release her until she was back on it. 'What happened?' she asked, needing to know the worst.

'That man?' Sergio asked.

She felt a sudden flash of irritation. What other man could she mean? 'What did he do?' she asked.

Sergio turned to the waiter and asked for a glass of white wine, anything he had. He looked at her untouched coffee, placed the back of his fingers against the side of the cup. 'Two glasses,' he said to the waiter and turned to Caterina.

'Tell me what happened,' she said, then added, 'Please.'

Sergio managed to smile, though she suspected it was to soothe her anxiety. 'I couldn't go until yesterday evening. I had to talk to some people in a hotel about metal reinforcements.' Involuntarily, Caterina clenched her teeth at the mention of this useless detail.

The waiter set the glasses down in front of them. Sergio handed her one but did not bother to tap his glass against hers or say '*Cin cin.*' He took a long drink, then scooped up a handful of peanuts and began to put them into his mouth, one by one. How long would she have to wait before he told her what had happened?

'I went in about seven. No one else was there. The store is full of crap, that stuff they get from China. Terrible, ugly things. *Robaccia.*' Was he wasting time to calm her down and prepare her for the worst?

'I went in, and he looked up and smiled, sort of waved his hand around the shop to tell me to take my time. As if any of that stuff would interest me.' Then he surprised her by saying, 'But some things did. He's got some of those butterflies the guy in

Calle del Fumo makes. Really nice. Only thing in the shop – except for him – that's Venetian.'

From wanting to hold him and protect him, Caterina had passed to wanting to put her hands around his throat to choke the information out of him. But she just picked up her glass and took a sip, tasting nothing.

'So I picked up one of them and went back to where he was sitting, reading the paper.' Sergio finished the peanuts and took another sip of wine.

'I figured I'd do it like the guys in the movies: be a tough guy, start right from the beginning and frighten the little creep.' The man who had followed her was ten centimetres taller than Caterina: only Sergio would see him as 'little'.

'So what did you do?' she ventured.

'I held up the butterfly right in front of him and asked him what he was doing following my sister-in-law around and frightening her. Then I broke one of the wings off the butterfly and let it drop on the page he was reading.' Having said this, Sergio looked at his feet, then reached for his glass and took a larger sip.

He held the glass up between himself and Caterina, his thick fingers easily capable of snapping the stem with the least of efforts. He set it down and took some more peanuts.

'What did he do?' she asked, needing to know the consequences of her own rashness.

Sergio put his handful of peanuts down on the napkin beside his glass and said, 'He pushed his chair back until it hit the wall and tried to stand up.' With his index finger, Sergio pushed at the peanuts, as if he were trying to straighten them into a single line. Caterina realized then that he wanted to have something to look at other than her as he spoke.

'But he couldn't stand up. He was shaking so hard he had to put his head between his knees.' Sergio lined up a few more peanuts.

'When his head was still down there and all I could see was the back of it, he said, "Please don't hurt me, please. My father made me do it. I didn't hurt her. I didn't even talk to her."' Sergio looked at Caterina for confirmation.

She could do nothing more than nod. He hadn't hurt her. He hadn't spoken to her. He'd followed her and terrified her, but he hadn't hurt her.

'What did he do to you? What did he say?' Sergio asked.

She shook her head. 'He frightened me,' she said. Then, realizing how inadequate that sounded, she said, 'He terrified me.'

Voice much lower, Sergio said, 'He started to cry. Not like people in the movies, with tears down his face and you know it's all fake. He was almost hysterical, sobbing and wrapping his arms around his chest and keeping his head hidden like he had to protect himself.' Sergio's voice came in gusts, like the November wind on the Lido. 'He kept saying, again and again, "I didn't want to do it. My daddy made me do it. I had to frighten her. He said she doesn't work enough." It was like he was a kid again. He really couldn't stop.'

'What did you do?'

Sergio threw his arms out to his sides; they were so long that one of the waiters had to dance away from his hand. Sergio apologized to him and the waiter smiled and said it was nothing.

When Sergio looked back at her, he seemed calmer. 'If it had been one of the kids I would have told him to quiet down and given him a handkerchief and told him it would be OK. But this was the guy who followed you.'

'So?'

'So I asked him his father's name.'

'And.'

'Scapinelli,' Sergio said. 'That mean something?'

'Yes,' Caterina said, realizing she had expected it. 'Then what?'

'Then, I felt so awkward, all I could think of was to ask him how much the butterfly cost.' Seeing her raise her eyebrows, Sergio said, 'I know, I know it was a stupid thing to say, but it was the only thing I could think of.'

'What did he do?'

Sergio smiled, or came close to smiling. 'I guess he was as surprised as you were, or I was, because he looked up at me and said it cost twenty Euros but I didn't have to pay for it. He'd tell his father it got broken by a client.'

'And?'

'I did what I had to do: I reached into my pocket for my wallet,' Sergio said. He paused and gave her a pained look. 'When he saw me move, he pushed away to the side like he thought I was going to hit him. Right along the wall, still in the chair. And this time he bent down and put his arms over his head.' Then, as though the story wouldn't be complete without this last detail, he said, 'And he made a noise. Like an animal. In a trap.'

Sergio picked up his glass, looked at it, then put it back on the counter.

In a calm voice, he said, 'I took out twenty Euros and I set them on the newspaper. Beside the wing. And I told him that nothing was going to happen to him and that he could believe me.'

'And?'

'And then I left the shop and went home.'

'Did you tell Clara?'

'No. I wanted to talk to you first.'

'Good. Thank you,' Caterina said, then, 'How did it make you feel?'

'Like a shit. I've never bullied anyone in my life,' Sergio said, then knowing how impossible that would be for anyone who saw him to believe, he added, 'Not since I was a kid, that is.' He raised his hands inwards and drew them repeatedly up and down in front of his body. 'I can't very well do that, can I?'

'So it's a handicap?' Caterina asked.

'What?'

'Being so big. It's a handicap?'

Sergio smiled, as if the question had suddenly set him free. 'I never thought of it that way,' he said, voice filled with new surmise. He took another handful of peanuts and put them all into his mouth. He washed them down with the rest of the wine, turned and signalled to the waiter, and gave her an inquisitive look, but Caterina shook away the idea of a second glass.

The waiter was quickly back with another glass of wine. Perhaps, having come close to Sergio's outstretched hand, he didn't want to keep this client waiting.

Sergio took the glass and waved it in Caterina's direction. 'What should I do about Clara?'

'You tell her everything, don't you?'

Sergio nodded.

'Then you better tell her.'

'I thought so, too.'

'But tell her you were doing it for me.'

'You think that will change anything?' he asked. Sergio, she knew from long experience, could be as hard on himself as she was capable of being when judging her own excesses.

'You were helping someone in the family. If she wants to get angry, she can get angry with me.'

'Wouldn't be the first time, would it?' he asked, then smiled. Caterina reached for some peanuts and thought about having a second glass of wine.

27

Although Sergio invited her back to dinner, Caterina was reluctant to go as far as San Polo. How easily the habits of the city returned, making her reluctant to leave her own *sestiere*, viewing an invitation to San Polo or Santa Croce as little different from a forced expedition to the Himalayas. What would happen if she had to cross Il Ponte della Libertà towards *terraferma*? Take her passport? Refuse to go because of her fear of strange food and exotic diseases?

She managed to shake off these musings and persuaded Sergio that it would be easier to explain things to Clara if she were not present.

When they left the café, he said he'd walk home, which meant he'd head back towards the Accademia.

He kissed her on both cheeks, told her to call him again if she needed him, and headed off towards his home and his family.

Caterina walked out to the water, noticed that the daylight was swiftly disappearing, and started along the *riva*, heading home. What a pair of failures they were. At the first sign of weakness, both she and Sergio capitulated. In her case, her dislike of confrontation was the result of size, not principle.

By the time Caterina was in university, Mina had long been a myth, and her discs could still astonish. How Caterina loved the cover of one of the old discs – it must be from three decades ago – with her head seamlessly airbrushed on to the body of a body-builder. A woman's head – and brain – on top of a hundred kilos of muscle and power: if Caterina had that body, she'd once believed, she'd be the head of the Music Department at the University of Vienna. Hell, she'd have been head of state.

But now, having learned that size and power could be a handicap, at least for a person as decent as Sergio, she had to dismiss even that illusion. The man had followed her because he was afraid of his father, and his fear now made him untouchable by her or Sergio. '*Mamma mia*,' she whispered.

When she got to the apartment, she spent another two hours hunting for the Abbé Montalbano, chasing him through scholarly books and journals in four languages, seeking some sign of his passing in the catalogues listing the hundreds of thousands of books now available online, even though she knew he was unlikely to appear. She searched for him in historical journals and musicological theses, in the diplomatic files of minor principalities and the memoirs of forgotten noblemen and women.

Occasionally she caught a fleeting glimpse. In 1680, he accompanied Friedrich August, the son of Ernst August, as tutor on a trip to Venice and Rome. A letter from a composer for whom he wrote libretti referred to him as an intensely religious man, though in a 'superstitious way'. Montalbano was believed to be Venetian, though she found no record of his birth in the city archives. He hung around the court in Hanover for years, always ready, it seemed, to help Ernst August with the embarrassing affairs of his family. Little was written about his salary until he was paid, and royally – Caterina smiled as that word came to her – the 150,000 thalers that came to him in the year of Königsmarck's death, though some sources cut it to 10,000. The only subsequent references that Caterina found appeared in a biography of Leibniz, where he was said to have returned to his native country and become the archdeacon of Mantova, where he died in 1695, and a reference to the account books of the court of Hanover, in which was noted a pension paid to the 'mistress of the Abbé Montalbano' for forty-seven years after his death. The money that was given to him, whatever its true quantity, might as well have evaporated for all that was ever known of it.

She switched files and found the words of Countess von Platen: it was the Abbé 'who gained from the fatal blow that sent him to his Maker . . . Did he not, Judas-like, enable the crime and profit from it? The blood money given to him bought the Jewels of Paradise, but nothing can buy him manhood and honour and beauty.'

'Pronoun reference, you fool,' she said out loud. Change the meaning of 'he' from Abbé Steffani to Abbé Montalbano, and the picture of Steffani changed focus. He ceased to be an assassin; he ceased to have been involved in a murder to curry political favour for himself or his religion. He went back to being a fine composer and a man busy advancing the interests of his church and family. 'Nothing can buy him manhood . . .' If this was not a reference to Steffani, then the writer was using 'manhood' as a synecdoche for all the manly virtues absent from a man like Montalbano and not for missing body parts.

The 'Jewels of Paradise', however, remained a mystery to her. What did Montalbano buy with his blood money and what became of it at his death?

Hunger reminded her that it was time to stop asking these questions and think of finding something to eat. She cut some courgette and put them on to fry, sliced tomatoes and added them, set it to simmer. The realization crashed in upon her that, in all this time, she had not done the obvious thing and listened to Steffani's music. She had read through it, sung through it in a soft voice, hummed a good deal of it. But she had not heard it in any real sense. She went over to the computer and connected to YouTube, typed in his name, and then selected *Niobe*, the work with which she was most familiar.

Turning down the flame under the vegetables, Caterina went back to the dining area and, glancing out the window, saw that the Bears were visible, having dinner. She switched off the light and moved back from the window, where she thought they would not see her, and studied the family. Niobe was the mother of fourteen children, and her boasting of their perfections had brought upon her the wrath of the gods, who slaughtered them all. The Bears had only two, both seated at the table with them.

Signor Bear opened the wine and poured his wife, and then himself, a glass. Caterina found that an excellent idea and went to the refrigerator and poured herself some Ribolla Gialla. The aria that came from the computer was, she thought, the lament by King Anfione, the father of the slaughtered children, sung by a countertenor whose voice she did not recognize.

Across the *calle*, Signor Bear turned to his son and slowly ruffled his hair, letting his hand linger at the base of the boy's skull for a second before returning to his fork. The singer's voice, accompanied minimally by lute and violins, sang to Caterina of the future, of his *pianti, dolor, e tormenti*. Did Signor Bear ever lie awake at night and worry about the safety of his children the way her parents, she knew, had worried about them? Did he have always at one step from him the fear of *il mio dolor*? Her father was a teacher, Anfione a king – and Signor Bear? What did he do to bring home the honey for his wife and babies? Did it matter? Grief was the great leveller.

The rhythm changed and Anfione was calling his troops *all'armi*. Almost by magic, as if the Bears had the music playing in their home, the son stabbed his fork at the food on his plate, glanced at his father for approval, waved a forkful of what looked like pieces of short pasta in the air a few times, and then, in perfect rhythm with the battle cry of the king, popped it into his mouth. Caterina laughed out loud and took another sip of her wine.

The young daughter, who sat opposite her brother, shot him a glance, the look every little sister gave to the older brother who got all of the attention. And love? Her face was a study in a child's version of tragedy, while from the computer the same voice announced '*Dell'alma stanca*', and, indeed, the little girl, in the manner of little girls, looked as though her soul were tired and dejected and abandoned. But then, just as the voice referred to '*placidi respiri*', the father leaned towards her, then leaned closer still, and kissed her cheek. Her glance as she turned towards her father was so filled with joy that Caterina looked away, telling herself it was time to check the courgette.

By the time she took her dinner and another glass of wine back to the table, the Bears had finished theirs and left the kitchen. Caterina, reluctant to read, turned her mind from the idea of children and considered, instead, the men, historical and actual, she had encountered since she came back to Venice. Her thoughts did not follow the chronological order as her speculations jumped from one to another, then leaped ahead three centuries, drawn by similarities between them: their effect on women, their loyalty to friends or causes, the seriousness of their desires.

At the end of considerable reflection, and to her great surprise, she discovered that Steffani was the man she found most interesting, although she failed utterly to form any clear sense of him or feel any emotion save pity. A priest, a proselytizer, probably a spy for the Vatican: Steffani was all of these things, and all of them were things she was historically conditioned to dislike. At the same time, she had found no evidence that Steffani had betrayed anyone, nor that he had suggested the burning of heretics. And he had written that music, the strains of which still haunted her.

As she washed and dried the dishes, she continued to think about him. He had been an insider, reared in the Vatican and familiar with the workings of Propaganda Fide. He knew what they were and worked to bring other people under their power. She stopped, a cotton towel running around the rim of her wine glass, realizing that she still had no idea whether Steffani believed it all or not. Was he a man of his era, as opportunistic as the next, using the Church as a means to accumulate power and hoping to convert people only to build up numbers? Or did he really want others to find the same salvation in faith he believed he might have found? Nothing she had read about him allowed her to decide. Was the Stabat Mater an example of glowing faith or an example of musical genius?

The next morning Caterina was at the Foundation at nine, bent on getting to work on the papers in the second trunk. She paused as she closed the door to the building, drawn, as if by the music of Parnassus itself, to the sound coming from Roseanna's office. Indeed, as she arrived at the open door, she found what she expected: Roseanna was typing. *Click* and *clack* and then *whir* and *slam* and *click, click click, thud, click click.*

She knocked on the side of the door, and Roseanna looked up, smiling when she saw her. 'Want to try?' she said and laughed.

Caterina shook her head as at the sight of mystery. 'No, thanks. But I would like you to give me a hand.'

Without asking what the task might be, Roseanna abandoned her task and got to her feet. 'Gladly.'

'Upstairs. The trunks,' Caterina said. 'I want to start on the papers in the second, but I don't want to have to lean over the first every time I have to get into it. Maybe you'd help me move them?'

'Good idea,' Roseanna said. 'Backs are terrible. You're sure to do something to yours if you keep leaning over like that, especially when you get to the bottom of the piles.'

Talking about bad backs and the people they knew who had them, the two women went upstairs to the Director's office. Caterina unlocked the door and let them in and was surprised to find the room warm, almost uncomfortably so. She looked around in search of the source, her mind flashing to the possibility of fire. Roseanna put her unease at rest by going over to open one of the windows and swing back the shutters, allowing the sun to flood into the room: cool spring air and birdsong entered with it. 'At last,' Roseanna said with palpable relief. She opened the other window and left them both open.

Caterina delighted in the fresh air and rejoiced in the sound. She unlocked the cabinet and pulled the doors open wide. For a moment, the women stood in front of the trunks, discussing the best way to move the first.

Having agreed, they each took a handle and carried the first trunk forward a metre or so, lowering it slowly to the parquet floor. They did the same with the second, which weighed more, and set it next to the other. Then they lifted the first one and replaced it in the back of the storeroom, where the other had been, and put the second trunk in front of it.

'Thanks,' Caterina said. Then, 'Curious?'

Roseanna, who had not had a clear view of the papers when the trunks were first opened, said that she was but remained at a polite distance, as if to acknowledge Caterina's right to open the trunk.

Caterina did just that, leaned over to peer inside,

and saw that the papers had shifted around so as no longer to be separable into piles. A few sheets of paper had worked themselves loose and now lay vertically between the piles. Thinking as a researcher, she realized that this would create a problem of chronology among any papers that were not dated and began to plan how to remove them systematically so as to maintain the right order.

Caterina crouched next to the trunk and leaned over the edge. She slipped her left hand inside at the point where the two stacks of papers must once have met. As she slid it down, the papers rubbed against her palm. She moved her hand slowly, hoping to find a place where the stacks were still separated.

Hearing Roseanna move behind her, she shifted her own weight in surprise. Her left foot slipped on the waxed parquet, and she lost her balance, sliding forward and falling across the open top of the trunk. Her left palm landed flat on the bottom of the trunk, and her right hand on the floor just in front. She braced herself, elbows stiff.

An inglorious, awkward figure, she crouched half in and half out of the trunk, her right knee on the floor, her left leg shot out behind her. Roseanna was immediately at her side, trying to help her back to her knees. 'Are you all right?'

Caterina did not answer, perhaps did not even hear the question, as she pulled her left leg forward and put her knee on the ground. But she didn't move away from the trunk. Instead, she remained kneeling, one hand inside and one outside the trunk, both palms flat.

'What's the matter?' Roseanna asked, squeezing her shoulder to get her attention.

'The floor,' Caterina said.

'What?' Roseanna asked, looking around.

'The floor,' Caterina repeated. 'It's lower than the trunk.'

Roseanna's look became troubled but she kept her hand on Caterina's shoulder, this time trying a squeeze that would provide comfort. In a consciously soft voice, she asked, 'What do you mean, Caterina?'

Instead of answering, Caterina rose up higher, still kneeling, supporting herself on both hands. She turned and looked at Roseanna, though her hands remained where they were. 'The bottom of the trunk is higher than the floor,' she said. Seeing Roseanna's confusion, Caterina could do nothing but laugh.

'There's a fake bottom,' she said. Some seconds passed. Roseanna looked at her, saw that one shoulder was higher than the other, and started to laugh.

It took a few moments for Caterina to decide what to do. Slowly, she pulled her hand from the trunk, and got to her feet. As if a message had passed between them, both women reached to the handles and pulled the trunk forward. 'I need a stick,' Caterina said, and Roseanna understood immediately.

'The carpenter,' Roseanna said. 'Across the street.

He'd have a metre stick.' Before Caterina could answer, Roseanna was out of the room.

Caterina returned her attention to the problem of getting the papers out of the trunk while keeping them in the order in which she had found them. She slid them with care to the centre of the papers, then moved her hands towards the sides of the trunk. Slowly, she lifted them upward. The papers came free and she stood, a slab of them in her hands. She walked to the desk and set the papers as far to the left as she could.

When she returned to the trunk, she could see the intermingling of small packets of papers continuing all the way to the bottom. She bent and repeated her motions, placing the next pile of papers to the right of the first. By the time Roseanna came back, there were five stacks on the table; enough had been removed to show that the rest of the papers lay in two separate stacks of neatly tied bundles.

Roseanna waved the segmented wooden stick above her head. 'I've got it,' she said, her voice as triumphant as her gesture.

Caterina smiled in acknowledgement. 'Let's get the rest of the papers out,' she said, kneeling to reach into the trunk. She picked up some bundles on the left and took them over to the table. Roseanna set the metre ruler on the table and went to the trunk. Monkey see, monkey do. Together they went back to the trunk and repeated the process until it was empty.

Only then did Caterina pick up the metre ruler

and pull open its first three segments. The trunk was no deeper than that, she thought. She put the end of the stick on the floor and ran her finger down the numbers. 'Fifty-nine centimetres,' she said aloud.

She lifted it and stuck it into the empty trunk until its end hit the bottom. 'Fifty-two,' she said. Out of curiosity, she pulled out the ruler and used it to measure the thickness of the wood used in its construction: one and a half centimetres. So if the true and false bottoms of the trunk were the same, there would still be four centimetres into which to place papers or objects.

'What do we do now?' Roseanna asked.

Caterina leaned into the trunk and felt all around the bottom with her hand. Everything felt smooth. 'Do you have a flashlight?' she asked Roseanna, who was suddenly kneeling beside her.

'No,' Roseanna said, then reached into the pocket of her jacket and pulled out her iPhone. 'But I have this.' She tapped the surface a few times, and a mini-spotlight ignited. Reaching in, she beamed the light around the bottom of the trunk. As she did so, Caterina leaned forward and they bumped into each other: Roseanna dropped the phone.

She picked it up and moved to the end of the trunk. 'I'll go around it slowly this time,' she said.

Caterina nodded, wondering if it was going to be necessary to shatter the bottom to expose whatever space was underneath. She ran her hand, more slowly this time, along the bottom, closing her eyes to let her fingers have more of her attention. When she had covered all four sides, she shifted the angle of her hand and began to move her fingers along the sides of the trunk, just above the seam where they met the bottom.

Only a few centimetres from a corner she felt it, though she didn't have any idea what she was feeling. Just at the seam: the smallest of imperfections, like a small chip on the edge of a wine glass, though so smooth that, unless one were feeling for it, it would pass undetected. 'Give me a pencil,' she said, keeping her finger on the tiny opening.

Roseanna placed the phone on the bottom of the trunk, went over to Caterina's desk, and came back with a pencil. Caterina took it with her left hand and reached into the trunk to make a small mark on the bottom, just below the place where she felt the hole. Then she continued to move her finger along the remaining three sides, but the wood was like velvet.

When she was finished, she took the pencil with her right hand and prodded at the place above the pencil mark. The point of the pencil penetrated a few millimetres and stopped.

Caterina got to her feet and went to her bag and removed from it, of all unlikely things, a Swiss Army knife.

'What are you doing?' asked a shocked Roseanna.

Caterina didn't answer as she came back and knelt again beside the trunk. She turned the knife around and examined the other side, then pulled out the cork-screw. 'Maybe this will work,' she said.

Roseanna picked up the phone and shone the light on the pencil mark. Caterina manipulated the knife until the point found the hole, then pushed the point until she felt it slip inside. Gently, gently, she tried to turn it, first one way and then the other, but it refused to move. There was only one thing left to do, which was to angle her fist so that the curved point would catch in the bottom panel and, if possible, lever it upward.

She gripped the body of the knife, which had now become the handle, and pressed her fist forward as she turned it up. At first she felt the same resistance that had met her attempts to move it to the side, and then it seemed that the point managed to penetrate something. The handle moved closer to the side of the trunk, and she had to push it with the flat of her hand.

The floor of the trunk began to move upwards. It rose steadily until the knife handle met the wall. The bottom had come loose in the corner, and she managed to slip her fingernails, and then her fingers, under it. Slowly, Caterina pulled at it until, as easily as if she were opening a box of cigars, the entire bottom panel slid up. As it reached the top of the trunk, they could both see that the board was slightly bevelled on all four sides. This allowed it to slip down easily and fit tightly into place. It could be prised up only by inserting a narrow, curved point into the hole in the side.

Caterina took the bottom, which was surprisingly thin – barely half a centimetre – from the trunk and propped it against the wall. Both women leaned into the trunk, and Roseanna shone her light into it.

They saw a piece of thick-woven cloth, perhaps a towel or small linen tablecloth. Unstained with age, it rested on the bottom. Caterina reached inside with both hands, took it at two corners, and peeled it back. Below it, resting in a thick nest of the same cloth, were six flat leather bags, the old-fashioned type with draw-string tops. Each was about the size of a human hand. A piece of paper lay atop them.

Caterina, her scholar's habits asserting themselves, picked it up with both hands and lifted it carefully from the trunk. Still kneeling, she rested it on the angle of the top of the trunk to examine it.

She recognized the back-leaning handwriting. 'Knowing my death to be near, I, Bishop Agostino Steffani, set pen to paper to make disposition of my possessions in a manner just and fitting in the eyes of God.'

She tore her own eyes from the text and looked at the foot of the page. The document was dated 1 February 1728: less than two weeks before his death.

'What is it?' Roseanna demanded.

'Steffani's will.'

28

'*Oddio*,' Roseanna said. 'After all this time.'

Caterina hadn't looked at the document closely, but she had noticed no witness signatures, though their presence or absence was rendered moot by the passing of three centuries. She looked across at the other woman. 'I think we have to call them.'

'Who?'

'Dottor Moretti and the cousins,' Caterina answered.

'Call Moretti first,' Roseanna said, then added, 'Unless he's here, there's no way to control them when they see those bags.'

Roseanna was right, and Caterina knew it. She had his number in her phone, and she dialled it. 'Ah,

Caterina,' he said by way of salutation. 'To what do I owe this pleasure?'

She worked at keeping her voice friendly. 'I've found something I think you and the cousins should see.'

'What is that?'

'I've found a statement of testamentary dispositions,' she couldn't stop herself from saying.

'Steffani's?' he asked, voice alert and louder than it had been.

'Yes,' she said, then added, 'and something else.'

'Tell me.'

'There was a false bottom in the second trunk, and there were six leather bags hidden there. Along with the paper, signed by him.'

'Are you sure?'

'I've seen other documents he wrote, and the handwriting looks the same.'

'Have you called the cousins?'

'No, we thought that should be left to you.'

'We?'

'Signora Salvi was with me when I found them.'

'I thought you said you needed to be alone when you read the papers.' An edge had come into his voice, one she had not heard before.

'I asked her to help me move the trunks.'

'You should have asked me,' he said, and she heard how hard he had to work to keep his voice level.

'I didn't know what I was going to find,' she said calmly. 'If I had known, I surely would have called.'

She let the silence after that grow for a while before she said, 'Could you call them? And come here?'

'Certainly. I'll do it now.' He paused and then added, voice very calm, 'I'd prefer you not to look in the bags.'

'I was hired to read papers, not look in bags,' she answered. She wondered if he heard the snap.

'I'll call them and call you back,' he said.

When Caterina switched off her phone, Roseanna said, sounding surprised, 'You didn't sound very friendly.'

'Dottor Moretti is only my employer.'

'I thought the cousins were.'

'Well, he's working for them, and they've asked him to oversee my work, so in that sense he's my employer.'

Roseanna started to speak, stopped, then began again. 'I'm not so sure he is,' she finally said.

'Not sure who is what?' Caterina asked.

'That he's your employer, or even what he's up to,' Roseanna said.

'How else could he be involved?'

Roseanna shrugged. 'I have no idea, but I heard them talking in the corridor outside my office the day the trunks were delivered.'

'All three of them?'

'Excuse me?'

'Was it all three of them you heard talking?'

'No, only the cousins.'

'Talking about what?'

'They insisted on coming, the cousins. As far as I could understand, he had already persuaded them to hire a researcher.'

'Why do you say that?'

'Because that was the justification they used to be present when the trunks came. They said they wanted to see if there was enough room for the researcher to work in.' Roseanna gave an angry huff. 'As if they cared a fig about that, or would even know how much room a person would need. Or what a researcher is.' Freed of her anger at the cousins, Roseanna said more calmly, 'At any rate, that's the excuse they gave for coming. But I don't believe it for an instant.'

'Then why do you think they came?'

'To look at the trunks, maybe even to touch them, the way people do with magic things, or the way they look in the newspaper every day to see what their stocks are worth.'

Failing to stifle her impatience, Caterina said, 'What did you hear them say?'

Roseanna bowed her head and pulled her lips together, as if to acknowledge her own long-windedness. 'They were leaving, all three of them, but Dottor Moretti had trouble with the lock of the door to the stairs, and the two of them came past my office while he was still back there.' She waited after she said this, but Caterina did not prod.

'Stievani said something about not liking Moretti, and the other one said it wasn't every day people got a lawyer like Moretti, and they should be glad that he was sent to them.'

'What does that mean?'

That shrug and smile. 'I don't know. I'm not even sure that's exactly what they said. They were walking past the door, and I wasn't really paying attention.'

Caterina wondered who would send Moretti to work for the cousins. It would be child's play to persuade the cousins to accept the services of a lawyer: if an undertaker offered them his services, they'd probably commit suicide to make use of the free offer.

Her phone rang. It was Dottor Moretti, saying he had contacted both cousins, and they would be there in an hour. She thanked him, hung up, and relayed the message to Roseanna.

'Time for a coffee, I'd say,' Roseanna declared.

'I think we can leave it,' Caterina said, waving a hand around the room and recalling the time she had failed to close up the papers and lock the room.

'*Va a remengo, questo,*' Roseanna said, consigning the trunks and the papers to hell or unimportance, or both. They went and had a coffee, and when they returned, they waited in Roseanna's office for the three men to arrive.

It was over an hour before they got there. Caterina was surprised that the three of them came together. She had foreseen the separate arrival of one of the cousins, who she was sure would say he could be trusted to wait upstairs in the office for the others. Dottor Moretti must have imagined the same possibility and arranged to meet them somewhere else, or perhaps he had not told them why he wanted to see them, had merely said it was imperative that they meet. She found that she didn't care any longer which it was or what he had done.

Stievani looked eager; Scapinelli looked unwell, like a man who had had bad news and feared hearing worse. Perhaps his son had called him; she hoped so. Moretti looked the same as ever, even to the gloss on his shoes and the all-but-invisible striping in his dark blue suit. He nodded at Roseanna and smiled amiably at Caterina. He was indeed a prudent man.

They all shook hands, but before Caterina could say a word, Scapinelli said, 'Let's go upstairs.'

So Moretti had told them, Caterina realized. Silently, she led the way up the stairs and down the corridor to the Director's office.

They all remained by the door, though it was clear that the attention of the men was directed across the room, as if on laser beams, to the open trunk that stood to the left of the cupboard. None of them, however, moved towards it, as though each needed the support of the others to break the spell that had fallen upon them.

Caterina decided the time of politesse was ended. 'Would you like to see the document?' she asked, not bothering to direct the question at any one of them in particular.

Like men released from an enchantment, they started towards the trunk at the same instant, only to draw up short of it, as if again zapped by some magic force. Caterina walked through them, the *maga* who had the power to unravel the secret signs. She picked up the document that she had left on top of the open trunk and held it out to Dottor Moretti.

He took it eagerly, and the cousins crowded to his side, looking down at the paper. Stievani tried to move Moretti's arm higher, as if to bring the paper closer to his own eyes, and Scapinelli took out a plastic box and extracted a pair of reading glasses.

As she watched, Moretti's lips began to move, as Italians' often did when they read. After only a few seconds, he moved his right shoulder in a gesture that reminded Caterina of a chicken fluffing out a wing to win it more space. Stievani moved a half-step away, and Scapinelli used the opportunity to move even closer.

Moretti, unable to disguise his exasperation, handed the paper to Caterina and said, 'Perhaps it would be better if you read it, Dottoressa.' He had slipped back into the formal '*Lei*', which suited her just fine.

She took the paper from him, saw the way the four cousin eyes followed it hungrily. And each of these men believed that the others would abide by their agreement to let the winner take all?

'"Knowing my death to be near, I, Bishop Agostino Steffani, set pen to paper to make disposition of my possessions in a manner just and fitting in the eyes of God."' Caterina looked up at the three men to see how they'd take to the idea of God's being mixed up in this. The cousins seemed uninterested; Moretti now resembled a hunting dog that had heard the first call of his master's voice.

'"My life has been devoted to service, to both my temporal and my Divine masters, and I have tried to give them my loyalty in all my endeavours. I have also served my other master, Music, though with less attention and less loyalty.

'"I have sought, and squandered, worldly gain, and I have done things no man can be proud of. But no man can be proud of the act that set me on my path in life.

'"I leave little behind me save my music, and these treasures, which are of much greater value than any notes of music that could be written or imagined. I leave the music to the air and the treasures . . ."' here Caterina looked up from the paper and studied the faces of the men in thrall to her voice.

She did not like what she saw and returned to the page. '". . . and the treasures I leave to my cousins, Giacomo Antonio Stievani and Antonio Scapinelli, in equal portions.

'"To eliminate all suspicions about my having accumulated such wealth as to allow me to purchase these Jewels . . ."' he wrote, and Caterina wondered if he had capitalized the word while writing in Italian because the Germanic influence on his language for

all those decades meant that he automatically capitalized all nouns '". . . I declare that the money was
given to me by a friend who became a Judas, not
only to me but to an innocent man. Judas-like, he
regretted his betrayal and came to me to be shriven
of his sin, forgetting that to forgive sins is not in my
power, as it was not in his."'

She looked at Roseanna, then at the men, and saw
the same confusion on her face and on Stievani's and
Scapinelli's. Moretti, however, seemed to be following
everything, the bastard.

'"The money came to me on his death, and I could
think of no finer, no nobler, use for it than to purchase
the Jewels of Paradise, which I leave here for the
edification and enrichment of my dear cousins in just
return for the generosity with which they have treated
me."'

There followed the signature and the date, and that
was all.

'So they're ours?' Scapinelli asked when it was
evident that Caterina had finished reading the document. He took a step towards the trunk and leaned
over to look inside. His cousin moved quickly to
stand beside him. Had the clear disposition of the
will put an end to the idea that winner would take
all?

To Caterina, it seemed like the moment of stupor
in a Rossini opera, just before the ensemble that
brought the act to a rousing finale. Would their voices
join in one by one? What duets would be formed?

Tercets? Would she sing a duet with Roseanna? She scorned the tenor.

'Dottoressa,' said Moretti, who had moved to the side of the trunk, 'I think it would be right for you to see to opening these bags.'

There was a long silence while the cousins considered the statement. Stievani nodded, and Scapinelli said, very reluctantly, '*Va bene.*'

Caterina walked over to the desk and set the document, face down, on the surface, then went back to the trunk. She leaned inside and, two by two, carried the bags over and placed them at the other end of the table.

'You're sure you want me to open them, Dottore?' she asked Moretti, also using the formal *Lei.* The three men had another silent conference, and when no objection was proposed, she picked up the first bag. The leather was dry and hard, unpleasant to her hand. With some difficulty Caterina untied the stiff knot that held the leather strings together and used the backs of her fingers to force open the mouth of the bag.

All at once she was overwhelmed by a reluctance to know what was in the bag and an even stronger repugnance to touch whatever it was. She handed the bag to Moretti. He reached inside, and his fingers delicately removed a slip of paper with a few words written on it in faded ink. He looked at the paper and, gasping, stood rooted to the spot.

Scapinelli, immune to presentiments or surprise, grabbed the bag from him and stuffed his fingers inside. A second later, his fingers emerged, holding a long, thin sliver that Caterina at first thought might be a decorative silver pin of some sort, tarnished with age.

Scapinelli transferred it to the palm of his other hand and studied it. 'What the hell is this?' he demanded, as if everyone else in the room had agreed to keep the information from him.

After long moments, Moretti broke the silence. 'It's the finger of Saint Cyril of Alexandria,' he said, holding the tiny scrap of paper towards Scapinelli. In a voice made low by reverence, he whispered, 'Pillar of Faith and Seal of all the Fathers.'

Scapinelli turned to him and shouted, 'What? Seal of what? It's a bone, for the love of God. Can't you *see* it? It's a piece of bone!'

Moretti reached out and took it from Scapinelli's hand. He removed his handkerchief and wrapped the tiny bone reverently, then, holding the handkerchief in his hand, he made the sign of the cross, touching his body in four places with the cloth.

Caterina thought of a time, it must have been twenty years ago, when she had been returning to Venice on an overnight train. Luckily, her compartment held only three people, she and a young couple. At about ten, Caterina had gone to use the toilet and, finding a long line of people waiting there, she had been away from the compartment for at least twenty minutes. When she got back, the door was closed and the light turned off. She slid back the door, thinking how lucky she was to have three empty seats on which she could stretch out and sleep, when the light from the corridor flashed across the naked bodies of the young people, linked in lovemaking on the seat opposite hers.

She felt the same shame when she caught a glimpse of the expression on Dottor Moretti's face, for there she read an emotion so intense that no one had the right to observe it. She looked away, allowed a moment to pass, and handed him the second bag. The paper described it as the fingernail of Saint Peter Chrysologus. And so it went until the six bags had been opened and the papers extracted. And each time Moretti handled the piece of dried flesh or nail or the bloodstained tissues with a reverence from which even the cousins were forced to avert their eyes.

When the bags were on the table, the document placed beside it, Caterina turned away from Moretti, who was leaning over them, his hands propped on either side of them, his head bowed. Addressing Scapinelli, she said, 'I don't see the sense of disputing any of this. His wishes are clear: you each get half of what's in those bags.'

A cunning look flashed across Scapinelli's eyes and he said, 'Aren't those things always surrounded by gold and jewels? What happened to them?' Suspicion seeped into his voice as he spoke, and the final words were all but an accusation of theft.

'Signora Salvi was with me when I found them.'
Roseanna nodded.

'I called Dottor Moretti, with her here, as soon as I read the first sentence.' Then, more forcefully, 'No one's stolen anything.'

'Then where did the gold and jewels go?'

'I doubt there were any,' Caterina said.

'There always was,' Scapinelli said with the insistence the ignorant always use when defending their position.

'Maybe he didn't want there to be any gold. Or diamonds. Or emeralds,' Caterina suggested.

Stievani broke in here to ask, 'What do you mean?'

'Maybe he wanted to leave only a spiritual gift to his cousins.'

'Then what did he do with the money?' Scapinelli demanded, as if he thought she knew and was refusing to tell him.

'The money went for the relics,' Caterina said. 'That's what had value.'

Waving his hand at the bags, Stievani said, 'It's only a mess of bones and rags.'

Moretti pushed himself away from the table and took a step towards Stievani. 'You fool,' he said in a tight voice. He raised his hands but lowered them slowly to his sides.

Caterina surprised herself by laughing. 'Fool,' she said, and laughed again.

Moretti turned his glance on her, and she asked herself what had happened to Andrea. 'He believed,'

Moretti said. 'He knew what they were worth. More than gold. More than diamonds.'

'And if he didn't believe?' she asked Dottor Moretti. 'If he thought they were just pieces of pig's bone and dirty handkerchiefs? What better way to free himself of the blood money he was given?' The cousins seemed to begin to understand, but she didn't want them to get off free, so she asked, 'And how better to pay back the cousins who refused to help him than by giving them things that had no value except that put on them by faith?'

'But he must have believed,' Moretti said, almost shouting. 'He must have believed these were the Jewels of Paradise.' He turned back to the table and ran his hand over the first of the leather bags.

Caterina, who had once thought of his hand running over skin of a different type, shivered at the sight. 'But maybe he didn't believe, Dottore. You're an intelligent man, so you have to know that's possible. Maybe he bought them knowing they were trash. And maybe he wanted that. Maybe it was time to pay everyone back. He was dying, remember, and he must have known that, so he didn't need money any more. And he didn't need the habits of a lifetime of patience.' She stopped then, already ashamed of some of the things she'd said and of the desire that had animated her in saying them. But she gave in to temptation and turned to the cousins. 'You've got your Jewels.' Then to Moretti: 'And you've got your Paradise.'

She walked over and picked up her bag. She opened it and took the keys out, all of them. She put them on the table and turned towards the door.

'You can't leave,' Scapinelli said. 'Your work isn't finished. There might be other things.'

'I'm not working hard enough for you, Signor Scapinelli, remember?' From his expression, she saw he understood. 'So find yourself another researcher, why don't you?' Then, because she felt like saying it, she added, 'Ask your son to help.'

She went to the door and did not turn around. She heard Roseanna's footsteps coming after her: click, click, click, just like her typing. She waited in the corridor. They went down the steps one after the other. In the *calle*, they felt that the warmth had increased.

Caterina felt the tiny shiver of her phone as an SMS came in. She flipped it open and read. 'Dear Caterina. It's the University of St Petersburg. They want me to be the Chairman of their Musicology Department. But I always refused to learn *Russki*, so I told them I will accept only if you come with me as my assistant, but with the rank of full professor. And they agree. So please come with me, and we will discover vodka together.' There was no signature.

Thinking that it was time the Romanian learned a bit of Russian, Caterina typed in one word, '*Da*', and she and Roseanna went off for a prosecco.

ALSO BY DONNA LEON

BEASTLY THINGS

When a body is found floating in a canal, strangely disfigured and with multiple stab wounds, Commissario Brunetti is called to investigate and is convinced he recognises the man from somewhere. With the help of Signorina Elettra, Brunetti soon realises he remembers the dead man from a farmers' protest. But what does this have to do with his murder?

Brunetti and Inspector Vianello's investigation eventually takes them to a slaughterhouse on the mainland, where they discover a whole world of blackmail and corruption.

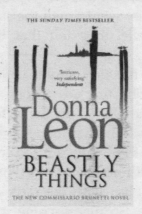

'*Beastly Things* is a perfect accompaniment to a hot day and a cool glass of white wine. Superb.'
Crimesquad

'Written with that depth of thought about crime and humanity that characterises the best of Leon's work.'
Independent